THE LIGHT EATER

BOOK TWO OF THE BAIRNS OF BREN

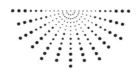

BY DENNIS JERNIGAN

SHEPHERD'S HEART MUSIC, INC.

Published by Dennis Jernigan/Shepherd's Heart Music, Inc.

7804 West Fern Mountain Road

Muskogee, OK 74401

Jernigan, Dennis: The Light Eater, The Bairns of Bren

ISBN (paperback): 978-1-948772-10-5

ISBN (epub): 978-1-948772-04-4

ISBN (mobi): 978-1-948772-03-7

Cover Design: Jones House Creative

Edited by: Darren Thornberry .

All songs (words and music) written by Dennis Jernigan unless otherwise noted.

To all my grandchildren for generations to come.

See life as an adventure—a journey—to be lived and enjoyed and savored and shared with those you love. Even the hardships and pain life brings are never wasted—depending upon your point of view. Stop here. Put down your logic. Put on your imagination, and proceed.

THE MAP

*I*t was the stormy time of year. Springtime in northeastern Oklahoma. The time when children were taught to watch the sky and pay attention to Mother Nature's warning signs. Darkening skies coming in from the southwest. Blustery winds followed by sudden stillness and calm. Rain falling sideways. Towering thunderheads and the dreaded lowering, spinning clouds that often became snaking twisters. The children had no time and no warning.

As usual, the grandchildren of Lee and Mellie Jennings—eight of the ten of them, as Ellie and Tillie lived in Australia—converged on the farm like a thundering herd. No sooner had they all piled out of their parents' cars and hugged the necks of their doting grandparents than they began begging to explore the forest Papa Lee called Bren. Papa Lee had spent many years creating the pathways that meandered through the small forest and just as many keeping them passable. He had taken great joy in naming the paths for the children.

Cullen's Lane is the entry point to the magical woods. Not easily recognizable as the entrance to the forest, the trees on either side of Cullen's Lane bow toward one another, giving the feeling one is walking into a deep, dark cave. This lane then makes its way to Elliott's Avenue. This path is over-grown on each side with the sweetest-smelling honeysuckle in the county and gives one a sense that anything is possible the further down this path they go.

Elliott's Avenue leads all the way to the campground Papa Lee calls Castle Aerie. This is the gathering place to which all paths eventually lead. It is Christmas all year round at Castle Aerie. The place where Papa Lee planted the little cedar tree when the family first moved to the farm. Not so little anymore, time has seen the small sapling grow into a magnificent towering tree. The children take great delight in decorating the tree and making sure it stays decorated all year round, filling Castle Aerie with a sense of wonder—of magic —that only the Bairns of Bren understand.

The first path leading away from Castle Aerie is called Warrior's Canyon. And it leads to the Forbidden Swamp. The Forbidden Swamp is only swampy after heavy rains, but is otherwise dry most of the year. Still, when it's soaked, it is almost impassable, except when the boys are brave enough to wade into the 8-inch deep waters in search of crawdads and tadpoles. And if the boys are not brave enough, Elliott often leads the girls out into the cold clear waters, much to the delight of Papa Lee!

Once one has traversed the Forbidden Swamp, the path turns northward toward the Sleeping Giant, a small rise running through the forest. This rise was once the pathway of an old-fashioned stagecoach trail running all the way to the Arkansas River way back in the 1880s! This trail is now called Mark's Way Parkway and takes the traveler farther into the darkness of the woods toward the Great Forest and Dark Mountains. Mark's Way Parkway is surrounded by dense undergrowth and vines, blackberry bushes, and thorny honey locust trees. There is nothing sweet about these prickly trees and, on more than one occasion, the children have stepped on fallen spikes, needing help getting them pulled out of their feet!

Mark's Way Parkway eventually morphs into Mia's Meander, a swervy, curvy trail that causes one to not know for sure which direction they are traveling. Rather than being a confusing feeling, it more often than not gives the children a sense of grand adventure ... as if they are exploring a never-before-seen land even though they have run and skipped and laughed down this particular trail hundreds of times before. It is as if, by some strange magic, the adventure down Mia's Meander is new every time!

As Mia's Meander comes to an end, the trail suddenly turns right or left onto Ronald's Roadway—a dark, tiny path through dense brush and rustling trees that leads through the

Dark Forest all the way to Menden Lake. Around the north side of the lake, it becomes more treacherous. The trees hang low. The vines seem to surround and crowd. And the thorns seem to reach out from both sides like dark and sinister monster hands! If this were not enough danger, the trail takes the traveler through the very edge of the lake itself, which means one has to be wary and keep vigilant watch for the beast they call the Red Dragon.

The Red Dragon is the big snake that makes Menden Lake—really a small tree-lined pond—its home. Papa Lee has always made sure the children keep their eyes peeled for the lurking serpent whenever they come near the lake's watery rim. Even though the lake is exposed to direct sunlight on the northern side, it still seems just as dark as the tree-covered southern side. (Papa Lee told the children it was because the Red Dragon was thought to be from the race of dragons known as Light Eaters, which made them shiver with fright whenever they neared Menden Lake. This part of Ronald's Roadway always made the children walk a bit faster and shudder in relief once they reached the other side turning southward again onto Matilda's Pike.

Matilda's Pike points south on the easternmost edge of Bren. Due to the dense trees and surrounding brush, not much vegetation is able to grow on the ground. This gives the beginning of the trail an otherworldly feel. From this portion of the trail, one feels a sense of foreboding. Although they would never admit it to one another, each of the children is always a bit glad whenever they get through this portion of Matilda's Pike and into the lush translucent green of the trees the further south it takes them.

Matilda's Pike leads eventually back to Mark's Way Parkway. As one travels the trail system all the way back to Ronald's Roadway, rather than going right from Mia's Meander, the trail leading left becomes Harold's Highway. Harold's Highway is a twisty, turning road through the forest that takes the trekker up and down over hill and berm. The Bairns always seem to laugh when they travel down this trail. It just seems to fit with Harold's happy-go-lucky attitude. Like being happy when one was with Harry because Harry was always happy, the up-and-down path made one feel light and happy! The children lovingly also call the up-and-down portion of the path Happy Trails.

As Harold's Highway turns west, it is intersected by two more trails. The first is Abigail's Avenue and the second is Annabell Boulevard. Both trails make their way through the forest, eventually becoming one as they near the old graveyard called the Hall of Heroes. The combination of these two trails has a way of making the children remember their own parents and grandparents—the ones who have given them life and given them so many memories—and to be grateful. Without fail, as the children pass by the old graves whose memorial stones are now so weatherworn as to be mostly illegible, they each grow more somber and respectful in their demeanors ... even to the point of being extra kind to one another. This trail once again merges with Elliott's Avenue and takes one either northward and out of Bren or straight back to Castle Aerie and Papa Lee's campground where it's Christmas all year round.

The final trail is aptly named Zella's Zigzag. Just like little Zella's running style, the trail zigs and zags, leading the children to chant "Zigging, zagging Zella! Runs like Cinderella!" Since the word "fella" did not really work well with a girl's name, Cinderella was the only word the children could think of to rhyme with Zella, which made them giggle as they thought about Cinderella running in a zigzag fashion! Intersecting with Cullen's Lane at two points, this trail is always a way to confuse and confound the children when playing hide and seek simply because they never know for sure which trail entrance to enter.

After greeting their grandparents and saying their hellos to one another, the children all turned to Papa Lee and began asking him if there had been any news from the land of Bren lately. Since their last adventure (spoken of in The Bairns of Bren: Hide and Seek) the children longed for more stories and more adventures and knew that Papa Lee believed them whenever they spoke of this adventure because he had lived it with them! With a smile and a wink, Papa Lee simply said, "Why, as a matter of fact, I do!"

As Papa Lee walked toward the road leading through the pasture to Bren, the children followed silently, all wonder-filled in anticipation of what their grandfather was about to tell them. Near the gate leading to the road to Bren, Papa Lee motioned for them to gather around as he took a knee and reached into his shirt. The children oohed and aahed as they saw the old, dusty scroll held reverently in the hands of their Papa Lee.

"Children," he began, "just this very day was I approached by an emissary of Bren."

Giddy with excitement, the kids felt as if their hearts would explode, such was the joy of this news to their souls.

"This map was handed to me with the simple explanation, 'Instruct the Bairns of Bren to follow this map. It will lead them to the long-lost treasure that is needed to free the land of Bren from the grips of the dreaded Red Dragon. There is no time to lose. Send them at once.'"

"Cullen, I leave this map in your hands as guardian of the map," said Papa Lee. "Children, I urge you to work together to do as the emissary instructed. The freedom of Bren is now in your hands."

Taking the map from his grandfather, Cullen boldly said, "Come, brothers and sister and cousins. To Bren."

As Papa Lee watched his grandchildren step into their destiny, he beamed with joy in anticipation of the adventure they would have and the maturity that would come to them as they traveled the path set before them. Little did anyone know of the storm that was brewing around them ... both literal and of the dragon kind.

7

2

INTO THE STORM

*A*s the children set off toward Bren, they began crowding around Cullen in order to get a look at the map. Of course, this made walking almost impossible as they tripped over one another's feet, bumping elbows and knocking knees with outbursts of "Ouch!" and "Watch it!" Jostling one another as they jockeyed for position, they fell over one another like dominoes when Cullen had finally had enough.

Pushing and shoving in an effort to get the children unraveled from on top of him, Cullen shouted, "Come on guys! Are you serious?"

This outburst, of course, made Ron snort out a laugh, which he immediately tried to squelch as he knew this would make Cullen all the more frustrated, which made the squelching quite impossible. As he untangled his legs from those of Harry and Mark and his arms from those of Mia and Abigail, and while he tried to get off of poor little Annabell, Ron could not stop laughing.

"Ron, I'm gonna let you have it!" Cullen blurted out, helplessly squished beneath the pile of wriggling children.

"And just how do you plan on doing that?" Mark chimed in with little boy snark.

"Yeah," giggled Mia. "How ya gonna do that?"

This, of course, caused Abigail to begin to snicker, which caused Annabell to snort and choke with laughter, which caused Mark and Ron and Harry to begin a tickle-fight with everyone else, which only enraged Cullen all the more. From a distance, Papa Lee shook his head and doubled over in a laughing fit. All he could see was a pile of writhing children and high-pitched squeals of laughter and what appeared to be a haze. Straining his eyes, Papa Lee realized the "haze" was merely grass and dust being stirred up and thrown into the air around the roiling clump of laughing kids!

Being the smallest and youngest of the children, Zella had not found the pileup nearly as humorous as the others. Struggling for air, she somehow managed to wiggle her way out of the jumbled mess. Tears brimming near the surface and exploding down her rosy little cheeks, she caught a glimpse of Papa Lee and headed back down the path toward him and his outstretched arms, her departure unnoticed.

The more the children giggled, the more entangled they became. The more entangled they became, the more raucous their sniggering. The more they sniggered, the more Cullen gave into the sheer and contagious joy. The more joy, the more tickling. The more tickling, the more intense the awareness of the children became. The more aware they became, the more they thought of their cousins in Australia, Elliott and Matilda. The more they thought of Elliott and Matilda, the more they imagined their girlish giggles.

While the giggle-pile grew and the imagination of each child focused on the joyful times spent with their Aussie cousins in the past, the sounds of Aussie-accented giggles and laughter began to swirl amidst the Okie drawl of the jumbled heap.

"Ellie, get your nose out of my ear!" shouted Mia.

"Mia, get your knee out of my bum!" shouted Elliott in return.

"Matilda, your elbow is in my nose!" laughed Mark

"Well, get your nose out of my elbow!" chortled Matilda.

And then the wriggling, roiling, laughing, snorting, mound of children gasped suddenly to a halt!

"Elliott?" wheezed Cullen.

"Matilda?" panted Ron, near hyperventilation.

"Cousins?" replied Elliott and Matilda, voices rising liltingly at the end of the phrase as Aussies often do.

"How? When? Wait ... what?" was all Mark could muster.

In wonder, the children, now nine in number, slowly and reverently untangled their limbs and noses and knees and bums from one another. Standing now in a dusty circle, they simply stared at one another for what seemed like an eternity. After a few moments of wonderment and silence, Mia broke the quiet as she rushed toward Elliott. Embracing her cousin, she cried, "Dear Elliott! How I've missed you!"

"And how I have missed you!" replied Elliott.

The kids morphed into a new pile, only this time, the pile stood tightly in a massive group hug. The laughs and giggles were replaced with tears of joy and snotty blubbering, the children greeting Elliott and Matilda as only the Jennings Clan could. Laughter and tears often go hand in hand at Jennings gatherings, whether planned or magical in nature.

After a few moments of exchanged greetings and embraces, Cullen once again drew the attention of the group to the map.

"Bairns of Bren," he addressed the children, who stood to attention at these words, as if reminded of their royal destinies and regal callings.

"We are children of Bren. We are the Bairns of Bren. I'm sure we are all thinking the same thing," continued Cullen.

"Yeah!" chimed in Harry, as little brothers are known to do. "How awesome it is to be *us*! It's magic!"

"And the Founders have something they need us to do," added Matilda.

"It means adventure!" said Mark.

"And unicorns and fairies!" chirped Abigail.

"Wolfen and ogres!" said Harry, bravely.

11

"Feasts and dancing!" laughed Mia.

"Wizards and riddles," said Ron.

"And swords and arrows!" squealed Annabell.

"It means danger and courage ... and demons and dragons," said Elliott, seriously.

"You're all right," assured Cullen. "Being the Bairns of Bren, we are called to the place of destiny. It is awesome to be us, but we are servants of the King and servants of the people of Bren. We may well find unicorns and fairies and wolfen and ogres and feasts and dancing and wizards and riddles and swords and arrows and danger and courage and even demons and dragons ... but more importantly ..." he paused. "More importantly, we must remember who and whose we are. Are we ready?"

At the posing of that question, Cullen extended his hand outwardly toward the center of the group. Without needing to be told what was happening, each child, in turn, placed his or her hand on top of Cullen's. As Cullen nodded, the children began the ancient, sacred chant of the Bairns of Bren.

Slowly at first and quietly in solemn affirmation, they said with one voice, "We shall surely overcome! Vict'ry ours when hearts are one!"

Over and over, the chant swirled upward from the children, like wisps of spoken smoke. Higher and higher the sound reached as the voices of the children grew louder.

"We shall surely overcome! Vict'ry ours when hearts are one! We shall surely overcome! Vict'ry ours when hearts are one! We shall surely overcome! Vict'ry ours when hearts are one!"

With each chant, their voices seemed to grow in volume and deepen in tone until outdone by rumbling and trumpeting rolls of thunder and streaking lightning and blustery, tree-bending winds. Like a twisting, turning column of power emanating from the circle of children extending higher and higher into the sky, the final chanting of "We shall surely overcome! Vict'ry ours when hearts are one!" exploded into a deafening thunderclap. A bolt of lightning crashed into the circle, sending them flying backwards. They sat in silence on the ground.

Cullen slowly untied the leather strap from around the scroll he somehow still held. One by one, the children reverently stood and gathered around him. Cullen knelt so all could see the scroll. The parchment—real parchment made from the skin of a sheep, not paper the moderns call parchment these days—was light brown in color. With the loosening of the strap, the thin leathery material released a musty, musky odor like the smell of a forest mixed with the wildness of a Bren horse after a long run. It smelled like adventure to the children.

While the smell of adventure wafted among them, the bold colors of the ancient words of Bren seemed to come alive on the page. Adorned with deep bright reds and ochres, blues bluer than the eyes of a Brennolinian maiden, purples more purple than the royal irises found along Cullen's Lane, and greener greens than the deep green of the Dark Forest, and all manner of colors known to man yet deeper than any known, the words seemed to dance and leap from the parchment. Matilda asked softly, "What does it say?"

In the most reverent tone he could muster (the children all say he sounded more like a man than a boy that day), Cullen read:

> With wind of storm and dark of night
> Enter the land and bear the light
> Stand firm on right or left, not middle
> Let truth of heart resolve the riddle

> Let hearts not fear the separation
> The way is found in contemplation
> Your way is set through the lone, through
> horde
> Your battles fought with fire and sword

> With boldness born of silver flagon
> Seek out the Eater of Light, the dragon
> Through fear and doubt, for Bren's dear sake
> Face the beast of Menden Lake

> Be bold, be brave, be love, be fierce
> Be humble, behold, 'til dragon heart pierced
> Return the land, restore the peace

Who would be greatest, be the least

Seek the treasure marked with gold
This treasure's worth the likes untold
Is found where death meets life, the measure
'Tis life laid down will find the treasure

Cullen faced the children. As they pondered the riddle of the map in his outstretched hands, Elliott posed the obvious question: "Where do we begin?"

As if to answer her question, the map began to vibrate. And sparkle. And beckon. Dumbfounded, the children looked at the parchment as the lines of the journey set before them on the page began to undulate like the movement of a snake! With the tiniest sparkly lights dancing from his head, the small gnome drawn at the beginning of the journey began to dance down the trail.

The children looked at one another and then back at the dancing gnome. Without missing a beat, Ron said, "I think we follow ... *him!*" The gnome, wearing a bright green gnome-hat, pranced into the road they all knew to be the road to Castle Aerie! And then the children realized they were no longer in Oklahoma. No longer in Papa Lee's homemade version of Bren. This was *the* land of Bren!

Without saying a word, the children turned and headed for Castle Aerie. The place they knew as home in the land. Confident strides turned into frantic running for shelter as the rain began to fall, the thunder began to roll, and the wind began to blow. The twister began to spin between them and the castle. They had no time. They simply ran into the first opening they came to. Ducking into the cave, the children smelled spoiled food, the sweltering humidity of a sweaty, summer day, and ... sulfur. They all knew it could mean only one thing. Dragon.

3

WHEN DARK EATS LIGHT

"What *is* that smell?" asked the usually quiet Annabell.

"Smells like dragon to me!" blurted out Ron in his matter-of-fact way as Cullen elbowed him too late.

"Shush, Ron! We don't want to scare the little ones!" Cullen loudly whispered.

"But it does smell like dragon! Like rotten eggs! Like your stinky toots!" giggled Ron without the slightest fear that a dragon could truly be nearby.

"Dragons? I'll check!" said Harry as he sped away in the blur the children had come to know him by when in Bren, so fast was he.

Cullen had no time to stop his little brother before he darted into the darkness. And before he could even respond, Harry darted back into their midst.

"No dragon here, brother!" said Harry, "but he's been here recently."

"How do you know?" asked Cullen.

"Because the ashes are still warm," said Harry.

"Ashes? What ashes?" asked the very concerned Mia.

"Why, the ashes we are standing in!" responded Harry.

The kids slowly looked down at their feet, their eyes adjusting to the dim light now emanating from the entrance of the cave, and they could see they *were* standing in ashes! And those ashes were indeed *warm*! Then Abigail stated the obvious: "These are not like normal ashes, sooty and soft. These ashes are shiny!"

"And crunchy!" said Matilda.

"They *are* crunchy, Tillie!" responded Mark.

As if they just realized their presence anew, the cousins of Elliott and Matilda all blurted out in one voice at the same time, "Elliott and Matilda! How did you get here?"

"Well," began Elliott, "our dad and mum were pulling us around the yard in a cardboard box and dad began to pull us around in a spinning circle, flinging us out of the box and onto the grass. But instead of the grass of our own yard, we found ourselves in the grass of Papa Lee's pasture ... in a heap ... with you!"

"That can mean only one thing," said Cullen. "Grandfather Leonolis—Bren—has some great deed or task only we can fulfill!"

"What could it be?" asked Abigail and Matilda simultaneously.

"It must have something to do with the map," replied Mark.

"And the riddle!" added Ron. "Don't forget the riddle!"

As only cousins and siblings can do, they all stepped as one, without being told what to do, toward the cave entrance in order to see the map more clearly. Once again, their eyes were drawn to the little drawn-on gnome with the green hat. Once again, the gnome began to move. Rather than dance this time, he simply jumped up and down, pointing to the first line of the riddle.

"What does it say?" asked Harry.

Cullen began to read:

> With wind of storm and dark of night
> Enter the land and bear the light
> Stand firm on right or left, not middle
> Let Truth of heart resolve the riddle

"Well, it obviously refers to the storm that sent us running into this cave," said Elliott.

"But what about the next line? We have entered the land, meaning Bren, but what is the light we are to bear?" asked Mia.

Instantly the light streaming in from the cave opening grew dim, even dark, the way a cloud covering the sun brings a sudden dimness. Abigail and Annabell were frightened. After all, it was their first time in Bren, having only heard the stories of the other children who were more accustomed to the many twists and turns of an adventure there.

"It's okay, little ones. It's only the clouds," assured Cullen.

"I've never seen a cloud ... with wings!" said Mark.

"Quickly! Back into the recesses of the cave!" ordered Cullen.

While the children scrambled for the darkness near the back of the small cave, the cavern went completely dark as the red dragon entered. Like a large stone rolled against the entrance, the dragon's massive body reduced the light to blackness. The children all noticed at once but dared not make a noise: It was as if the light were still there, yet was being consumed by the beast! As they peeked from behind the boulders and crevices where they had found refuge, they noticed something like crystal snow falling. Ashes! Not sooty. Not soft. Crunchy ashes. The children all realized the ashes were the residue of the light being eaten by the terrible beast! Without thinking, Ron held out his hand to feel them. As the other children gasped, Ron blurted out, "They're *crunchy*, guys!"

Even before the words had echoed through the chamber, the dragon heard! Spinning in the direction the voice had come from, the dragon lurched for Ron while shouting, "Who dares violate the realm of the mighty Luminaud?"

As the dragon waited for a response, the children noticed a very strange thing. When the beast inhaled a breath, the light would dim, and with each exhale, the darkness grew less ... dark.

"I said who dares violate the realm of the mighty Luminaud?" demanded the dragon.

Again the light grew dim with the monstrous creature's every inhalation and returned with each exhalation. When it was light enough to see, the kids were confronted with a massive scaly lizard whose scales were deep red, like the color of dried blood on a scraped knee. And around the dragon's head arose a misty fog, yellowish in color the older children knew as dragon's breath. And they knew that dragon's breath smelled like rotten eggs. Thus, the smell of sulfur.

Leaning back on his massive haunches, the dragon waited for the children to speak. Mia dared to look out from behind the rock she had hidden behind and wished she hadn't! The dragon's claws jutting out from his front paws appeared as daggers—long, sharp, and menacing. Holding her breath, she slid slowly back down behind the rock, hoping the dragon had not seen her or heard her quiet gasp at the sight of his talons!

"I see you, girl!" hissed Luminaud. "And I smell you... others...all nine of you! Come out at once or I absorb the life of the girl."

Each child heard the dragon's strange threat and wondered what the phrase "or I absorb the life of the girl" could possibly mean. Even the youngest, Tillie and Abbie

21

and Harry, knew it could not be good! So, without thinking about their own safety, the children left their hiding places and stepped into the dim light that now emanated from Luminaud's red, red eyes and said, "Leave her alone!"

Chuckling at their bravery, Luminaud spoke. "Ha! Ha! Ha! Ha! What brave children you are, but you are merely children! You know no better!" smirked the beast.

Of course, Elliott could not hold her tongue. "Who are you to declare the realm of Bren your own?"

Hissing and spitting, sulfurous mist wafting around his head, the dragon shouted, "I am Luminaud, Eater of Light! Master of the Realm! Bringer of Darkness! The Lord of the land you call Bren!"

"Since when?" demanded Elliott.

"Since I defeated the one they call High King Leonolis! Since then!" hissed the beast.

With those words, the children gasped aloud in disbelief at the possibility that their dear grandfather could have been defeated as the dragon boasted.

"Ah," seethed the dragon. "Do I sense ... fear? Do I sense dismay? Do I sense love for grandfather?"

Bursting into tears, everyone ran to surround Mia as tears streamed down their faces.

While still clinging to his cousins and brothers, Cullen raised his head toward the dragon and asked, "How could you possibly have defeated the High King when he commands the entire and massive forces of Bren?"

"I am glad you asked, boy!" sneered Luminaud. "It was as simple as night and day. I grow and survive by consuming light. Having been born in the fires of the volcano they call Envy Mountain, I was created to consume what I cannot have ... to destroy what I cannot enjoy ... to be what I cannot be ... to bring suffering to those who enjoy peace ... to absorb the light of life!"

"What do you mean when you say 'absorb the light of life'?" asked Cullen.

"It is easier shown than spoken," said Luminaud, "but since you are children, I will try to explain the new reality of Bren before I demonstrate to you what is inevitable. I thrive on the light of others. Each human in the land you know as Bren is endowed with an inner light. I cannot exist apart from the consumption of—eating of—such light. With one breath breathed in, I taste the wonderful life-giving elixir of life."

"And what of the one you absorb light from? What happens to them?" asked the boy.

"Well, I am afraid I have some bad news for you," chuckled the dragon. "When the light of life has been absorbed from a man or woman of Bren, that man or woman is no more!"

"You mean they *die*?!" said Cullen with great disgust.

"Yes, they *die* as you say! But I *live*!" laughed the beast. "And what's more, since many of your kind lose a bit of the light of life as they grow into what you call adulthood, I receive more light from absorbing the light of children than I ever do when absorbing the light of a grown person! All the more reason I am glad to have found you traipsing around this day in my private lair! Now, who would like to go first?" asked the dragon as he licked his lips.

At those words, the children huddled all the more tightly together, except, that is, for Abigail (who, from that day forward, was always referred to as Abigail the Awesome in the lore of Bren). Standing just beneath the awful head of the beast, she lifted her little hands and looked straight into those red, red eyes and stopped him dead in his tracks as her Brenolinnian power was discovered in that very moment! Abigail had mesmerized the mighty beast with her gaze. As she did, she began to search the dragon's thoughts for a way to lead her and the other children to escape.

"We can get away through the tunnels behind us!" Abbie shouted.

"We can ... wait ... what?!" asked Cullen, stupefied.

"You heard me! We can escape through the tunnels behind us!" shouted Abbie, forcefully.

"How do you know this? And why is the dragon just staring into space?" asked Mark

"I don't know how or why, but he seems to be frozen in my gaze, and I am able to hear his thoughts!" said Abbie, now quivering in confusion at the discovery of her Brenolinnian gifts.

"Trust your gifts, Abbie!" shouted Cullen. "Trust her gifts, brothers and cousins!"

But Annabell had already stepped from the middle of the huddle. Reaching into her pocket, as if commanded to by some unspoken voice, she retrieved a small bell! Lifting it high above her head instinctively, she rang it. As she lifted her free hand toward the head of the dragon, a shudder went through the entire cavern, shaking the children from one another's grips and causing the locked gaze between Abbie and Luminaud to be broken. The children stood quietly in awe as the shudder resolved into utter stillness. Annabell stopped ringing the bell and said, "We must go. I am not sure what I am doing, but I feel we may make our escape behind us as Abbie has said."

"What about you?" asked Elliott.

"I will hold him even as I move with you. Ellie, take my shoulder and guide me to the tunnels. I can hold him until we are safely inside. These tunnels are too small for him to be able to follow. Now!"

While Ellie led Annabell from behind, she and the other children made their way further into the rear of the cavern. Sure enough, they found a tunnel and quickly entered!

"What now?" asked Mia.

"The map!" exclaimed Elliott. "Open the map!"

With Annabell holding time still in her lifted hand, the other children looked to the map. The trail had magically extended into the cave in which they now found themselves. The gnome was jumping up and down as he pointed to a three-way split in the trail farther down the escape tunnel. To the amazement of all, a pack of nine tiny wolves suddenly appeared on the parchment. As they watched, the wolves all ran through the map and headed toward the split in the trail. Once they made it to the split, five went left and four went right. At that very moment, the gnome began to speak the words of the riddle:

With wind of storm and dark of night
Enter the land and bear the light
Stand firm on right or left, not middle
Let Truth of heart resolve the riddle.

"What does it mean, Cullen?" asked Mia.

"I'll tell you what it means," said Elliott. "We are to bear the light of what we have discovered of the dragon's plans to the leadership of the realm of Bren. The wolves represent *us*! We are to avoid the trail in the middle. We are to go either right or left!"

"But how will we know who should go right and who should go left?" lamented Ron.

"We will let Truth of heart resolve the riddle just as the riddle says!" Mark chimed in.

"He's right!" said Cullen. "We will trust our hearts when we get to the split. The light of Truth is in us. We will just 'know' when we get there!"

Having stepped backward and out of sight of the dragon, Annabell broke her connection with the horrible beast, and shook in disgust at what she had just endured. As she turned to follow the gang down the tunnel, she heard the fury of the beast raging behind her.

"Where are you?!" raged the beast. "By what vile magic have you made your escape?!"

While the ground beneath them quaked at the terrible force of the dragon's fury, the children made their way through the tunnel toward the split, following the tiny wolves as they bounded down the trail of the map, the tunnel ablaze with the light produced by the power of Ron's ability to conjure up fire. At last and at least they were safe ... for now.

4

A PARTING OF WAYS

With the sound of Luminaud's anger dying behind them, the children did not lessen their pace though they knew the tunnel was much too short and narrow for the dragon to follow. With Ron's fire lighting the way, they quickly navigated to the spot where the trail divided into three tunnels just as the map had shown. As the troupe came to a stop, they gathered around Cullen, who was already unfurling the rolled-up parchment of the map.

"What now?" asked Mark.

"We follow the map and we let Truth of heart show us the way," said Cullen.

"What does that even mean?" asked Elliott.

"It means we listen to what our hearts tell us to do," said the soft-spoken Mia.

"But what does the map say? And what about those tiny wolves?" asked Matilda.

"If the wolves represent us, then how do we know which wolf is which child?" asked Abigail.

"I know! I know!" said Ron, very excited. "Look at the map! See the collars around their necks?"

"Why, there *are* collars around their necks!" replied Harry.

"And look there!" exclaimed Annabell. "There is a symbol emblazoned on each one!"

Sure enough, there on each collar of each tiny wolf was a tiny symbol. As the children strained their eyes for a closer look, the animated images of the tiny wolves became quite apparent.

"There! I see mine!" said Cullen. "See? There on the side of the collar of the dark blue wolf ... a mountaintop vista ... like another point of view ... like an ability to see visions and dream dreams!"

"And I see mine!" responded Mark. "On the collar of the grey wolf, a tiny herd of deer because I can speak with animals!"

One by one, the children began to recognize the symbol identifying which wolf represented them. Elliott saw a wisp of cloud disappearing from one part of the collar of the orange-ish wolf to another, like her ability to transport herself to distant places. Mia recognized hers—the brown wolf—because of the little lightning bolt on the collar. Of course, everyone recognized Ron's due to the flaming fire on the collar of the white wolf. On the pinkish wolf was the symbol of a bow and arrow representing Matilda. On the red wolf's collar, a swoosh of wind—like something speeding by at supersonic speed—that could only mean Harry. On the blonde wolf's collar was one solitary blue eye all knew to symbolize Abigail. This left only Annabell. Her wolf was not colored but clear, like a shimmering light. And on its collar? A teeny, tiny bell!

"What about Zella?" asked Ron. "Where is her wolf?"

Finally, the last wolf came into view. Silver with a tiny lightning bolt in the shape of the letter zee, or zed, as they say in Australia! "The silver wolf must be Zella!" exclaimed her big brother, Cullen. As the children watched the silver wolf, it ran back in the direction they had just come from and faded completely away!

"Speaking of Zella, where is she?" asked Mia.

"Oh, no! Did we leave her in the dragon's lair?" lamented Annabell.

"I thought you all knew!" chimed in Elliott.

"Knew what?" asked Cullen.

"Just as Tillie and I were joining the giggle fest, I saw Zella run to Papa Lee. She is safe with him."

"She's probably better off with him since she is the littlest," declared Mia.

"Now that we know Zella is with Papa Lee and now that we know which wolf represents us, all we need to do is watch which way they go on the map ... right?" asked Harry.

This sounded reasonable to all the children. So they watched and waited. And nothing happened.

"Why are they just standing there in front of the tunnels on the map? Why won't they choose a way to go?" asked, who else, but Elliott.

"I think this means *we* must choose which way we go," replied Cullen.

"Why bother with a map if the choice is ours?" asked Mia.

"It's like Papa Lee always says, 'We may not have a choice as to our circumstances in life, but we always have a choice as to how we will respond to those circumstances.'"

"Okay, but how do we know what tunnel to choose?" asked Elliott.

"The riddle says to let Truth of heart solve the riddle. We must trust the Truth, and the Truth is this: Bren needs us. Brothers and cousins, what does your heart tell you?" asked Cullen. "Let us trust the wisdom of the Founders to guide us."

After a few moments of silence, Ron stepped toward the tunnel to the left and said, "Something in my heart tells me I am to go to the left. Who is with me?"

"I am," replied Annabell as she stepped to Ron's side.

"I am to go right," chimed in Harry with a big smile.

"Me, too!" exclaimed Abigail.

"To the right," said Mia as she stepped to her sister's side.

"And I will go to the left with Annabell!" declared Mark.

Without hesitation, Matilda bravely said, "I am to go to the left!"

"Well, you're not going without me!" proclaimed Elliott. "Mum and dad would not be happy if I let you go without me!"

"I guess that leaves me," said Cullen. "And I feel I am to go to ... *right!*"

Standing there for a few moments as Ron's fire illuminated their faces, Cullen broke the silence. "Well, what are we waiting for? We must be about the business of freeing Bren from the grip of the Light Eater, Luminaud! Let us go at once!"

Mia took Abigail by the hand and headed into the tunnel to the right. She used her free hand to produce a stream of small lightning (extending from her fingertips) to light the way. As Harry followed the girls to the right, Cullen waited to see the others off to the left. He wanted to make sure they all made it in together. Watching his brother Ron lead the other group into the left tunnel, he waited until he saw them all safely in before he turned to the tunnel to the right. What he had not noticed was that Mia, Abigail, and Harry had gone on ahead without him. And Cullen suddenly found himself in total darkness! Alone!

Trying not to panic, he began to search for the opening of the tunnel to the far right. Feeling his way toward the wall in the direction he assumed was to the right, he became confused about where he was in relation to the three openings. Feeling a tinge of fear coming over him, he stopped and whispered a plea for help into the darkness: "Oh, Founders, I need your help!" Before the words left his lips, a tiny light appeared right in front of him.

The tiny flickering light seemed to fill the entire place where he stood. In wonder, he reached out his hand. The light flitted around his head and then away. Once again, Cullen reached for the light, and once again it darted away from him and then back again as if it were playing with him!

"What are you?" he asked. "Are you a fairy? Or a sprite? Or a firefly?"

While Cullen followed the path of the flitting little light-bearer, he could see it was more like an insect than a fairy. "You *are* a firefly, aren't you, little one?" he exclaimed. He'd seen fireflies before (the adventure written about in the Bairns of Bren book, Hide and Seek)!"

Cullen's fear was gone as suddenly as it had arisen once he realized his prayer had been answered. "You were sent by the Founders to guide me like before!" he rejoiced as the little insect began to dart back and forth in excitement all its own!

"Lead the way, little friend!" said Cullen.

Cullen followed the glowing insect as it flitted and floated ahead of him into the *middle* tunnel!

While Cullen was distracted by the glowing insect, the tunnels to the right and the left had disappeared! Only the middle tunnel remained open. And what had led Cullen down the wrong path was actually a ... *dragonfly*! And that could only mean one thing! A dragon was near. Cullen had haphazardly fallen right into the trap set for him by Luminaud. As he'd sung a lilting song of contentment, thinking he was being led by the Founders, Cullen was on his way to disaster right down the path the riddle had warned him to avoid!

Meanwhile, the children who had ventured left—Ron, Annabell, Elliott, Matilda, and Mark—followed the tunnel for several miles until they came to a dead end ... or what they *thought* was a dead end. The tunnel had led them to a large cavern with stalactites hanging from the ceiling and stalagmites rising from the ground.

"What do we do now?" asked Annabell.

"We find the way out," said Mark, matter-of-factly.

"Easier said than done," said Elliott.

"The Founders would not have led us to a place where they could not reach us," said Matilda. "The way out is here... somewhere. I just know it!"

"She's right, cousins," said Ron. "After all, this is Bren... and we all know what that means."

"Of course!" replied Elliott. "That means the Founders have made a way, and it's up to us to figure it out!"

Silently, the children began to search high and low for the way out. Climbing around the boulders that littered the floor of the cavern, shinnying up and down the stalagmites, they searched every nook and cranny. After several fruitless minutes of scouring, the children seemed on the verge of giving up. In frustration, Mark picked up a small pebble and threw it against the stone wall at the far side of the cavern. As the stone struck the wall, the children all looked at one another. An echo!

"Did you hear that, guys?" asked Mark.

"Yes!" exclaimed Elliott. "That was the sound of stone striking wood—like a wooden door!"

The kids ran toward the wall and stopped in amazement at what stood there before them: A massive oak door, ornately decorated with the signs and symbols of Bren! It was much like a grand doorway that reminded them all of the entrance to the throne room of Castle Aerie.

Ron pulled with all his might on the massive ring used to open the door. It would not budge. "Help me, guys!" he shouted.

While Ron held the mighty ring, Mark stood behind him and wrapped his arms around his cousin's waist ... as Elliott did his ... as Matilda did hers ... and as Annabell pulled on hers! Slowly but surely, the mighty door began to creak and groan as if awakening from a long, deep sleep! The more they pulled, the more the door moaned. The more the door moaned, the more the children pulled! With much sweat and exertion, the door began to open, bits of dust and rust floating in the air as the hinges gave way to the efforts of the children.

The door swung open and the darkness of the cavern was

replaced with bright light streaming in from the windows lining the grand hall the children knew to be the throne room of High King Leonolis! And seated there on the thrones in the middle of receiving people of the realm were none other than their grandfather, King Leonolis, and their grandmother, Queen Abila, mouths agape and eyes agog at the sight of the children.

With both incredulity and great joy, High King Leonolis asked, "What are *you* doing here?"

5

WHAT ARE YOU DOING HERE?

*T*he children ran toward their grandparents, all shouting frantically, and Leonolis and Abila could not get a word in edgewise! With bewildered looks at the guests they were receiving, their eyes conveying "So sorry but these are our grandchildren," the King and Queen simply embraced the swarm!

After a few seconds of uncontrolled, high-pitched chatter, Leonolis rose from the giant bear hug and said, "Quiet, children!" Silence immediately filled the throne room, the young ones knowing the tone of voice their grandfather used to express the need for respect and reverence. They knew he loved them in spite of the intensity of his words.

Turning to Mark, Leonolis asked, "Son, how did you come to be here?"

"In the other realm we were given a map and told to embark on a quest to save the land of Bren!" began the boy.

"What is this quest?" asked Leonolis, while giving a side-glance to Abila.

"We were given a map and told to follow it!" said the boy, excitedly.

Leonolis nodded, "Go on, boy."

"On the map is a riddle, and there is a little gnome that lives in the map. And as we tried to solve the riddle, a storm came. We were driven into a cave as we looked for shelter! And while trying to solve the riddle, he appeared!"

"Who appeared?" asked Abila.

"Luminaud," said Mark.

"The Eater of Light," said Leonolis, again looking at Abila, who responded with a look that said, "I know."

"And then what?" asked the Queen.

"Annabell stopped the beast in his tracks and we were able to escape into the depths of the cave where the dragon could not follow."

"Because he was too big to fit!" chimed in Elliott, a giggle in her voice.

"He was kind of fat," snickered Ron.

"But he was still scary, and when he breathed in, the light dimmed," said Annabell.

"Oh! Oh! And don't forget the tiny wolves!" shouted Matilda while pulling on her sister's shirt. "Tell 'em about the tiny, pretty wolves!"

"Wolves, you say?" asked the King.

"Yes! Tiny wolves. One was brown and one was dark blue! And one was red ... Oh! And mine was pink! A *pink* wolf! So awesome! Another was blonde and Mia's was brown and Elliott's was orange, but my favorite was Annabell's! It was *clear*, and on its collar was a teeny, tiny, cutie-patootie little bell! That's how we knew it was hers! It was *clear*, grandfather! Clear!"

"And where were these tiny wolves?" asked Leonolis.

Stepping in front of Matilda, Elliott replied as if her grandparents should have figured that out by now: "They were in the map! And they represent all ten of us ... well ... the nine of us who entered Bren, since Zella ran back to Papa Lee!"

"All nine of you?" asked the Queen, counting them. "But I only see five! Where are the others?"

"They went down the tunnel to the right," said Ron.

"And where does that tunnel lead?" asked Leonolis.

"We have no idea," replied Mark.

"No idea?" gasped the King. "Then why did they not come with you to find us?"

"The riddle told us to follow the truth of our hearts. We had no idea the tunnel we chose would lead us to you. We simply trusted what our hearts told us for the sake of Bren," explained Mark.

"Of course. Of course," said the King, rubbing his beard. "We had just consulted with the seers of the land, asking them for the word of the Founders in regard to ridding from the land of Bren the menace of Luminaud, Eater of Light."

"And what did the seers see?" asked Ellie.

"They saw menace and mayhem and a great dimming, but nothing concerning the actual appearance of Luminaud. Yet his appearance is not surprising since they foresaw a great dimming, and he is called The Eater of Light."

"What would you have us do, grandfather?" asked Mark.

"I will summon the seers at once and compare their sight with the riddle of the map," declared Leonolis.

After the seers had been ushered into the throne room, King Leonolis instructed Mark to tell them all the children had experienced since entering Bren that day and all he could remember of the riddle. While he told the tale, the five seers of Bren went into a trance-like state, as if meditating on the boy's every word. With a flurry of words and with great detail, Mark weaved a very clear picture of all that had taken place. No sooner had he concluded than the seer, Adolphus, began to speak.

In a hushed tone, yet full of passion, Adolphus said, "Even now, Luminaud goes about marauding, eating the life of the Bairns of Bren. Lo, he doth dim the light from the north, but I see this darkness he would spread from north to south and from east to west ... quenching the very light and life of Bren..."

His words trailed into silence. Leonolis waited for Adolphus to continue. He waited ... and he waited ... and then he could wait no more. "Good seer, Adolphus! There must be more! Surely this cannot be all you have seen."

The five wise men of Bren whispered in their tight circle. A few seconds later, Adolphus turned to the King and opened his mouth as if he were about to speak, but nothing came out.

"What is it, Adolphus?" implored Leonolis. "What is it?"

"Good King, I ... I ... hesitate to speak what we have seen in the presence of ... in the presence of ..." He glanced toward the children. "In the presence of your precious grandchildren."

"Dear Adolphus, these indeed are my grandchildren, but they are much more than that! These are the mighty Bairns of Bren—those who were foretold of in the echoes of heroes past. They have been summoned by the Founders for such a time as this. They *must* hear. So speak, good seer. Speak."

Reluctantly at first, Adolphus spoke. "Sire, this day have we seen the light of children being consumed by the evil one —by Luminaud. Though we have not seen faces of particular children, no children—not even the grandchildren of the King and Queen of Bren—are safe. Many will be lost should the children of the land not be protected."

"And how might we protect the children of Bren from such a beast?" asked the King.

"What we have seen, sire, is that to consume the light of a child, the dragon must be in close proximity to a child. We must do whatever is necessary to ensure that no child comes within breathing distance of the beast. We advise that the children of the land be taken into hiding."

"Where do we hide the children of Bren that would be safe from the beast until we have found a way to defeat him?" asked Leonolis.

"We have discerned that Luminaud cannot consume light through stone. Yet mere stone houses will prove no match for nor can they withstand the sheer size of the beast and will prove defenseless against the massive strength of the monster and will be crumpled by one swipe of his mighty forepaw!"

"Please tell me there is a way to protect the children beyond fortifying an entire nation's stone houses," implored the King.

"There is a way ..." began Adolphus.

"Yes! Yes! Please go on!" urged Leonolis.

"There is only one way to defeat the beast. Only one way to slay the monster."

"Please tell us, good Adolphus! Time is of the essence where the lives of our children are concerned and where the future of Bren is concerned!" said the King.

"Luminaud is the Eater of Light and can only be defeated if he himself is consumed with light. And that light can only be wielded by one with the faith of a child. This was prophesied in days of old by Christophe the Atoner, who said, 'On the day of the Eater of Light, one will rise up from the unseen realm with the Sword called Lumen's Hammer, the great sword of victory, that which was used to send the Liar back to the Pit of Darkness, that which was wielded by the Victor, the Light-bearer, the one called Lumen. Only a child may bear this sword. Only a childlike faith may find the sword. Only by a child can the armor of the Great Dragon be pierced."

Adolphus continued, "There is a way to protect the children until the day of Lumen's Hammer. Actually, there are several steps in the process, each providing but a portion of what is needed. Luminaud cannot consume what he cannot smell. We have seen this. Since he cannot consume life through solid stone, we have seen that the refuge of our children is to be found in the depths of the Great Cavern of the North."

"The Great Cavern of the North?" asked King Leonolis, incredulously. "That is precisely where Luminaud is said to be! We will never be able to get all the children there safely, Adolphus! We will be leading them right to their demise ... right into his realm!"

"Sire, there is a way through. A way around, if you will," continued the seer.

"How so?" asked the King.

"We will lead the children by night in the cover of darkness."

"Will the beast not sense their presence?" asked Leonolis.

"Not if their scent is disguised. It has long been known that the very scent of the orchid called Dragon's Breath Lily can be used to mask human odor. I will instruct the Royal Chemists to produce vials of the elixir throughout the realm, to be taken to the household of every child in the Kingdom. And there is one more thing that may be of use, sire. The very essence of Bren's own Phrygian crystal has been proven to diminish the powers and senses of such a beast. With each household's delivery of Dragon's Breath elixir, we will also distribute a bag containing a piece of Phrygian crystal to further diminish the senses of the dragon."

Facing the other wise men, Leonolis asked, "Do you agree with the plan?" Each of the four seers nodded in silent approval of what Adolphus had spoken.

"Make it so, Adolphus!"

With that command, the five seers of Bren set about concocting the Dragon's Breath elixir while Leonolis instructed the head of the Royal Mining Corps to set about devising a national plan for delivery of a stone of Phrygian crystal to each child-rearing household in the land.

They had stood silently until all instructions had been given, but now the children began to speak. "Grandfather, where do we look for Lumen's Hammer?" asked Mark.

"Grandfather, we need to find the other children!" demanded Elliott.

"Grandfather, we must go at once and collect Dragon's Breath Lilies!" pled Matilda.

"Grandfather, I can ring my bell and summon help!" said Annabell excitedly, reaching for it.

"Grandfather, I'm hungry, and I need to pee!" chimed in Ron.

Laughing even in the midst of the dire circumstances, the King once again reached out with open arms and beckoned the children in for a group hug. "I am so grateful to the Founders that they gave me grandchildren like you! You make me very, very happy!"

"Why do we make you so happy, grandfather?" asked Ron.

"I'm so happy because ... just because."

"Just because why, grandfather?"

His eyes glistening with tears, Leonolis said, "Just because you exist."

After a few seconds of awkward, wonderful lovey-dovey-ness, the King and his grandchildren went to work. Leonolis commanded them in the use of their gifts.

"Annabell! Ring that bell!"

"Mark, ask the animal realm of any news of the dragon!"

"Matilda, prepare your arrows!"

"Elliott, prepare to transport us to the last place you were with the other children!"

As the kids set about to comply with the wishes of their grandfather, they joined hands, Elliott taking Ron's, Ron taking Annabell's, Annabell taking Matilda's, Matilda taking Mark's, and Mark taking his grandfather's. When Leonolis was ready, he looked to each child for a nod of readiness. One by one, they all gave their consent. Elliott looked to Grandfather Leonolis, he gave her the go-ahead, and they were gone!

6

THE PEOPLE OF LIGHT

*T*he children who had ventured down the tunnel to the right—Harry, Abigail, and Mia—had set out tentatively at first. Mia led the way since she could send out small bolts of lightning from her fingertips to illuminate the path. Rather than having to keep sending out individual bursts, which required very intense concentration, she quickly discovered out of necessity that she could simply focus her index finger and produce a small steady beam of light. With that realization, Mia's confidence began to soar, which bolstered the confidence of Abbie and Harry.

"Where do you think this leads, Mia?" asked Abigail.

"I have absolutely no idea, but this is our only option," replied Mia.

Harry, feeling cheerful and as happy as the girls knew

him to normally be, said, "Cousins, we have nothing to fear if you think about it."

"What do you mean?" asked the girls.

"Well, if we have been summoned to the land of Bren, we are meant to be here. If we trust the Founders and the map and the wolves and the gnome of the map, we were led down this path for a reason. And that reason is to ... somehow save Bren, so why worry when we are being led by the magic of the Founders?" replied Harry with little-boy seriousness.

"Let's keep walking," urged Mia. "We won't get there if we don't take the next step."

"And the next and the next and the next ..." teased Abigail.

"Wait a minute! I thought Cullen was coming with us!" exclaimed Harry.

"Didn't his wolf lead down the tunnel to the right? Isn't he supposed to be with us?" Mia asked, worriedly.

Running back the direction they had just come from, Harry began to cry out for his brother. "Cullen! Cullen! Cullen!" He listened intently for his brother's response. Nothing.

Again he shouted, "Cullen! Where are you? Cullen! Cullen! Culllllllllllll-ennnnnnnn!"

"Could he have run ahead of us?" asked Abigail.

"No! He was the last to choose, and I *know* he chose the right passageway. I definitely heard him say, 'And I feel I am to go to the *right*!'" said Mia.

"Why isn't he here? Why would he not be with us?" implored Harry.

"I do not know," began Mia, "but I do know we should not go back any further. Listen. Do you hear that?"

Straining to hear what it could be that Mia was hearing, Abigail and Harry exclaimed in unison: "Luminaud!"

Echoing from the lair of Luminaud all the way down the tunnel system and the three passageways, the snorts and snarls and gnashing teeth and scraping talons of the ranting and raging beast could be heard, sending shivers up and down the spines of the children.

"What do we do?" Harry asked.

"Remember what you just said, Harry? 'If we have been summoned to the land of Bren, we are meant to be here. If we trust the Founders and the map and the wolves and the gnome of the map, we were led down this path for a reason. And that reason is to somehow save Bren, so why worry when we are being led by the magic of the Founders?' We have no choice but to believe Cullen has been summoned to another mission. That makes the most sense. I say let us believe that until we are told otherwise. Let's continue. Come on."

With a heavy heart yet determined in purpose, the trio made their way deeper into the recesses of the tunnel, and their eyes grew accustomed to their surroundings. When they had first entered the hollow passageway, the walls seemed rough yet smooth, the way a canyon wall looks after millennia of the effects of wind and water eroding away solid rock and leaving the emptiness of the tunnel in its place. The farther their feet carried them, the more the tunnel surfaces appeared to change.

The children thought *how odd that the water could have created a series of steps ... how odd that the water eroded the rock into the shape of a bench ... how odd that the cave walls appear to have been smoothed so completely as to appear purposely shined ... enough to reflect one's face back at them like a mirror.*

"Is anyone else seeing what I am seeing?" asked Harry.

"If you mean the roughness of the pathway being replaced by a hand-carved walkway, complete with steps, then yes!" said Mia.

"If you mean how every few steps there is a bench seemingly chiseled purposely into the cavern wall and that the wall itself seems to have been polished so well as to see my reflection, then, heck yeah!" exclaimed Abigail.

While the children marveled at the transformation of the cave around them, Harry sat on one of the benches and said, "Come on! Let's rest a bit!"

Without a moment's hesitation, the girls joined their cousin on the bench and took a much-needed break from their travels. As they sat there, they began to talk of all they had just experienced, from the initial hugs from Papa Lee and grandma Mellie, to the tickle-pile and tangled limbs with the other children, which made them giggle and snicker all over again, to the events surrounding their escape from Luminaud.

After a few minutes of conversation, their attention came back to the present.

"I wonder where the other tunnels led to?" asked Abigail.

"I hope the others are safe," said Mia.

"Maybe they have found help by now," added Harry.

"I wonder why we were not supposed to take the middle passageway," pondered Abigail.

" I wonder who built this bench," Harry said.

"I wonder why it is still light enough to see since Mia stopped with the lightning routine," said Abigail.

Mia, mouth open in shocked amazement, said, "I didn't even realize I had stopped! What? How?"

Pointing toward the source of the light ahead, Harry excitedly shouted, "There! There! There!"

As the girls turned to look, the light suddenly began to bounce around the cavern, spinning and twisting and turning and spiraling and careening from side to side, the way a laser pointer darts about the room when teasing a cat! While they watched, the light headed toward them as it continued its cavorting about the cave, the shiny wall giving the affect of a fireworks display on the Fourth of July or that of a strobe light at a dance! Suddenly, the light came to hover just in front of and slightly above the children.

"What is it?" asked Abigail.

"It looks like a tiny star," said Mia.

"It *does* look like a star!" said Harry.

"What should we do?" asked Abigail.

"I say we watch it and wait," added Mia.

Before Mia could reach out to stop him, Harry stood and said, "I want to touch it!"

"No, Harry!" said Mia.

"Stop, Harry!" cried out Abigail.

While the girls reached for their cousin, Harry's finger brushed the outer aura of the light. The trio was suddenly knocked back onto the bench! Stunned into silence, the children felt as if they had been picked up by an unseen hand and placed on their behinds. Though the fall had taken place in the blink of an eye, they had felt no pain. Only comfort, peace, security and ... welcome?

Before they dared utter a word (they were too shocked to say anything anyway), the light began to grow. Before their eyes, the most brilliant light any of them had ever seen began to dazzle and glow and grow! Dumbfounded, not by fear, but in amazement and wonder, the children sat, eyes fixed on the light. If they had not been to Bren before, none of them would have believed what was unfolding. Still, they had never seen anything like this—not even in Bren!

Like an exploding star, yet contained in the smallness of the cavern, the little light grew and grew and grew! In its expansion, the light began to take shape. At first, it appeared to form a star, but then began to take the form of a person! Back and forth, from star shape to person shape, from person shape to star shape, the light went! After several moments of shape-shifting glorious brilliant display, the light froze in the shape of a girl! Though now glowing with blinding brilliance, her form seemed to fill the room with light, yet the children could gaze upon her and see her clearly!

For a few seconds, the girl simply stared, as if in wonder herself at the sight of the children, while the children stared back in wonder at her. Breaking the silence and startling the children, she said, "Welcome, daughters of Bren! Welcome, son of Bren! Welcome, Bairns of Bren!"

As if following some formal protocol, Harry awkwardly bowed and said, "Greetings ... light-person ... cave girl ... daughter of ... the tunnel. I am Harry, son of Bren."

Giggling at their cousin's boyish awkwardness, Abigail and Mia stood and said in unison as if rehearsed, "Hello, we are Mia and Abigail, daughters of Bren."

"I am Ariel, star child of the enchanted land of Galaxia—the world within the world, the land within the land of Bren. We have been expecting you, Bairns of Bren."

Unable to stop himself, Harry blurted out, "Star child! Your parents are stars! Whoa! How cool is that?!" Turning to his cousins, he said, "So cool, right?! So cool!"

"Harry!" scolded Mia. "Not the time! Not appropriate! Remember your manners! What would Grandfather say?"

At that, Harry composed himself, but Ariel broke into the awkwardness of the moment and saved face for the now red-faced and put-in-his-place boy. "Indeed, I am the child of the stars. I am of the race of stars called The Nova. We Nova are given breath in the heavens, the outer realms of the universe, and we are light-beings. We are also known as light bearers. We carry the light of the Founders to dark places in need of light."

Feeling confident once again, Harry blurted out, "Man, are we in need of light *now!*"

"More than you know, Bairn of Bren. More than you know," responded Ariel. "And what do they call you, boy."

"Harry, er, Harold is my real name, but just call me Harry."

"Come, Harry. Come, Mia. Come, Abigail. The place you have ventured this day is the Portal of Light. You call it a tunnel or a cave, but we fashioned this passageway as a portal between our two worlds. Our world within the world is called Galaxia. It is the home of The Nova in the land of Bren, much like Bren is the world within the world you call Earth."

As they followed Ariel, the children asked many questions.

Abigail asked, "Are you a fairy? You seem like fairies we have known in Bren!"

"No, but we are often mistaken for fairies," chuckled Ariel. "Actually, we are more like what you might call shape-shifters. We are able to take on the form of any being we come in contact with in order to set others at ease. We find people or beings relate better to their own kind. We hope to be all things to all kinds."

"Do stars have their own language? You speak English quite well," added Mia.

"Yes, a language of sorts. What you call beams or rays of light are actually words spoken in our language. One of the abilities of being a light bearer is the ability to understand and speak the language of those we meet. The only language we cannot and do not and will not speak is that of darkness. The Nova cannot speak the words of darkness."

"How is it that you speak only light but you know of the darkness in the land of Bren?" asked Harry.

"Although The Nova cannot be consumed by darkness, there has come one—a Light Eater—who threatens our land..."

Before Ariel could complete her explanation, Abigail interjected, "Luminaud!"

"Yes! Luminaud, Eater of Light! Although we cannot be consumed as a people, the red dragon is slowly consuming the light we bring to Bren. The Founders summoned us to bring light to the land of Bren very long ago. As a symbol of that light, a warrior of Bren, Lumen the Victor, was given a great weapon called Lumen's Hammer. This sword was endowed with the power of the stars. Lumen used that weapon to liberate the land of Bren long ago. Though he gave his own life to save the world, the sword remains. It is said that Lumen rose to life and passed the power to wield the sword to the Bairns of Bren. Only Lumen's Hammer can defeat the power of this present darkness."

"Where is the sword? We are Bairns of Bren! Where is it?

54

Show us and we will use it to take down the dragon!" said Mia.

"I am afraid the Bairns of Bren lost the sword long ago. The sword still remains. We Nova sense it but cannot wield it since the Founders forged it for the Bairns of Bren. It has been spoken of among my people that one day three Bairns of Bren would seek passage through the Portal of Light, and here you are," replied Ariel.

"Where was it lost?" asked Abigail. "How do we find it?"

"It will be found by the spoken word," said Ariel. "It will be wielded by the firstborn child of a Bairn of Bren. A grand-child of a King. A servant of men."

The wheels of her mind turning wildly at the words of the light bearer, Mia began to try and solve the mystery of the prophecy out loud. "The firstborn of the firstborn of the Bairns of Bren? Could it be King Leonolis? My grandfather?"

"It cannot be Leonolis since he himself is King," said Ariel.

"Could it be my father?" queried Mia.

"The prophecy says he will be the son of the King, perhaps the son of a son, perhaps the son of a daughter of the King. It is for the Founders in their wisdom to unravel the mystery. He or she who finds the sword will be the one and same who is able to wield the sword," responded Ariel.

"Where do we even begin searching for something that has not been see for thousands of years?" asked Abigail.

"It will be found in the darkest of times, in the darkest of perils, beneath the darkest of hearts, in the midst of darkness itself. Whoever finds and is able to wield the Hammer will be the one who dares face darkness itself. It will be found when the proper word has been spoken. Only the proper word can find and release the power of Lumen's Hammer," prophesied Ariel.

"Then tell us the word and we will speak it!" declared Harry.

"The word is in the heart of those who seek the Founders. The word will be written upon the heart of the Bairns of Bren. The word will be revealed in the darkest hour. The word, though unknown, is known," said the light bearer.

As only Harry could do, he uttered, "What the heck?!"

Suddenly, Ariel spoke, "Zella comes. We must go to her and to your grandmother at once!"

7

OVER THE DARK MOUNTAINS

*A*riel led the children out of the tunnel and into a land of brilliant light. The sky was vividly blue as one would expect after having been confined to the dim light of a tunnel, but this sky was even more vivid and blue than the children had ever seen. Like a colorblind child who puts on special glasses and sees color for the first time, Mia, Abigail, and Harry saw the sky and felt a bit overwhelmed — as if they had never seen the sky before!

As their eyes adjusted and they gazed toward the heavens, the sky was not the only thing that appeared more vivid to them. They saw trees and hills and flowers and deer grazing in a meadow and people milling about the pathway they walked along, but everything had an aura about it. A glow. Wherever they looked, they saw it.

Harry broke through the silence and wonder. "Everything glows! The trees glow! The grass glows! The hills and deer glow! The stream over there glows. And the people! The *people* are glowing!"

"Yes! Yes! Yes! I see it, too!" exclaimed Mia.

"Me, too! Me, too! I see it! Everything glows! It's simply *beautiful!*" said Abigail with a shout.

"Why is everything so bright?" asked Mia.

Laughing to herself, Ariel said, "Welcome to Galaxia, land of The Nova. We are the people of light. Long ago my ancestors came to the land of Bren, summoned by the Founders to be guardians of the light—a sort of buffer between the darkness and the people of Bren. Especially to and for the Bairns of Bren."

"What does that even mean?" asked Mia.

"Well, it means that we are to be conduits of and vessels of light to the world and to the land of Bren. We are created by the Founders for the specific purpose of reminding Bren to always seek the light," explained Ariel.

"You mean, you are like angels?" quizzed Abigail.

"I suppose, for lack of a better term, yes! We are like what you might call angels. Yet, unlike angels, we are a race of beings that marry and have children and families just like the people of Bren. We are mostly unseen by humans."

"So how are we able to see you? We are humans!" interrupted Harry.

"Yes! Yes! Of course you are humans! But we only reveal

ourselves as needed, and I am afraid in times like these, it is needed," replied Ariel.

"What do you mean 'times like these'?" asked Mia.

"Dear Bairns of Bren, in times of threat of darkness. Luminaud is a child of the darkness, feeding on the light of life. You are children of the prophecies of old. You see me—us —now because the Founders have willed it," said Ariel. "As part of that prophecy, it has also been foretold that the Bairns of Bren would one day recover and restore Lumen's Hammer and overcome the darkness once again. According to all I have seen this day, since you first entered the Portal of Light, it can only be as part of the fulfilling of that ancient word that you are even here ... that you can even see me now."

"Then what are we to do? What does the prophecy say we are to do?" implored Mia.

"As I have already told you, a child will lead them. A word spoken will reveal and release the Hammer. A word unknown yet known. A word written upon the heart of the child," said Ariel.

"Which of us is the child? How will we know the right word? How can we know something that is unknown?" queried Mia.

"In time, dear children. In time it will be revealed. The word is life and the word is born of light. You will know what that word is when the time has come, when the word is spoken in faith," said Ariel. "Come, Bairns. We have no more time to waste. I sense Zella has need of us. Need of you."

While the children stood there, mouths agape in wonder at what those words truly meant, Ariel gently scolded them. "What are you doing standing there?! We must find Zella at once!"

Running after the Nova girl, Mia called out, "We are coming, Ariel! We are coming!"

While they walked along the path through the countryside of Galaxia, each child wished and hoped they could linger and take in all the sights and sounds and smells and wonder of the fantastical land they now journeyed through. Yet their desire to save the land of Bren and to find their cousins and siblings compelled them to keep moving. While they followed Ariel, the children continued to ask her questions.

"How do you know we need to find Zella? She is back in Oklahoma with Papa Lee!" shouted Harry.

"I have heard her true name," responded Ariel, matter-of-factly.

"What do you mean you 'heard her true name'?" asked Abigail.

"Do you not know? Each human, every Bairn of Bren that has ever been or ever will be, was spoken into existence by the Founders. Each person has their own unique name."

"What is my name?" asked Harry.

"What is my name?" asked Mia.

"And mine? Don't forget my name, Ariel!" shouted Abigail.

"You each already know your true name. It was written upon your heart the moment of your conception. Search your hearts, dear Bairns of Bren. Search your hearts," said Ariel earnestly.

As if the children had suddenly been placed in a walking trance, they began to search their hearts for the name that spoke them into existence. Magically, each was fully cognizant and aware of Ariel and able to fully fix their eyes on her and follow, yet they were somehow able to walk along the pathways of their minds and memories back to the moment they first became aware they were alive.

"My name is Peace-Warrior!" exclaimed Harold.

"You have heard well, son of Bren," assured Ariel.

"And mine is My-Beloved-Daughter!" shouted Mia.

"How did you do that?!" said the exasperated Abigail. "I can't hear anything!"

"Be patient, dear Abigail. It is there, even now. Don't try so hard. It is indeed there," assured Ariel.

Taking the advice of the star girl, Abigail simply trusted that she would hear when the time was right. And within seconds she exclaimed, "I heard it! I *heard* my name!"

"What is it?!" asked both Harry and Mia, excitedly.

"*My* name is Daughter-of-Joy!" exclaimed Abigail.

And just like that, the children walked with greater confidence than they ever had before. It was as if they had suddenly become aware of something they had somehow known all along —something from somewhere deeper inside they had ever

61

thought conceivable or possible! It was as if speaking the name spoke in volumes of life! Of light! As if somehow, some way, their words and names and declarations had leapt from the written pages of their hearts right into the reality of whom they were!

While they pondered these things in their hearts, Ariel stopped. "Let us rest here."

"Rest?" asked Harry. "We just started!"

"Son of Bren, we have been walking for hours," Ariel said. "Even now we have begun our ascent up the passageway through the northern Dark Mountains of Abysstine. We have much farther to go once we have reached the summit. To the south we must go.

"We've been walking for hours?" asked the confused Abigail.

"No way!" exclaimed Mia. "You just told us to listen for our true names!"

"That is to be expected," laughed Ariel.

"What does that mean?" asked Mia.

"It simply means that when exposed to the light of Truth, the human mind transcends time for brief amounts of ... time," Ariel tried to explain.

"Huh?" sighed Harry.

"When infused with the light—when the word written on one's heart is finally spoken—that truth tends to overwhelm the human mind ... in a good way," Ariel said.

"In an *amazing* way!" agreed Harry.

"In the most *beautiful* way!" agreed Abigail.

"In a *timeless* way!" punned Mia.

"Yes. One could say that you have been operating on two levels at the same time. The levels of time and the level of the absence of time the level of human eyes juxtaposed with the eyes of the Founders. You have been here while you have been there," responded Ariel.

"Wherever 'there' is, I *like!*" said Mia, and the other children nodded their agreement.

"You can do this anytime you like, children. Anytime you need, you can operate between the world of Bren and the world of the timeless. The Founders are not hindered by either, choosing to step into the world of Bren from time to time, but always maintaining a foot in the timeless. This is another reason we Nova are here. We are always waiting for and watching over the Bairns of Bren, ready to speak words of light into the atmosphere through a dream or through a breeze or through the occasional 'I-wonder-where-that-thought-just-came-from' kind of thought."

"I've *had* those!" exclaimed Harry. "I've *had* those!" He looked at Ariel in astonishment. "That was *you?!*"

At Harry's words, Ariel burst into a fit of laughter, joined by the girls and Harry too! "It was not always me, but there have been a couple of times when it *was* me speaking words of light into your dreams and even one of those 'I-wonder-where-that-thought-just-came-from' kind of thoughts!

Remember the time you heard, 'Do not eat the cookie. Give it to the sad girl'?"

"Yes! yes! I gave the little girl my cookie, and it made her feel better. You mean *that was you*?!"

"Indeed, that was me!" laughed Ariel.

After their laughter at Harry's outburst died down, Ariel urged the children to resume their trek. Upward and upward and ever more upwardly, the Nova girl led the three young children. The higher they trudged, the steeper the incline and the more difficult it became to breathe. The higher they climbed, the mistier and the foggier the air became, making it difficult to see much of anything other than a few feet in front of their faces. If the path had not been well worn, they would not have known if they were even on the trail.

By now, the four travelers had stopped talking except for the occasional "Watch your step" or "Are we there yet?", giving an eerie silence to the scene. Trudge, trudge, trudge, trudge was all the children could hear besides the sound of their own labored gasps for breath. And then they heard something silently float above their heads. More than hear it, they could sense they were suddenly not alone. Like the sound of a cape flying behind one's shoulder on a breezy autumn day, the sound fluttered somewhere above, again passing directly over their heads.

Ariel stopped. Having already sensed something was not right, the children crowded around the star girl and froze,

THE LIGHT EATER

silently straining their ears to hear. They waited. And they waited. And they waited. Finally, Ariel spoke.

"Who goes there? Reveal yourself!"

And they waited again.

"I said, 'Who goes there? Reveal yourself!' I know you are there. I sense it!"

With a sudden flurry and flutter, the misty fog above their heads began to swoosh and swirl as if a small tornado had descended upon them. As the children cowered closer toward Ariel, the fluttering and flurrying drew closer and began to take shape. Watching in horror, having never seen but having heard the tales, the children recognized the being before his talons had even touched the ground.

"Chiroptera!" shouted Mia. The children had all heard the stories of this bat-like race of the northern mountains and their taste for owls and children, although the chiroptera would deny ever having eaten one child.

While the children crowded in behind Ariel, the creature began to speak in a birdlike, chirpy voice. "It is I, fair star maiden. My name is Averichi, watcher of the heights of the Dark Mountains. I should be asking *you* who goes there!"

"Who we are is of no concern to you," replied Ariel, curtly.

"Then who I am should be of no concern to you, should it?" reasoned the creature.

"Good and noble Averichi, watcher of the heights," said Ariel as she tried to appease the beast, "we are about the busi-

65

ness of the Founders. Please grant us safe passage to the southern route toward Castle Aerie. Even now, the throne awaits word of the darkness close at hand."

"What darkness do you speak of?" chirped the chiroptera.

"Even now, the land is being laid to waste by the ravages of a Light Eater..." began the star girl.

Interrupting Ariel, Averichi gasped, "Luminaud! It is true then! Luminaud is risen from his slumber and even now this way comes!"

"Yes! Luminaud!" agreed Ariel. "But how do you know?"

"Our young have been vanishing. One moment they are with us and the next—without warning—they are no more! Our elders have discerned the signs and the signs all point to Luminaud! Such evil could be by no other hand than that of the Light Eater!"

Stepping out from behind Ariel, Mia boldly said, "It is true, good Averichi. Even this day have my sister and cousins borne witness to the red dragon! This very day have we barely escaped his evil light-eating clutches. We are sent of the Founders to alert the High King Leonolis even now! All children of the land, both beast and human, are at peril. We must be allowed to continue our journey, sir, and would dare ask you to take word to your elders that what they have seen is..."

But Averichi was already gone. All the children heard was the flapping of wings and a faint echo, "You may pass..."

Without wasting another moment, the four set off again,

not realizing they had merely been a few steps from the summit of the pass. What had taken so much of their energy and breath in the uphill climb was now quickly replaced by the steep downhill grade and the quickening of steps in the downward trajectory, spirits buoyed by the knowledge they would have no more trouble with the dreaded chiroptera this day!

8

WHAT ABOUT CULLEN?

$\mathcal{W}$hile the other children had found their ways to Castle Aerie and to Galaxia and were relatively safe, Cullen had no clue where he was or where his siblings and cousins might be. All he knew was that his prayer for guidance had been answered. His heart cheered by the welcome light of the tiny flitting creature, Cullen sang aloud, almost skipping along the tunnel as he sang.

> Joy! Joy!
> I just spoke the word!
> Joy! Joy!
> Somebody heard!

Cullen found himself buoyed by the seeming answer to his prayer as he sang the words to his little made up ditty over and over, again and again, until the tiny glowing creature stopped in midair, hovering directly in front of the his nose. The creature lunged at the tip of his nose and spit at him. Cullen could have sworn he spoke the faintest raspy "Stop!" as if to say, "Stop that infernal singing, boy!"

It still didn't occur to Cullen that the creature he was being led by was not a firefly until the next moment when the creature spit again, only this time the sound came out in the form of a tiny burst of fire, striking Cullen right on the tip of his nose!

"Ouch!" exclaimed Cullen. " Why did you do that?"

Rather than answering the boy, the creature turned and flitted ahead once again.

"Wait!" insisted Cullen. "I am not taking another step until you tell me why you spit fire at me!"

Stopping once again, the creature flitted back toward the boy at full speed, stopping once again just before his nose, and spit fire! But this time, Cullen was ready. He swatted the creature, sending it crashing to the cave floor.

"What is wrong with you, firefly?" asked Cullen.

Shaking its tiny head, the creature slowly flapped its wings and spoke in the tiniest raspy voice Cullen had ever heard.

"I am no firefly, silly boy! Do not *ever* call me such a disgusting name again or ... I'll..."

"You'll what?" dared the boy.

"Or you will see soon enough, vile Bairn of Bren!"

"Why, you are not a firefly at all! You're ... you're ... a ... *dragonfly!*"

Cullen's joyful, cheerful attitude suddenly became fear and dread and hopelessness. How could the Founders have led him astray like this? Why would the Founders do such a thing? Even as his mind raced, he forced himself to think, "What would Papa Lee do?" and his mind immediately began to calm. He knew, first of all, that Papa Lee would never believe the Founders were anything but good. He knew his Papa would never believe the Founders wanted anything but what was best for him. And above all else, He knew Papa Lee would say, "Son, we may not get to choose the things that tempt us and we may not get to choose our circumstances, but we *always* have a choice as to how we should respond to them, so choose wisely. What you think will determine how you feel. Choose truth."

Even as Cullen encouraged his own heart, the dragonfly righted himself and tried to get airborne again. Flapping and flitting and grunting and groaning, the dragonfly could not manage to fly. Rather pathetically, he was only able to make it a few inches before crashing in a heap on the cavern floor.

Calmly and matter-of-factly, Cullen said, "One of your wings is broken."

"*You* broke it, you human imbecile! *You* did this to me!" shouted the dragonfly in an even higher pitched voice.

"I was only defending myself from your angry little outburst! *You* burned me, insect!" came Cullen's retort.

"You will pay for this! You will pay, boy!" returned the dragonfly. "Just wait until he hears of what you have done! Just you wait! You're going to be so sorry you ever laid a hand on me, vile boy!"

"Just who is the 'he' you are referring to? asked Cullen.

As if he had mistakenly shared a secret he had been sworn to keep, the dragonfly said, "Oh, I meant, I meant to say ... uh ... er ... um ... I simply was referring to the one I work for."

"And just who do you work for?" asked the boy.

"That is not your concern!" replied the creature.

"I suppose it is of great concern if the one you work for is the one you lead me toward," responded Cullen.

"I do nothing of the sort!" replied the dragonfly. "I merely saw you floundering for the entrance to the tunnel and thought you needed my ... guidance ... yes! You needed my guidance! I am only trying to help you."

Thinking quickly, Cullen said, "Then I have you to thank for guiding me down the right-most tunnel!"

Sensing the boy had fallen for his lie, the dragonfly proudly corrected him. "Oh no! No! No! I led you down the tunnel in the middle just as he told me to..."

Before he could catch himself, the creature gasped at his own mistake and covered his tiny dragonfly mouth with his tiny dragonfly forefeet in bewilderment.

"Oh! Oh my! What have I done?!" groaned the dragonfly.

"You work for *Him*! Don't you?" quizzed the boy. You

were sent by Luminaud! I mistakenly assumed you were a firefly sent to guide me. You are just doing the evil bidding of an evil creature! The Light Eater sent you for me, didn't he?!"

The little dragonfly just sat there stunned, his tiny dragonfly mouth opened wide in shock and amazement at the boy's words.

"Say something, creature! Don't just sit there. You might as well be honest with me because I am not taking another step until you tell me the truth," said Cullen.

Hesitating, the dragonfly quietly began. "Yes, it is true. Luminaud, Eater of Light, summoned me to persuade the Bairns of Bren to follow me to a place of his choosing, but even that I have failed at. I was supposed to lead you all to him, but was only able to bring you along while the others eluded me."

Feeling a tinge of compassion for the dragonfly and remembering the words of his grandfather, "Kindness goes a long way in reaching the heart of another," Cullen gently spoke to the creature, anger now gone from him.

"Dragonfly, do you have a name?" asked the boy.

"Why, yes I do," spoke the wounded creature.

"What is it?" asked Cullen.

"They call me ... they call me ... Little White Lie," responded the dragonfly.

"Why do they call you that?" asked Cullen.

"Because I love to play jokes on others, pretending to be hurt or pretending to be in trouble or pretending to be someone else only to spring out in surprise at whomever it is I am trying to trick. It is all quite in fun, but after a while, that was how my name became Little White Lie."

"So, Little White Lie is not your given name?" asked the boy.

"Why, no, it is not," said the creature sheepishly.

"Please tell me your given name, creature," said Cullen.

As if embarrassed or perhaps because it had been so long since he had even heard his real name spoken by another, Little White Lie answered, "My given name is Verona."

"And do you know what the meaning of your name is?" wisely asked Cullen.

"It means 'True Image' in the language of my people," said the dragonfly.

"Then I shall call you Verona. Verona is a very good name, and where I come from, there is a saying that goes, 'A good name is more to be desired than great riches,' so there! It is settled."

Instantly, the attitude of Verona went from anger and embarrassment and frustration to peace and humility and acceptance of the boy. "You are not at all as I was told," said Verona.

"What were you told?" asked the boy.

"Only that you of the human race were vile, wicked, stupid creatures who needed to be completely rooted out and eradicated. Nothing more, nothing less," said Verona, matter-of-factly. "But now I see you are capable of wisdom and kindness. Do you know how long it has been since I heard my name called? Do you know what it means to be treated with simple kindness?"

Without waiting for permission, Cullen bent down and scooped up Verona in both hands, holding him gently as he brought the tiny fire breather toward his face. Holding Verona near the nose he had just brought so much pain to, the boy said, "Let me get a closer look at that wing." Eyeing and squinting and examining the little wing by the light of the dragonfly, Cullen said, "I don't think your wing is actually broken, Verona. It appears to be simply bent."

"This is wonderful news! This is good news!" squeaked Verona. "This means I will be able to fly after a few hours of rest. The wonderful thing about a bent wing is that, with rest and plenty of fluids, it will mend itself! Wonderful! Wonderful ... uh ...er," he stopped at the realization that he did not know the boy's name. "What do they call *you*, Bairn of Bren?"

"My name is Cullen," replied the boy.

"And what does the name Cullen mean?" asked Verona.

Laughing out loud, the boy said, "My name actually means 'handsome lad'!"

Taking a serious look at the boy's face, Verona simply shrugged and said, "Hhhmph! I don't really see it, but to your race I suppose that may be true."

Laughing, Cullen asked, "What do we do now, Verona?

Where were you to lead me, and better yet, why were you to lead me there?"

"I am afraid I was sent to lead you to his northern lair. A place beneath the waters of Menden Lake, reachable only two ways. The way we go now leads to one entrance while the other can only be entered by way of a swim ... an entrance submerged near the easternmost shore."

"Then let us go back from where we came, Verona," implored the boy.

"I am afraid we cannot, Cullen. When I led you in, the tunnel was sealed by dark magic behind us. I am afraid we can go but forward."

"There must be another way," insisted Cullen.

"If there is, I do not know of it," replied Verona.

"To go ahead is to lead me to certain death, Verona."

"To not go ahead leads me to mine," said Verona, sadly.

"What do you mean?" asked the boy.

"I did not wish for nor did I ask for this assignment. Though the race of dragonflies is associated with the nearness of dragons, we were created, according to the legends of old, to be sentries, those who warn the world about the presence of the terrible beasts. We were never intended to serve them. No! No! No! And even now, I do not do so willingly. You see, dear boy, Luminaud has taken my wife and eleven children captive, promising to release them unharmed only if I deliver the Bairns of Bren to him. I am afraid I will be considered a failure simply because I was able to only seduce one to follow me. I am doomed if I do and doomed if I don't deliver you to his wicked hand. But my greatest grief is over what this will mean for my own family!"

As Cullen thought about what Verona had just told him, he had a vision. He saw himself and Verona entering the northern lair of Luminaud that lie hidden beneath Menden Lake. He saw the wife and children of Verona locked away in a recess in one of the walls of the lair, directly behind the place Luminaud stood. Though he saw these things, he was not frightened at all. He knew this was merely a vision coming as a result of his gift. Then he heard a voice from somewhere around him. It simply said, "What is meant for evil, I will use for good."

"Did you hear that, Verona?" asked Cullen,

"Hear what?" asked the dragonfly.

"The voice!" exclaimed the boy.

"I heard nothing," replied Verona, eyeing the boy with a look that said 'Is he losing his mind?'

"It's going to be alright!" said Cullen. "We have nothing to fear."

"Nothing to fear?!" asked Verona, incredulously.

"We have only the most evil, vile, need I say, *giant* beast of a dragon to fear!" exclaimed Verona.

"I have seen that we are to proceed down the path you lead us on. I have seen your family being led to safety. I have seen this," replied Cullen.

"Are you mad? Have you lost your human mind? I see

nothing but darkness lying ahead! I see nothing but the anger and venom and death at the hand of the beast ahead, boy! How can you see anything other than this?!" implored Verona.

"Trust me, dear Verona. Trust me. I do not understand it myself, but somehow, some way, the Founders have bestowed to me the power to see visions and dream that help others through their own darkness. Even in the midst of chaos, I have come to know I can trust what I have seen."

"What do we do? How do we defeat him? How will my family be rescued? What do we do?" asked Verona.

"That part I have not seen, but I do know we must forge ahead. We have no reason to fear," said Cullen.

"Now it is I who will not be taking one more step forward. What you have seen is not even possible! I am but a tiny helpless dragonfly and you are merely a boy! He is a mighty beast who lives to draw the light of life from other creatures! I will not move! How do we know we can even trust the vision you have seen? How do we know we can trust the Founders?"

"If I tell you something you have not told me, something only known to you, would you trust me then?" asked the boy.

Thinking he had the boy cornered with logic, Verona said, "I will trust you ... then and only then."

In the darkness illuminated by the tiny light of the Dragonfly, Cullen sent his thoughts toward the Founders, and simply said, "Show me."

While Verona sat waiting in Cullen's palms, he expected Cullen to come to his senses. His smug demeanor was reduced to tiny dragonfly tears when Cullen simply said, "Your wife's name is Fidelia. And her name in your language means trust."

Verona sighed and replied, "Forward, brave Cullen. Let us go forward." And the two headed north toward Menden Lake.

9

THE ZEST OF ZELLA

$\mathcal{E}$ven though Zella had run back toward the outstretched arms of Papa Lee, overwhelmed by the pile of writhing cousins and siblings, she had determined she would rejoin the other children. She had run back to Papa Lee because she loved being with him ... loved the way his unconditional love made her feel ... and because she knew Grandma Mellie would do the same. In fact, truth be told, she had a special place in her heart for her grandmother. Not only did Mellie make her feel loved, but she also made her believe she could do anything.

Grandma Mellie was a strong woman. Strong in her faith and strong in demeanor. Nothing ever seemed to rattle grandmother; she never allowed fear to rule her choices or her identity. Mellie was strong emotionally and strong physically, yet she was the most feminine woman Zella knew. Deep in her heart of hearts, Zella longed to be just like her Grandma Mellie!

After a long embrace in the arms of her Papa Lee and after he had wiped away her tears, she opened her eyes and saw her G-ma—as her grandchildren fondly called her — standing there with *that* look in her eye. The look that spoke volumes without saying a word. The look that said "Zella, you've got this! Face your fears and dry those tears and go and find the other children." Running into her G-ma's arms, she hugged her tightly and said, "I've got to go, G-ma!"

Mellie replied, "I know, dear. Your task is at hand."

Running with all the speed her little legs could muster, Zella was already so much more like her Grandma Mellie than she realized. She had not given a single thought to fear as she ran through the pasture and through the gate and into the Forest of Bren. Knowing she had a "task at hand" filled her, once again, with a sense of wonder and destiny and purpose. Her eyes and her heart were so focused on the splendor and wonder of the magical land of Bren that she had no time for fear! In the forest set aside by her grandparents, her Papa Lee had instilled in her and the other children that it was Christmas all year round!

As she ran into the tunnel created by the canopy of the overlapping branches above her head, she did not even have to think about which way to go. Having been through the forest of Bren many times already, her imagination was set on the place she loved the best. She felt magical every time she saw it. She was filled with a sense of wonder and mystery whenever she set foot there. She ran down Cullen's Lane and onto Elliott's Avenue and around the twisting, turning path through the trees. Not caring about or even seeming to notice the storm clouds that were swirling above her now, the zestful glee Zella felt as she ran toward her favorite place of all carried her above and beyond and through the fear until she saw it!

There it stood. Like a beacon of light breaking through and overwhelming even such a dark, foreboding, cloudy day stood the most beautiful sight she had ever seen. There stood the proof of why Papa Lee said in his forest it was Christmas all year round. Papa Lee had told them how he and his children had discovered the lone cedar tree long ago ... how he and his children—their parents and their aunts and their uncles—had first decorated the tree when it was only a few feet tall.

Like looking back into the past, the higher her eyes gazed upon the tree, she could tell the ornaments upon those high branches appeared to be older and more weatherworn, less bright than those on the lower branches. Seeing the ornaments that had been placed there years before they were born made all the children feel they were a very real part of history. Part of something bigger and grander than their eyes could see or their minds could truly fathom. Seeing the wear and tear of the older ornaments never caused them to seem less beautiful in Zella's eyes. She saw past their ragged exterior into the beauty of the legacy of her past. And this legacy filled her with a deep longing to leave a legacy of her own! She recognized decorations on the lower branches that she had put there.

As the memories of decorating the tree unfolded in her mind, she could not help but see the mingling of the old and new as a reflection of her own life. In that moment, she looked into both the past and the future and gratitude filled her heart with joy. Just as she thought she would explode with the feeling of sheer unadulterated joy for joy's sake, she heard a familiar voice calling her name. It sounded at once like Grandma Mellie and Queen Abila!

"Zella! Zella, is that you?" asked Queen Abila.

"Grandmother! It is me! What are you doing here?" asked Zella.

"What are you doing here, dancing around Castle Aerie?" queried Abila.

So full of zest and joy at the feeling of Christmas all year round, Zella had not even noticed when she pranced around the cedar tree that that the tree had become the well in the courtyard of Castle Aerie! Sure enough, she was dancing around the well! She was in Bren! She was where her heart longed to be!

"Where are the children, Grandmother?" asked Zella

swaying in a standing still sort of dance, her legs unable to stop moving.

"They have joined your Grandfather, King Leonolis, for a quest!" replied Abila.

"What quest, Grandmother? What quest? I must join them!" exclaimed Zella.

"Even this day, a great beast has threatened doom upon the land of Bren. A great darkness has arisen in the form of a dragon called Luminaud—a Light Eater," explained her grandmother.

"A dragon that eats light?" responded Zella.

"Yes, he is a most terrible beast. He consumes the light of life of any living creature he comes in direct contact with, especially the light of children!" explained Abila.

"What is my task? You told me ... uh ... G-ma told me my task is at hand! This must be what you ... she ... meant!" said the girl.

"Just moments ago, Ron, Annabell, Matilda, Elliott, and Mark suddenly appeared in the throne room," said the Queen.

"Where are the others? What about Harry, Abigail, Mia, and Cullen?" Zella asked, worriedly.

"That is the question, dear Zella. That is the question," said Abila.

"I will join Grandfather and the children with him and search for them!" said Zella with zestful emphasis.

"That will not be possible, as they have already left on this quest," Abila replied.

"Then I will join them! Where have they gone?" implored Zella.

"I am afraid you cannot, dear Zella. They have transported by virtue of Elliott's gift to the last place the children were all together. Your quest appears to be of a different sort," replied the Queen to her granddaughter.

The conversation was interrupted by the voice of the seer, Adolphus. "Zella, come at once."

Without hesitation, Zella took the hand of Abila and followed the wise man of Bren into Castle Aerie and directly into the chamber of counsel—the place the King and Queen always gathered the wise men and women of Bren whenever there was a national emergency requiring it. A place Zella regarded with great reverence, since she had never been invited in but always knew important things were happening there. That sense of reverence was very heavy upon her heart as she walked in. The sense of reverent awe grew even greater as it dawned on her that she—a little girl—was about to be sent on a very important quest for the Kingdom of Bren!

"We have not much time, Zella the Zestful. Even this day have I heard the voice of the Founders saying, 'One comes who will carry the key. Full of courage and zest she will be.' It is of no surprise that you have appeared, little one. Great things are about to be placed upon your shoulders. Do not fear. The Founders have granted you great wisdom and have sent one to go with you on your quest," said Adolphus.

As he stared directly into the eyes of the little girl, Adolphus said in the most tender yet stern voice, "Stay near and trust the traveler assigned to you, Zella. Stay near and walk in the light of the one sent to come alongside."

Zella immediately noticed someone or something standing next to her. Still mesmerized by the words being spoken to her, she felt the weight of the task being placed upon her shoulders but somehow felt completely at ease. As if the burden had somehow just been shared with another ... the way sharing a terrible secret with someone you trust makes the secret a bit more bearable.

"Zella, meet your traveling companion, Abel. She will walk with you through the course of your quest," said Adolphus.

Bowing slightly as per the protocol when in the midst of royalty, Zella extended her hand to greet Abel, saying, "It is my honor to travel with you for the good and for the sake of the land of Bren, good companion, Abel."

Doing likewise, Abel bowed and extended her hand toward Zella, speaking in what could only be described as a whisper, yet with an unmistakably clear voice, "It is my honor to be your traveler, good and faithful Zella."

Wide-eyed at the power exuded by this whisper of a voice, Zella felt at once peace-filled and courage-filled and encouraged to begin the quest, saying boldly to Adolphus, "We go at once! What is the task? What is my quest?"

"The quest the Founders have granted you is a journey through darkness, through treachery, through chaos, and through turmoil. You will enter places where up will appear down and right will appear wrong. This is why you will need to draw near to Abel. By her still, small voice, you will find surety when confused. By her still, small voice, you will find guidance when the way seems impassable. By her hand, she will light the way through both storm and dark, through both day and night," said Adolphus.

"Your brother, Cullen, has been led astray, but even now relies on truth. And that truth is preserving him even though darkness is all around him. Your task is to assist him in his task."

Speaking boldly again, Zella said, "For Cullen and for Bren, I will gladly do as you say, good Adolphus!"

Reaching into the folds of his robe, one of the billowy robes of the seers of Bren that the children always teased one could get lost in, Adolphus pulled out a strange looking piece of metal. Not shiny or ornate as one might expect of a relic of Bren, the simple piece of iron was about five inches long. It was a key with a simple loop on one end and a two-pronged key-head on the other. A rustic, simple key.

"This key is your charge," instructed Adolphus. "Only you may bear it. Only you may wield it. It will unlock the way between you and your brother, Cullen. With this key, you may unlock that which is hidden. It will unlock what eyes cannot see and open what ears cannot hear. With this key, words will be given meaning and mysteries will be opened. Guard it with your life. Once you have reached Cullen, give it to him. Without this key, the Hammer cannot be wielded. He will know what to do once it has been placed in his hands."

Holding out her hand, Zella began to shake slightly, as much from sheer awe and reverence as sheer excitement and wonder. As her hand felt the coolness of the metal, she wrapped her fingers around it and was immediately full of courage and encouragement. Faith in the words she had just spoken suddenly became a very real part of her. Holding on as if her life and the lives of an entire nation depended upon her completion of the quest assigned her, Zella started walking out of the counsel room.

"Where are you going?" asked Adolphus.

"I am going to my brother!" insisted Zella.

"Are you not forgetting something?" asked the seer.

Zella immediately ran to her Grandmother and hugged her, saying, "I am sorry I forgot to say 'goodbye,' Grandmother!"

"Wait, child!" said Adolphus. "What of your traveler ... your companion?"

"Oh, yeah!" replied Zella with a sheepish yet contrite grin. "Come on, Abel! Let's go!"

But Abel did not budge. "What's wrong, Abel? There is no time to waste."

"You are headed in the wrong direction, child," whispered Abel.

"I am sorry, Abel. Where should we begin?" apologized the girl.

Abel's reply?

"In darkness."

10

ABYSSTINE AND THE AGENTS OF DARKNESS

bigail, Mia, Harry, and Ariel of the Nova made their way from the dark northern mountains and their brief meeting with Averichi, the chiroptera, to the outer realm of the fortified city of Abysstine. Coming down the mountain trail leading directly to the northern city gate, they occasionally passed people, mostly small groups of farmers with wagons either loaded full of goods headed for sale in the Abysstine markets or those headed back up the mountain trails with empty wagons. The children felt somewhat apprehensive each time they passed a farmer or a group of tradesmen or random travelers. Were they who they appeared to be or were their innocent-looking exteriors hiding something more sinister?

As they cleared the final few yards of the foothills and

onto the main road leading into Abysstine, the quartet passed by more and more people. The closer they drew to the massive northern gate, the more hustle and bustle surrounded them. A grand bazaar lined each side of the road, booth upon booth and bin upon bin of goods and wares meeting their senses. The vivid colors of the spices alone sent their minds into a splendid frenzy of imagining dishes the color of the rainbow! Bright red saffron! Brilliant red paprika! The glorious yellow of turmeric! The wonderful green of curry! The cobalt blue of the rare mountain-grown blue sumac! The rich flamingo-pink of the spice of the paradise plant! The shiny off-white metallic sheen of the spice of pearl freshly harvested from the southern shores of the Sea of Arabon.

As if the colors were not overloading their senses enough, the smells! Oh, the smells! Sweet unmistakable pomegranates and mangoes! The wonderful sourness of yogurt and fermented sticky rice! Salty seaweed and salted nuts! The bitter aromas of herbs and dark leafy greens! Astringent yet somehow desirable odors of raw pumpkin and squash and soya beans! And, ahhhh, the wonderfully pungent spicy chili peppers, garlic and wild onions!

Such was the overwhelming nature of the smells and sights of the fruits and vegetables and herbs and spices that they became quite lost in the beauty of the goods surrounding them. Though they came from a more modern world, the wonder and simplicity of the goods and necessities of life in medieval Bren added a sense of gratitude to the sensory mix!

Beautifully carved wooden utensils and bowls crafted with great care and artistry. Some ornate, some plain. All made to last a lifetime.

Blankets and tapestries and cloaks and shawls, meticulous in detail and practical in use. Simple furniture like tables and small three-legged stools. Hutches to hold the utensils. And then there were the blacksmiths and their constant clanging of metal upon metal, producing pots and pans and daggers and swords and plows and bridle-bits and all manner of necessary goods the children would've normally taken for granted.

Women surrounded clothes and brilliant cloths, haggling for the best price. Men gathered around a small pen where hogs and goats and chickens and guinea fowl were being auctioned. The sounds of people making deals, of children playing tag, of metal clanging from the bell-peddler's stall, women laughing, men boasting, a small band of minstrels making merry music all made the children forget their worries for at least a little while. As they neared the northern gate, the immensity of the large structure brought them out of their sensory overload to the reality of the task at hand.

Sentries were on either side of the gate. Each child hoped the kind-looking sentry on the left would be their first contact with the authorities of Abysstine, but that was not to be. The gruff, muscle-bound, harsh-sounding sentry on the right asked, "Who goes there?" The very tone of his voice told the

children there was no way any of them would make it
through Abysstine that day!

Placing her hand in front of the children, Ariel answered,
"I am Ariel of the Nova and the children are in my watch and
care. We seek passage through the grand city of Abysstine to
our intended destination of Castle Aerie."

The guard bristled at her words as if something she said
offended him. This caused the children to draw close to Ariel,
behind her and as much out of the guard's sight as physically
possible! Obviously agitated, the burly man stepped toward
Ariel and placed his hand on the hilt of his still-sheathed
sword! While the children ducked and winced in preparation
for whatever was coming next, Ariel placed her hand—palm
forward—toward the guard and looked him squarely in the
eyes!

What happened next was extraordinary, to say the least!
As bristled and agitated as he appeared to be, upon locking
eyes with Ariel, his bristling turned to a relaxed stance, as if
greeting a long-lost friend, and his agitation turned to
peaceful welcome!

"Good Lady Ariel, welcome to the city of Abysstine!
Passage to Castle Aerie you seek! Passage to Castle Aerie you
shall have! And those in your charge, the three children, are
guaranteed safe passage as long as they are under your
watchful care. If you will, allow me to summon one of the
royal guardsmen of Abysstine to escort you and your precious
cargo through the city. Do you require food? Would you care

for a cool refreshing drink of the pure waters of the northern mountains? I am at your service, dear lady!"

Astounded and nervous, the children began to giggle. Nudging Mia, Harry asked, "What just happened?"

Assuring her sister, Mia said to Abigail, "We are going to be alright, sister!"

Looking at her sister and cousin, Abigail giggled, "That is *not* what I thought he was going to say!"

Ariel assured the guard that she knew her way around and through the city, and he sent the little band on their way, cheerfully waving farewell as they walked through the gate and into the city as quickly as possible! All four felt a sense of "whew" as they made their way into the crowded streets of Abysstine. The hustle and bustle would obscure them from spying eyes that were surely lurking somewhere in these dark streets.

Walking quickly, the children all began to calm a bit from their encounter with the guard. "What just happened back there, Ariel?" asked Mia.

Her answer was short. "The power of the spoken word is what happened, dear Bairns of Bren."

"But it seemed there was more to it than that," instead Abigail. "It was like ... like ... magic!"

"What some call magic is actually much simpler than that," Ariel began to explain. "The Founders have ordained it as such. With one word the universe was spoken into existence. What is not spoken aloud remains unrealized, relegated to the whims of feelings. When truth is spoken, the atmosphere changes. Sometimes the change is instantly apparent, but more often than not, the change works its way out in time. A word spoken aloud is like the planting of seed into the atmosphere. When the planting is released, the seed must be given adequate time to grow. Just because a seed is covered with soil and disappears from sight does not mean it is not growing. So it is with the words we speak. That is why I urge you each to cling not only to the words of the Founders, but to the personal and specific words spoken to your own hearts."

Those wise words began to take root in each child's mind even though they had not a clue how it would all come to pass. There were still many miles left in their quest, but the fear and nervous tension of the encounter with the guard had been quelled by the truth of Ariel's words. Though wary as they walked the crowded streets, a kind of peace filled their minds and put them at ease.

Ariel led them through the city at a modest clip. Not so slow as to dilly-dally and waste time and not so fast as to draw unnecessary and unwanted attention. The four travelers walked two by two, Abigail beside Ariel leading the way, Harry and Mia trailing close behind, holding hands so as to not be easily separated as the crowds ebbed and flowed around them. Knowing the children would require food and rest, Ariel led them down a side street lined with coffee and chai vendors among charming little cafes serving the normal lunchtime fare of Abysstinian ham and eggs and toast and jam and sweet pumpkin pie.

Taking a small table nearest the most obscure cafe they could find, Ariel and the children placed their orders with the young girl who had greeted them. She returned with wonderful Abysstinian chai, and they gleefully drank cup after cup of the sweet goodness. While they waited for their meal, Ariel spoke. "Do not fear, but we are being watched."

"Watched?!" asked the startled children.

"By whom?" asked Mia.

"Let not your hearts be troubled, dear Bairns of Bren. Even now, those who are watching us are being watched by ones who have been sent to protect you on your quest," replied Ariel assuredly.

"Is it the old lady standing near the corner?" asked Abigail.

"Is it the man seated in the cafe across the street? The one who keeps looking our way?" asked Harry.

"Is it the tradesman working on the well in the small square among the cafes?" asked Mia.

"No, children. The watchers are none of these. Those who watch are smaller. More unnoticeable. More ... dragon-ly," said Ariel.

"Dragon-ly?" asked Mia. "What do you mean?"

"Have you noticed any insects in the city this day?" asked Ariel.

"Come to think of it, I expected the animal auction to be

fly-infested, yet there seemed to be not even one fly," said Harry.

"And the flower vendors ... normally I am afraid of the bees that always seem to be attracted to the flowers, yet I did not see a single scary bee today," replied Abigail.

"Did anyone notice the lack of butterflies on the wild-flowers growing alongside the roadway as we traveled down through the foothills? There were none! Not even one!" exclaimed Mia.

"So, what *did* you notice about the insect world today as we made our way to where we now sit?" asked Ariel just as the buzzing sound of a hovering insect somewhere nearby became very obvious to them all.

"Shhh! Shhh! Shhh!" whispered Ariel as she placed her finger on her lips, signaling silence. "Do not let them know we are aware of them."

The children calmly began to eat their meals even as the spy grew silent, perched on a nearby fence. The children knew. Those who watched were of the kind that struck fear in the hearts of other insects—like flies and bees and butterflies. The kind of spy sent by and always associated with the most fearsome of beasts! Eating their meals so as to not give their spy any indication they had been discovered, the children knew. Their watcher was a dragonfly.

Knowing they were being watched was one thing. Knowing the ability of a dragonfly to hear things even from a distance made it next to impossible to plan their escape without being heard. But Mia noticed something wonderful coming their way. The melodic and grand notes being played and sung by the traveling group of minstrels gave her an idea. Motioning for the musicians to come close to their table, Mia asked them, "Do you know the song 'The Merry Maids of Menden'?"

Without missing a beat, the minstrels broke into a most boisterous and raucous rendition of the popular song of Bren. As the singers sang and the players played, men from the surrounding tables began to stand and politely ask the ladies at their tables to dance. Before the dragonfly knew what was happening, a party—a grand dancing affair of joy—broke out in the small square and grew from one cafe to another until the entire city block was filed with music and dancing and laughter and merriment!

There once was a maid of Menden Lake
Who danced for joy for dancing's sake
She danced and jigged and leapt and spun
'Til every maid danced 'round as one!

Dancing! Dancing! Merrily!
Dance for joy and dance with glee!
Dance for joy of dancing free
The dance goes on unenden

Dancing! Dancing! Merrily!

Dance for joy and dance with glee!
Dance for joy of dancing free
The merry maids of Menden!

While the song was short and merry indeed, the more the crowd danced, the louder the musicians played and the louder the musicians played, the louder the singers sang! Joy led to merriment! Merriment led to laughter! Laughter led them to start the song and dancing and laughter all over again and again. So loud and so wonderfully confusing and so joyful and merry the crowd had become, the dragonfly never saw Ariel and the children leave!

With the sound of laughter and dancing wafting wonderfully through the streets of Abysstine, the quartet made its way toward the southern gate of Abysstine. Ariel knew they would not be safe to try and escape through the gate by day. Their chances would be better at night. If there was one watcher, Ariel knew there would be more. The foursome made their way from one alley to the next, listening for the telltale sounds of flitting dragonfly wings as they ventured though the busy streets.

Afternoon would soon give way to night and the cover of darkness. At least that was the hope. Squirming and fidgeting and trying to hold off as long as he might, Harry finally broke the silence. "Sorry, cousins! Sorry, Ariel. I really need to pee!"

"You're just like Ron!" exclaimed Mia.

"Boys!" chimed in Abigail.

Not wanting to cause any undue embarrassment, Ariel replied, "We could all use a break now, couldn't we? I know just the place."

Ariel led the group to a small out-of-the-way inn called The Nodding Nova. The sign that hung above the door was a star nodding toward the ground as if to say "Rest here, weary traveler." Once inside, the Nova introduced the children to the innkeeper, Arnoldo.

Arnoldo was of the Nova race. The children just knew it, such was the friendly and knowing countenance of the innkeeper. After directing Harold to the outhouse, he then showed them to a room they used as a resting place until night fell.

Once darkness had settled in, Arnoldo took Ariel and the children to the stable. There, he instructed them to lie down in the back of a wagon he had already hitched to two horses. He then covered the children with blankets and a few bundles of cloth and various other lightweight items. Once they were sufficiently hidden, Arnoldo sat in the wagon seat and prompted the horses to giddy up. A few minutes later, they came to a halt. The children knew they must have come to the southern gate of Abysstine. A few minutes of muffled voices and nervous waiting later, the wagon lurched forward.

Finally, the wagon made its way out of Abysstine and to the shore of nearby Menden Lake. Coming to a sudden stop, the children held their collective breath as the bags and blankets were lifted off of them. As the last blanket was removed, the smell of fresh air and freedom filled their lungs! As their eyes adjusted to the dim moonlit night, they could see the mist rising from the waters of beautiful Menden Lake. They had made it and gone unnoticed!

Or had they?

11

TO THE CAVE AND INTO THE RIVER

o sooner had King Leonolis given the go-ahead to Elliott than he and Ronald, Annabell, Matilda, and Mark found themselves in the cave where the children had all decided to separate. Rubbing his hands together, Ron produced a fire illuminating the three tunnels— or what should have been three tunnels.

"I see only two tunnels," said Leonolis.

"There are, er, were three, grandfather!" said Mark.

Pointing to the tunnel on the left, Matilda said, "Here it is! This is the one we used to get to you, grandfather!"

"And there," said Annabell pointing to the one on the right, "is the one used by Cullen, Harry, Abigail, and Mia!"

"But there is no other tunnel, children. Are you sure there were three?" asked the King.

Bewildered, Ronald said, "Of course there are three,

grandfather. See here," he said as he pointed to the ground. "There are five sets of footprints heading down the tunnel to the left. We made those footprints! And see there?" he continued. "Three sets of footprints heading that direction!"

"But I thought four children took that tunnel. Did you not say that while your group went to the left, Cullen, Harry, Abigail, and Mia all went right?" asked the King.

Nodding, the children did not understand the King's point.

"There are five in your group and four in Cullen's group. There should be nine sets of footprints, but there are only eight here!"

A sudden shock of disbelief went through the minds of the children as they realized what this might mean.

"Oh, no!" exclaimed Annabell. "What if the dragon..."

"The dragon would not have been able to squeeze through the small tunnel leading to the three," reasoned Mark. "One of his henchmen must have taken one of the children!"

"Or one of them became frightened and confused and ran back toward the dragon's lair!" said Matilda, fearfully.

"Wait, children! Let us not allow vain imagination to overshadow what we know to be true and real," said their wise grandfather.

"What else could it be if not something evil, grandfather?" asked Mark.

"Even if evil is somehow at work here, let me remind you

of the truth of the Founders. Long before the time before the most ancient of days, a truth was established. It says: What the darkness intends for evil, the Founders can use for good and Light. What do your gifts tell you, children? There is always more than one point of view.

"Of course!" exclaimed Mark. "I will call out to creatures that make this cave their home and see if they can tell us anything!"

"I will brighten the light in the room and expand the search, grandfather!" exclaimed Ron.

"Or we can follow these footprints that lead directly into this wall where the middle tunnel should be," said Elliott in a somewhat snarky manner.

"Evil is surely at work here, grandfather," she said. "And by the size of the print in comparison to the others, it could only be Cullen who made these footprints. And he has the map."

Challenging his grandchildren, Leonolis asked, "And what does this tell us? What is another point of view?"

Tillie jumped in, "The Founders have led him through! This is part of his mission. It may appear as evil to us, but the Founders may have led him alone down this path for a certain task. A certain reason!"

"That's more like it, Tillie!" exclaimed Leonolis. "So, what should we do, children?"

Mark made a shushing motion, placing his finger to his lips and whispering, "Quiet!"

Stirring ever so softly, a creature could be heard scurrying along the tunnel wall directly toward Mark.

With the ability to converse with animals and having just sent out the question in mind-speak to any creature within hearing distance, Mark said, "Who goes there?"

The others—except for his grandfather with whom he shared this particular gift—could not hear him, but they knew from prior experiences that Mark was communicating with ... something.

"It is I!" came the reply from the darkness. Of course, the other children only heard tiny squeaks, but Mark heard the distinct voice of a rat.

"And who is asking?" asked the rat.

"It is I, Mark, grandson of King Leonolis."

"I sense more present than just you, good Mark! I assume you are good since you purport to be the grandson of good King Leonolis," replied the rat.

"You sense correctly. You are among friends here. Come into the light where we might see you," urged Mark.

"You may see me but I cannot see you," came the rat's squeaky reply. "My race has lived so long in the darkness of these caverns that we have no need of sight as you know it. But our other senses are highly developed."

"And what is your name, dear friend rat?" asked the boy.

"I am called Nigel," said the rat.

Nigel stepped out of the shadows and into the light produced by Ron's outstretched hands. Sniffing loudly, he said, "I smell five others, and I hear five children and the breath of one adult."

Cocking his head from side to side as if listening to the silence, the rodent's eyes were not dark and beady as one might expect, but were rather large and milky white. As if he were "gazing" into the eyes of each child, he nodded in recognition of their presence. But when he came to King Leonolis, Nigel stared into the King's face as a sighted rat might do. He became very still, reverently bowed his head, and placed his right paw over his left, saying, "Your highness, the great and wise King Leonolis of Bren. I am honored to meet you, sire, and want to be of service to you and the realm."

"Rise, good friend Nigel. We do have need of your service," replied the King. After hearing of the day's occurrences and the threat of Luminaud, Nigel asked, "How may I help?"

"We must find Cullen and the map he bears," said Leonolis. "I fear he is in grave danger since he alone went down the middle path."

"And the three others? The ones who ventured to the right?" asked Mark.

"Among my race, news has come of the three you speak of," Nigel answered. "Even now they have ventured into the safe realm of Nova. At least that was the news I last received on the matter."

At that moment, Annabell began to tug on the coat of maille beneath her grandfather's breastplate. "Grandfather!

Grandfather! I know what to do!" Annabell took the bell from her pack and began to ring it loudly while walking toward the place where Cullen's footprints ended at the wall. With one mighty last fling of her wrist, she pealed the loudly echoing bell where the tunnel should have been.

The sudden boldness of his sister caused Mark to step out toward the other children and spread his arms, beckoning them silently to give her plenty of room. Like a flashlight pointed into a dark place, the tone of the bell seemed to ring on forever. As the sweet tone began to fade away, a deep groaning, moaning, rumbling, shaking began to resonate in the cavern. Normally, one would have feared the walls to be caving in, but by now the children were so used to the power of the Founders and so expectant of magic that they all simply waited for whatever was about to happen! And happen it did!

Like the way a sugar cube melts in one's mouth, the solid rock where the middle tunnel should have been began to do just that. It melted away! Though darkness had forged an evil blockade to the entry, the light of the magic of the Founders had once again made a way where there had seemed to be none!

Once the opening was completely clear, Matilda readied an arrow and pointed it into the tunnel! Reaching to stop her, Leonolis was too late. She let it fly directly into the darkness. "What are you doing, Matilda?" asked her grandfather.

While his question lingered in the air, the children all

waited, expecting to hear the arrow strike the cavern wall. What they heard was a gravely, ogre-ish voice shrieking, "Ouch! Why have you shot me?"

What the children saw and heard next caused them each to jump back several feet. Something big was coming their way. Something that kept saying "Owie!" and "Oof!" and "Oomph!" as if it were bumping its head on the cavern ceiling and stubbing its toes on unseen stones and ramming its shins into unseen boulders! And then it rolled out into the light of the cavern where the group stood, weapons at the ready, and came to a sudden stop in a heap!

King Leonolis recognized the common cave ogre. Smaller than the mountain-dwelling ogres of the northern reaches of Bren, yet barely small enough to fit into the tunnel from which it just came. The King asked, "Why do you lie in wait for us, ogre?"

Breathing heavily and gasping for air, the creature mumbled and muffled and miffed unintelligibly, "Mmph! Rigga! Tigga! Mumlbety! Pumblty! Mmph!"

"You must speak the truth, ogre! The arrow was not intended to bring you harm, but it was infused with the magic of the wisdom of Bren! You are commanded to speak the truth!" Matilda coldly proclaimed. "Because real wisdom is truth!"

The ogre had just received a command he could not disobey. He struggled to sit upright and dust himself off. Pulling at the arrow protruding from his left shoulder, he said,

"I am Oliver the ogre of the cave-dwelling ogre clans. I was commanded by Lord Luminaud to guard this tunnel from intruders—especially of children. It is my charge to do whatever is required to impede your forward progress."

Matilda immediately put another arrow into the right shoulder of the bewildered ogre. "It would be wise for you to see from the Founders' point of view, Oliver the ogre!" declared Matilda.

"You go, girl!" exclaimed Elliott proudly to her sister.

"Yes! Yes! I declare allegiance to the King and to the realm of Bren! I only did as Luminaud demanded out of fear! Your arrow has revealed to me the truth and the wisdom of the Founders ... and ... and..."

"And what?" asked Ronald.

"And I have been led by fear for far too long. I am weary of it. Thank you for setting me free this day, dear child," said the ogre.

"Oliver, we will do no harm to you, but we must find the boy who made his way into the hidden tunnel from which you came. Help us find the boy. We search for him not out of fear, but out of love, and love conquers fear. If you are truly weary of being led by fear, then help us find the boy and conquer that fear!" said Elliott.

"My granddaughter speaks wisdom, Oliver," assured Leonolis. "I, as King of the realm of Bren, have always done right by the race of ogres, have I not?"

Nodding sheepishly, Oliver said, "Oh, good King. This

day I will help you find the boy. All I know is that I was sent to keep others out and that a trap had been set for him."

"Where is the trap? What kind of trap? urged the King.

"What kind? Not the good kind. Where? All I know is that one lies in wait for him beneath the waters of Menden Lake," said Oliver.

"Oliver, how well do you know these caves?" asked the King.

"Like the back of my hairy hand!" responded the ogre.

"Will you lead us?" asked the King.

"Grandfather, how can we trust one who was sent to bring us harm?" asked Mark.

"We do not trust him," said the King. "We trust the wisdom of the Founders within him. Trust that same wisdom within yourselves, children. We have no time to waste!"

Running ahead of the group, Ronald held his flaming hands before him and shouted, "Grandfather! Cullen's tracks! He went this way!"

Oliver pulled the arrow from his right shoulder and ran after the boy. Leonolis lunged toward the ogre with his sword, but he was too late! Just as Ronald was about to round the first bend in the tunnel, Oliver jumped on top of him. Ron tripped over a string that set a falling rock plunging from the ceiling of the cavern! The trap, meant to crush whomever wandered across that string, fell onto Oliver as he shielded Ron's body from the massive weight of the stone slab!

Acting like nothing had just happened, Oliver rose onto

his hands and knees and lifted the slab of stone onto his own back and away from Ron. Sliding the slab safely to the side, he helped Ron up and dusted him off, saying, "Oh, yeah. Forgot to tell you. There may be traps along the way."

"No duh!" Elliott replied.

While Ronald stood, Annabell began to shake and point her finger at the walls of the cavern directly in front of them. "Grrrr ... andddd ... fath ... er! The walls ... the walls ... are moving!"

Like a massive army of hairy little eight-legged soldiers, thousands of spiders began to move toward them from below and above and all around. Not just any old garden variety spider, but the most dreaded of all Brennolinnian spiders: Spotted spitting spiders! Although their bites were deadly, they did not need to bite to kill. They needed but to spit their venom on their prey, which would be rendered paralyzed and unable to breathe! They could spit up to three feet, and that distance was about to become reality for the tunnel travelers until Ron rubbed his hands together and produced such an intense ball of flame it caused everyone, even the ogre, to cover their faces from the intense heat!

Suddenly, the dark, dank cave was cool again. "Okay, done," said Ron. "Come on guys. Let's find Cullen!" Stepping into what appeared to be black dust, the children soon realized it was actually the ashes of the once-mighty spiders Ronald had burned to the ground!

Each child secretly thanked the Founders for once again

giving them the wisdom and the gifting to make their way through. Each was filled with the wondrous feeling that they were truly not alone on this journey—that perhaps the Founders were with them. Somehow. Some way.

Rounding the next bend, the dread and fear returned. Standing between the troupe and the bridge to their next passageway was a hissing, snarling, twitching, twirling dragon with *three* heads! Mark leapt into action, plunging his sword into the neck of the first head and lopping it off! Then he chopped off the head on the right! And then the one in the center! But the children all gasped in horror as the dragon instantly grew three new ones!

"What do we do, grandfather?" asked Mark.

"Wait a minute! Just wait one minute!" said Elliott matter-of-factly as she walked right past Mark and onto the bridge and directly up to the center head of the beast. Pointing her finger at the creature, she said, "You are *not* real!" and walked across the bridge.

Everyone saw that the dragon was still there, yet somehow Elliott had made it across.

"How did you do that, Ellie?" asked Matilda.

"Simple. It's not real!" came Ellie's reply.

"Not real?! Are you seriously crazy?" asked Ronald.

"It depends on your point of view, guys! While Mark was fighting the beast, I transported to the other side and saw from that point of view that there was no dragon there. It's an illusion meant to cause fear and stop us in our pursuit of Cullen!

Point of view is everything! Have faith! Trust me! This dragon is not real!" declared Elliott. "I simply walked across to prove the truth to you. Come on! Let's get on with this!"

"She is right, children. Follow me," said King Leonolis as he walked right across the bridge and through the dragon. The kids followed, and then only Oliver was left, paralyzed by fear. Elliott walked back across the bridge, took Oliver by the hand, and said, "Come on, big fella. Let's get on with it."

Seeing that big ogre led by such a diminutive yet bold little girl sent yet another wave of faith and wonder through the hearts of the children. By now, they were less concerned with fear than with the wonder of what adventure might lie around the next bend! An entirely new perspective was informing the collective mind of the children. It was quite intoxicating and somehow splendid!

After several minutes without incident, the children came to an unexpected dilemma. The tunnel had suddenly become impassable. A massive hole stopped them in their tracks.

"What do we do now, grandfather?" asked Matilda. "I can see Cullen's footprints on the other side, yet I see no way across."

"What does wisdom tell your hearts, children? What would your gifts tell you to do in this moment?" asked the King.

Once again, Annabell took her bell and began to sling it back and forth, sending out the sweetest tone any of the children had ever heard. When she sensed it was time to cease her ringing, the sweet hushed tone of the peal echoed into the darkness and everything became still.

All stood motionless, waiting for whatever answer would come. As sweetly as the bell's tone had called out, the echoing response was the sweetest little song sung by the sweetest little voice emanating from the sweetest little light streaming from the wings of the sweetest little fairy that came flitting across the dark chasm:

> The way across no solid ground
> But through the storm the way is found
> Listen now and what you hear
> The sound of life to dampen fear
>
> Falling! Lilting! Lifting! Dreaming!
> River's rescue this way streaming!
> Truth the love and not the fear
> Love, the way, is near ...

The fairy floated past them, then turned and beckoned them to follow, which they did, singing their new song all the while. After a few more refrains, the fairy led them down a previously unseen break in the tunnel. As they followed, they listened intently to the song, somehow knowing it would tell them what to do next.

Falling! Lilting! Lifting! Dreaming!
River's rescue this way streaming!
Truth the love and not the fear
Love, the way, is near ...

Matilda heard it first, exclaiming, "Listen, everyone! Do you hear that?"

"I hear water! Running water!" exclaimed Ronald as he led the way toward the sound, fire still streaming from the palms of his hands. "Look! A river!"

Ronald leapt in and shouted, "Come on in! The water's fine, boys and girls! This is the way out! Don't be afraid!"

Elliott jumped in next, followed by Matilda. Mark waited for Annabell and then he jumped in after her. Next came King Leonolis! And the next thing they knew, a mighty wave was sweeping them toward an opening in the cavern that could only mean the outside world of Bren! That wave? That was Oliver leaping into the water in a full-fledged cannonball! And with that, they were outside on a moonlit night in Bren.

12

CULLEN AND LUMEN'S HAMMER

*H*aving just heard Cullen speak the name of his wife—a name he couldn't know—Verona the dragonfly sat up boldly in Cullen's outstretched palms, his faith and resolve bolstered. Even though Verona's bent wing meant he could not fly for several more hours, the little dragonfly bravely encouraged Cullen. "Onward, good Cullen! Onward we go!"

Cullen was about to take a step when a thought occurred to him. *Check the map.* Being a boy of good manners, Cullen simply replied, "There is one more thing I must do before we plunge onward, dear Verona. I must consult the map."

Gently placing the confused dragonfly on a stone outcropping, Cullen took the parchment from the leather pouch attached to his belt where he had been safeguarding the precious document. Stepping closer to Verona as he quickly unfurled the map, he asked, "Verona, would you mind shining your light a bit brighter?"

"Of course, good Cullen," said Verona. "Where did you get this map, and just where is it leading us?"

"This map was delivered into the hands of my grandfather in the realm from which I came. My siblings, cousins, and I were dispatched to the realm of Bren for the purpose of a mission I am only now beginning to understand. Somehow, we are to thwart the evil plans of Luminaud and his minions. But we became separated by some evil devised surely by the great beast himself. I am hoping the map will reveal more to me now in this most dire time of need."

"Reveal more of ... itself?" asked the dragonfly.

"Yes. It seems the map is a living, breathing, growing picture of the tasks we are to fulfill, as if the document itself is somehow alive," replied Cullen.

Even as Cullen said the word "alive," the map began to glow. While Cullen's eyes adjusted to the brightening of the map, his heart was instantly lifted as he saw the little green-hatted gnome jumping joyfully while simultaneously pointing in two directions. To the east, Cullen saw three tiny wolves running into Galaxia—the land of the Novae!

"See! See! See!" said Cullen to the now even more confused little dragonfly. "The wolves! Three wolves running safely through the tunnel to the right!"

"Wolves? Surely you do not intend for us to pursue such vicious creatures!" exclaimed Verona.

"No! No! No! Not vicious creatures! The red wolf ... Harry ..." said Cullen.

"You know their *names!*" shouted the dragonfly in his own tiny way of shouting.

"Yes, of course! The red wolf represents Harry, my youngest brother. And the blonde wolf represents my little cousin, Abigail! The brown wolf is her big sister, Mia! And the white wolf represents my brother, Ron. This means they are safe! They're *safe*, Verona!" said Cullen, his words spewing out joyfully a mile a minute!

The gnome of the map was still jumping up and down, but was now pointing west.

Now Cullen began jumping up and down for joy himself in a sort of happy-dance with the gnome of the map. "And look, Verona! A white wolf—that would be my brother, Ronald! And a grey wolf—my cousin Mark! And the bright orange wolf, that would be my cousin Elliott. She's a girl! And the pink wolf," giggled Cullen, "the pink wolf is Elliott's little sister, Matilda! We call her Tillie!"

Suddenly, Cullen's joy was very subdued when he realized one was missing. "But where is my cousin Annabell? Mark's little sister. Oh, no! She is not on the map, Verona!"

"Then why is the little green-hatted man laughing and pointing in the same direction? He must see something you cannot!" replied Verona.

"Of course! Annabell's wolf is the *clear* wolf! Her color, or lack of color, is my very favorite because you can't always

117

see where she is going or know what she is actually up to—at least as far as the map is concerned," said Cullen as if he were about to tell Annabell's life story.

"She is fine then, right?" asked Verona, wisely cutting him off and helping him focus on the map at hand.

"Yes, it seems she, Ron, Matilda, Elliott, and Mark have made it to Castle Aerie and have embarked on a mission of their own with our grandfather!" replied the boy.

"Why have they set out on a mission with your grandfather? Why not employ the help of the high King of Bren rather than—pardon my honesty—seeking the help of an old man?" asked Verona.

"That old man—my grandfather—is no ordinary old man. My grandfather is the one of whom you speak. My grandfather *is* High King Leonolis of the realm of Bren," said Cullen, proudly.

"Well, I guess that settles that," said the now-embarrassed dragonfly.

While Cullen continued to jump for joy, Verona glanced back at the map. "Why is he doing that?"

"Why is who doing what?" asked Cullen.

"Why is the gnome pointing north toward the beast?" asked Verona.

There on the map, on what Cullen knew to be the path he and Verona were now following, was the moving image of a giant red dragon, yellow mist floating around his massive serpent head. Even the smell of sulfur emanated from the image. With each inhalation of the beast's lungs, the light of the map dimmed, and with each exhalation, the map's light grew a bit brighter.

"I shudder to think about what the beast will do to my poor dear wife and children when he hears of my failure to lead the Bairns of Bren into his lair," said Verona.

"By the Founders, I assure you help is on the way and that even what you consider failure, the Founders will mean and use for your good," replied Cullen. "Take heart, dear Verona. Someone got you this far, did they not? Someone revealed to me the name of your wife, did they not? Let us move now. Onward!" replied Cullen.

"What is he trying to tell you now?" asked Verona, pointing at the gnome.

The gnome was trying to get Cullen to look to the cavern ceiling on the southward portion of the map. There, Cullen noticed two figures. One was the shape of a woman Cullen had never seen before, but the other was a wolf. A silver wolf with a curious z-shaped symbol on its side. That could only mean one thing!

"Zella!" shouted Cullen. "It is my sister, Zella! And she is not alone!"

"But what does the gnome mean? Why does he point to her?" asked Verona.

"She and the one she travels with are about to enter the Forbidden Swamp! We, the grandchildren of Leonolis, have been warned many times about the dangers of crossing this eerie place. We know of only one other crossing by a child. When my grandfather was a boy, he crossed the swamp safely on a mission set forth by the Founders! Surely Zella has been summoned from our realm into Bren for just such a mission!" explained Cullen.

"You keep speaking of another realm, boy. What is this other realm? Where is it? Is it of the land of Bren or further to the south?"

"It is a long story, one we do not have time for right now. After we rescue your family and rid the land of Luminaud, perhaps I will tell you of my realm," said Cullen with wisdom beyond his years. "For now, we must focus on the mission at hand and allow the Founders to carry the others to their own tasks. No time for worry now. It is time to face our fear and trust the Founders to use even our fear for our good."

Cullen glanced once more at the map to get his bearings, but everything on it disappeared except for the tunnel leading them directly to the lair of Luminaud somewhere below Menden Lake. Carefully rolling the map back up and gently placing it back in the leather pouch, Cullen extended his right hand, palm upward, toward Verona, who gingerly walked right onto it. "I think there is only one way, dear Verona! Onward it is!" The boy and the dragonfly, now bolstered in their faith and filled with resolve at what the map had revealed, began to surely and steadily follow the tunnel they knew would lead them right into the realm of Luminaud.

After a few minutes of Cullen carrying Verona in the palm of his hand, it was decided that it would be easier and more efficient for both the boy and the dragonfly if Verona simply sat on his shoulder! This was welcome relief for Cullen, who was afraid to admit that he was getting a bit tired. So on they went in this manner.

At times the tunnel took them upward. At other times, down. Sometimes they seemed to spiral in circles while at others the pathway seemed to zigzag aimlessly to nowhere. Always leery of who or what might be lurking in the tunnel, they moved as quickly and quietly as possible. After several hours of this tedious trekking, they came to a most welcome sight. Actually they heard it before they saw it. They could even smell its fresh sweetness.

Upon hearing and smelling the water and the pleasant gurgling of the stream running out of the cave and down into some unseen chasm, Verona flitted from Cullen's shoulder and lightly skimmed the surface of the water. He sipped happily and danced through the air.

Cullen fell to his knees, cupped his hands and pulled handful after handful of the sweet water to his mouth. For several minutes the two just drank and drank and laughed and laughed and finally fell over into heaps on the cavern floor next to the stream for a much-needed rest.

While they rested there, Cullen sat upright suddenly and laughed at Verona. "You flew! You can fly again! Your wing, Verona! Your wing is well enough and strong enough for you to fly! Not that I do not mind carrying you, but you are well, friend!"

Verona buzzed excitedly around the cavern, gleefully shouting as only a dragonfly can, in a teeny tiny yet surprisingly loud way, "By the Founders, I can fly! I can *fly*!"

Suddenly, a rumbling, like the shaking of boulders in a cavern during an earthquake, brought the glee to a very abrupt end as the boy and the dragonfly held their breath. While Verona alit on Cullen's shoulder, the two held as still as they possibly could until the rumbling stopped. But that was no earthquake. What they had felt—the rumbling, earth-shaking sound—could only be coming from one source. Luminaud!

As stealthily as possible, the boy and the dragonfly crept around the next bend of the tunnel just in time to see the tip of the tail of the massive beast as he left the cavern. He was up to no good and headed for the outside world above! When the dragon left, Cullen and Verona both expected absolute darkness. But it didn't happen. An ever-so-faint but distinct light was coming from somewhere near the center of the dragon's lair ... from beneath and behind the place where the dragon obviously slept.

Something deep inside Cullen told him to look at the map. Before he had even unrolled the parchment, it was glowing once again. Expecting to see some sign of direction, Cullen was disappointed when the only portion of the map that seemed to be glowing contained the next part of the riddle:

> Let hearts not fear the separation
> The way is found in contemplation
> Your way is set through the lone, through
> horde
> Your battles fought with fire and sword

"What does that even mean?" asked Verona.

"I am not exactly sure," replied Cullen, "but I do know each word is important, so let us simply do as it says. I suppose we may need to separate from one another. Perhaps, since the beast has gone, you may search for your family."

"Where would I even begin?" asked Verona.

"Look at the next line. 'The way is found in contemplation.' If you were the beast, where would you hide and hold your captives?" asked Cullen.

"Why, I would want them in a hidden place so as to threaten harm and keep me doing his bidding. They must be somewhere nearby!" exclaimed Verona.

"But the next line, 'Your way is set through the lone, through horde,' what do you suppose that means?" asked the boy.

"Knowing the beast as I sadly do, this can only mean my family is guarded by a horde of dragonflies ready to do the

bidding of Luminaud. I think it means I must go alone. The dragonfly horde will think I only appear so as to give a report of my
mission's progress!" said Verona as he began to flutter his wings
excitedly in preparation of zooming away to search for his family.

"Wait!" whispered Cullen, "what of the next line? 'Your
battles fought with fire and sword.' What does that mean?"

In that instant, the map again began to glow, as did the
wall behind the dragon's sleeping chamber. Something began
to take shape on the map in the spot where the dragon slept—
a symbol of some sort ... the form of a sword! And this sword
kept shifting shapes from a hammer to a most magnificent and
kingly sword! Even as the map began to reveal the sword
hidden beneath the dragon's chamber, the dragon's chamber
itself began to glow. And the same symbol began to appear
within the stone.

What had once looked like granite now appeared to be
actual crystal, a mixture of quartz and diamond and opal and
ruby, at once opaque yet clear as day! The sword—the
hammer—could only be one sword and one hammer:
Lumen's Hammer, the sacred sword of the Victor.

"You know what this means, Verona?" asked Cullen

"This is the sword Luminaud searches for!" replied
Verona.

The boy and the dragonfly had not heard the slithering.
Had not smelled the sulfur presence. Had not noticed the
yellow mist surrounding his evil eyes. But they were certainly

sure whose voice they heard as the massive dragon suddenly filled the room.

"So, you have found the one they call Lumen's Hammer, have you, human scum?" seethed the beast. "Well done, Verona, my pet! Well done! I see you brought the would-be wielder of the sword. You can tell me later how you dispatched the other human vermin, but well done, dragonfly! Well done!"

While the beast spoke and pranced around the room in arrogant pride, Cullen quickly rolled the map and placed it in its pouch. The map stopped glowing and so did Lumen's Hammer. It was obvious to both boy and dragonfly that Luminaud had no idea that what he was searching for was right beneath him every night!

The dragon noticed the sudden dimming of the light. "What do you know of the sword, boy?"

"I know only that its power can be wielded by innocence and not evil," answered Cullen.

"And of its location?" asked Luminaud.

"I cannot say," replied the boy.

"Cannot or will not?" asked the dragon, his nose now inches from Cullen's. As Cullen turned his face from the fiery eyes of the dragon, he could not help but look toward the place he knew the sword to be hidden.

"There?!" exclaimed the beast. "The Hammer of Lumen is *there*? Of course! Hidden in plain sight beneath my own bed! Stupid boy, your thoughts betray what you consider holy and sacred."

Violently and with evil glee, the beast turned toward the place of the hidden sword and began tearing away at the stone. He clawed and ripped so violently that his talons began to bleed. Not a happy dragon.

Finally, in exasperation, the beast slashed one last time at the stone and his talon became lodged in the smallest of slits. As he pulled, it actually broke his claw, leaving it lodged in ... a keyhole.

Turning viciously toward Cullen, the dragon demanded, "Where is the key, boy? Give it to me *now!*"

"I do not have it," said the fearful boy.

"Your thoughts once again betray you, boy. You speak the truth. You do not have it, but there is one who even now carries it to you."

"Sssssssssssssister."

13

ZELLA AND THE DARKNESS

Once Abel had convinced Zella to follow her into the darkness of what Zella knew to be the secret northern passageway out of Castle Aerie, Zella was fully intent on one thing: finding Cullen and delivering the key that had been entrusted to her by Adolphus. All she knew was that this key would unlock something Cullen needed to defeat the dreaded Luminaud. Little did she know of the power of that one small key to unlock not just weapons but mysteries she had not yet encountered.

Zella, being strong-willed and single-minded in her task, found it difficult to follow the slow but steady pace of Abel, her traveling companion. Ever patient, Abel continued her pace in spite of Zella's obvious impatience. "Little girl, be not in such a hurry. Haste has a way of bringing confusion where clarity is needed."

Quite offended at being called a little girl, Zella lit into her guide. "Little girl! You call me little girl? I will have you know I have three older brothers who I tend to. In fact, if truth be known, it is I who help them make much more mature choices than they would otherwise make on their own! I'll have you know my parents trust me because of my maturity and because of my ability to see a certain situation or problem and find a way to bring a sure and wise conclusion! I may be small but I am no little girl!"

Stopping in her tracks, Abel turned toward the still-ranting Zella, who promptly ran right into her, causing her words to become muffled and then silenced within the billowing folds of Abel's robe. Stepping silently back from Abel, Zella was at once defiant and embarrassed at the abrupt interruption of her very important and informative speech.

"You are not as mature as you think," Abel said softly but boldly. "You are not as wise as you assume. Your words are not as persuasive as you insist. The words I use—'little' and 'girl'—do nothing but convey the simple truth of your stature and your gender. Nothing more. Nothing less. The very fact that you take offense at my use of such terms tells me what you truly think of yourself—who you really think you are.

"Of course your parents trust you. Of course your brothers need you from time to time, but do not place more on your shoulders than they are able to bear," she continued.

"What do you mean?" asked the contrite child.

"Your shoulders were never intended to carry the weight of the entire world," declared Abel.

"But I don't carry the weight of the *entire* world," said the now-not-so-sure-of-herself little girl.

"Just the weight of all of Bren. Just the weight of the care of your brothers. Just the weight of everyone else's needs but your own," said Abel. "All you have been asked to do, your only task and assignment, is to carry a small but important key to your brother. Yet you think too far beyond your own realm and assignment, worrying about and thinking about the thoughts of others you were never assigned to worry of or think about."

Tears trickled down Zella's face as the truth of Abel's words met the weight of the world she carried on her shoulders. Falling into the open arms of her guide, Zella sobbed, "You are right, dear Abel. You are right! I worry about my brothers, my parents, my grandparents, and the entire world of Bren, not to mention the world and realm of reality in which I mostly live in my natural realm! I do not know how to *not* do such things! I cannot carry such a burden, yet I do."

As Abel tenderly wiped away Zella's tears, she took the girl's face into her hands and looked into her eyes with the clarity of love and said, "Burdens are best carried when shared. Burdens best carried are only those we have been tasked to carry. You cannot carry another's burden for very long without collapsing under its weight."

"So how do I know the difference between my own burden and those of others?" asked the girl.

"You are a girl of faith, are you not?" asked Abel.

Zella nodded.

"Where does your faith lie, Zella?" Abel asked.

"My faith lies in the Founders," replied the girl.

"If that is so, I suggest you share your burdens, your worries, your fears, and your thoughts with them. Whenever you are feeling overwhelmed, share that thought with them. Whenever you are feeling afraid, share that fear with them. Whenever your thoughts are confused, share them. Every feeling you have is attached to some thought you are thinking. If you want to change the way you feel, change the thoughts you think," said Abel.

"But how?" asked Zella.

"One thought at a time. One moment at a time. One burden at a time. Carry only what you have been tasked to carry and then trust the Founders to carry the burden of the rest of the world. After all, it is they who spoke the universe into existence. Does that not tell you something about their power?" asked the guide.

"It tells me they are stronger and more able than anything I could ever do alone. It tells me they have nothing but my best in mind. It tells me they have not asked me to carry more than I can bear. It tells me they are the Founders ... and I am not."

Zella knew in the depths of her heart that she had

allowed pride to replace her humility and that Abel had rescued her from much heartache. She knew that pride leads only to downfall and destruction and that her true strength would come through humility of heart.

"Come, now. Your task is at hand. Carry only what you have been asked to carry, Zella."

"I am a little girl," began Zella, only to be interrupted by Abel. "You may be little and you may be a girl, but you are mighty in spirit that evil dare not reckon with. And one day you will become a mighty woman that evil dare not reckon with!"

Zella grew quiet as Abel led her out of Castle Aerie and into the shadow of Counsel Hill. The two walked on in silence around the eastern end of the massive hill and right to the edge of The Forbidden Swamp she had seen on many occasions but had never ventured into or through. Walking right up to the edge of the shallow reed-filled waters, Abel held out her hand, signaling Zella to wait.

While the girl and her guide waited quietly at the water's edge, they heard a gentle stirring. From several hundred feet in front of them, they could hear the rustling of reeds and hear the rippling of water. Someone or something was heading straight for them. It was dusk, so they could only see what was nearby. Soon, the sound moved to within a few feet of the pair. Zella saw reeds moving directly in front of her and heard the sloshing of feet. Sensing the girl's fear, Abel said, "Friends. We are here."

"Here! Here! Here we are!" said two friendly voices in unison.

"Good Sniffum and good Snuffim, meet Zella," Abel began.

"Granddaughter of High King Leonolis!" declared the two creatures.

"Sniffum and Snuffim! Dear Sniffim and Snuffim, helper of my grandfather many ages ago! He has told me of your adventures together many, many times! Oh, how I have longed to meet you ... let alone talk with you!" exclaimed Zella. "*Talk* with you? I am talking with you! How is it I can hear and understand the language of ... of turtles?" asked the confused but happy girl.

"The Founders have granted you the ability for such a time as this. That could be the only explanation, dear one. Do not try to conjure thoughts of 'why.' Just believe and receive the gift," responded Abel.

"You are so much bigger than the way my grandfather has described you!" said Zella, excitedly.

"We have known your grandfather for many, many years. Much time has passed since the days of our youth and that of your grandfather. We have grown; indeed we have!" said the turtles in tandem.

"On you go!" said the turtles, pointing their heads back the way they had just come.

Zella climbed on the back of Sniffum while Abel climbed atop Snuffum. Slowly but surely, the turtles carried their charges across The Forbidden Swamp in silence. Soon, they caught the faint but definite glow of a flame near the center of the swamp, and it was apparent that this was exactly where the turtles were carrying their passengers. Zella figured it out before they arrived at the shore of the small island near the center of the swamp.

"Jidgel! Jidgel! Are you home?" shouted Zella. "Jidgel! Jidgel! Quickly this way come!"

In a small mud-covered ogre's dwelling along the swampy shore, a gruff giggle could be heard.

"Welcome, granddaughter of my old friend, Leonolis! I have been expecting you!" said Jidgel, the small plump, dwarflike creature and friend of her grandfather.

"As with your grandfather before in the days of old, you shall have a short rest and a meal," said the now-not-so-gruff little ogre. "I have plenty of marsh figs, fresh catfish, and flour from the marsh reeds from which I will stir up a batch of reed cakes. After a meal and a short rest, you must be on your way," replied Jidgel.

Eating a meal she had long dreamed of after hearing her grandfather speak of them, Zella felt as if she was living a part of history. So consumed with wondrous thoughts, she fell asleep and slumbered until she felt the gentle nudges of Abel rousing her. "We must be on our way, Zella."

Zella groggily said goodbye and hugged her grandfather's old friend, Jidgel. Then she and Abel once again climbed onto the backs of Sniffum and Snuffim, who quietly carried them to the northern shore of the Forbidden Swamp and into the looming shadow of the Sleeping Giant rising from the center of the Canyons of Callay.

Saying their goodbyes, Sniffum and Snuffim mentioned something curious to Zella and Abel: "You will find what you seek—the place of the key—beneath the waters of Menden Lake." Abel simply nodded in acknowledgement and headed down the road leading around the Canyons and directly toward the Oaken Fork. Once at the place where the ancient oak divided the road, Zella asked, "To the Dancing Meadow or to the Great Forest?"

"You have great knowledge of the land of Bren, Zella," "Abel reasoned. Bearing left, Abel led them northward. "To the Great Forest it is," Zella said. Knowing full well the lesson she had learned concerning pride and the bearing of burdens, Zella could not help but think of what might await them within the environs of the Great Forest. Rather than allow those what-ifs to direct her feelings and thoughts, she turned the thoughts around to *What wonderful vistas await us within this wondrous place?* Perspective is everything. Point of view can mean the difference between despair and hope. Zella was choosing hope!

Onward they walked into the darkness of the woods. The farther they went, the steeper the climb became. The deeper the darkness became, the creepier the sounds of the night seemed. With such thoughts beginning to overcome her, Zella imagined things that were not real.

At the sound of a twig in the distance being snapped by a doe, she imagined a swine rat making its way for them. When an owl silently glided somewhere above, gently filling the air with a gentle swoosh, she imagined a chiroptera coming her way. With each step and with each new sound, Zella's fears overtook what she knew to be true and caused her to suddenly stop dead in her tracks, frozen by dread.

"What is it, Zella?" asked Abel.

"Do you not hear? Can you not sense the dreadful creatures now surrounding us in all directions?" asked Zella, her voice trembling.

"What do you hear, Zella?" asked Abel.

"Snapping twigs!" whispered the girl.

"And what might cause a twig to snap?" asked Abel.

"A swine rat, of course!" said the girl.

"If it were a swine rat, do you not think we would have heard more than a simple snap of a twig? Would we not hear the shrieking, squeaking marauders long before that? What is true, Zella? What would truth say to you concerning the sound you heard?"

"I ... I ... suppose ... it might be a ... deer ...?" said Zella half asking, half declaring.

"And what else, dear Zella?"

"Did you not hear the swooshing sound just above our heads a moment ago? What if it's a chiroptera?" she said, her voice still quaking in fear.

Abel asked, "What does truth tell you?"

135

"The truth? The truth is I may have heard that sound before, like the sound of a bird gliding through the air ...?"

"Zella, until the truth tells you otherwise, do not allow fear to replace wonder and do not allow despair to replace hope. You have a choice. You always have the choice as to how you will respond to any temptation, to any circumstance, in any moment.

"You have a choice to make right now. You can hide. You can turn back, or you can go through. What will you choose?" asked wise Abel.

Just as she had done when they set out on this quest, Zella had a reckoning of heart. More like a reckoning of mind and a wrestling of thoughts. She decided to choose to believe the best and allow the Founders to carry the burden she could not. Her choice? To go *through* the forest. Immediately, worry drained from her and fear was gone like a wisp of smoke driven away by a strong wind. And a light appeared directly in front of her!

Peering into the eyes of the now fearless little girl was a small creature hovering in midair, its transparent wings aflutter, fairy dust creating an aura around her tiny little fairy face, announcing in the teeny-tiniest of fairy voices, "I am Rania! Follow me! I have been tasked by the Founders to lead you through the Great Forest of Bren and to the shores of Menden Lake. We have not much time before the beast makes another attack on the children of Bren. The key you now carry must be delivered or far too many children will be lost!"

All Zella could say was, "I *know* you! I *know* you!" Her grandfather had told her stories of his childhood adventures with the same little fairy! Zella followed Rania, and Abel had a difficult time keeping up! Through the woods they went at a steady pace. Over each rise and down the other side, past grazing deer and right under the nose of a stalking lion, the tiny creature stealthily showed them the way. Under giant fallen trees and through gently flowing streams, through beams of pleasant moonlight and in spite of the occasional howl of a wolf or scream of a wildcat, the fairy showed them the way. And before Zella and Abel knew it, they had done it. They had made their way *through* the dark woods of the Great Forest!

Just as they were about to step into the great meadow between the edge of the woods and the still misty-covered waters of Menden Lake, Rania stopped glowing and said abruptly, "Not another step! Not another sound!"

While Abel and Zella stood frozen, Rania hovered without fluttering a wing, buoyed by the power of fairy dust, as they all watched the giant reptilian dragon slither from beneath the eastern edge of the lake's depths. Like a great sea serpent, the beast glided through the water, head barely exposed, but undulating behind him like a slithering slimy snake trailed his great dragon body!

Although the girl and her companions were frozen in

absolute fearful silence, the beast seemed to be headed in their direction. The closer he came, the bigger he appeared. Once clear of the lake's waters, the entire dragon could be seen. Red scales. Yellow mist emanating from his fearsome dragon-nostrils. Red glowing, piercing eyes that Zella believed were staring at her! And then there was no doubt. Luminaud called out, "There you are, sister of Cullen ... the one they call, I believe ... Zella? Though my eyes do not yet see you, I smell something familiar ... the same smell I sense from your brother. I smell your fear."

Zella began to tremble in fear and turned to run back into the dark depths of the forest, but Abel stepped into the meadow, extended her right hand toward the beast and began to speak.

"Oh, great beast of dark and pride

What you sense cannot coincide

Sense of smell and sight's perfection

Lead the darkness the opposite direction"

Instantly, the beast stood still and thrust his massive scaly head into the air as if trying to pick up a scent. Zella's scent! Then Luminaud leapt into the air and flapped his awful, mighty wings and was gone! Abel had cast a spell on the dragon.

"Come quickly, Zella," Abel cried. "I do not know how long it might take for the beast to realize he has been duped. To Cullen's aid we must go!"

Zella and Rania ran—and flew—after Abel, who ran with

the grace of a gazelle and leaping ability of a leopard toward the eastern edge of the lake where the beast had first appeared. Once at the edge of Menden Lake, Zella felt a bit less fear because of the covering of trees the forest surrounding the lake afforded them.

"We must find the entrance," Abel said.

"But the beast came from *under* the water, Abel! And this is a deep lake! Who knows how far below the surface the entrance might be!" replied Zella.

"There is another way. A drier way, but we must go at once," said Rania.

While the fairy, Abel, and Zella made their way through the eastern woods surrounding Menden Lake, they heard the great and terrible roars of the Light Eater snarling his frustration and bewilderment in the distance, confused at not being able to locate the girl. Even the distant thrashing of the beast caused Zella to shudder in fear as she followed Rania and Abel to the hidden entrance to his lair. Known only to fairies, this entrance was a mere crevice between two boulders that appeared to lead nowhere, but Rania flitted easily through and into the cavern's narrow opening, beckoning Zella to follow.

Zella rushed in but didn't notice that Abel had not done the same. After almost a minute of squeezing her way through the very narrow passageway, Zella squeezed her way back to the entrance, where she found Abel waiting for her.

"Come, Abel! We must go at once!" pleaded Zella.

"I am afraid the passageway is much too small for me to enter, Zella! You must make this part of the journey without me," said Abel, sorrowfully.

"I cannot do this alone, Abel! I cannot! I *will* not!" declared Zella.

"What is truth, Zella? What does truth tell you?" asked Abel.

"The truth ... the truth. Truth tells me I am to be about the task set before me, to deliver the key to Cullen," replied Zella, solemnly.

"And what else?" replied Abel.

"The truth is..." she hesitated, "the truth is I am not alone. I am never alone. I have Rania and I am sent forth by the Founders. They are *with* me even now. I ... I sense their presence."

Knowing she would soon be facing the dragon, Zella made a decision that would come back to haunt her. While embracing Abel, she slipped the small pouch holding the key into the outer pocket of Abel's robe. Her reason? Even though she had been instructed to carry the key and allow no one else to do so, she felt it might be wiser to search for Cullen in the dragon's realm without the key. After all, she reasoned, "I am but a little girl."

Zella made her way to where she had last seen Rania. Seeing the girl, Rania implored, "It is your brother. He is in need."

14

LUMINAUD'S RAGE

*T*he great beast could smell the girl and feel her presence, but something had misdirected him and he had flown away from Menden Lake and away from Zella and Rania. Like a bat growing frustrated at not being able to locate his desired prey, the dragon flew wildly to the north, toward Abssystine, but having lost all sense of and scent of the girl, turned west, heading straight for Treacherin.

Flying low over the city, he sniffed and strained for any sign of Zella, but once again was unable to pick up even the slightest trace. His anger growing with each moment, Luminaud's rage grew so intensely hot that he began to glow. And as he glowed, the light of life began to seep from his heart. Like fuel to a fire, he needed the light of life—the life-force of others—to keep his own life from ebbing away.

Seething now, great puffs of yellow, sulfurous smoke

streaming with jet-like force from his nostrils, Luminaud realized he had not eaten in quite some time, focusing on finding
the King's grandchildren more than his need for light. With
lightning speed and with thunder-inducing power, the
mighty creature let out a roar so blood-curdling, it had sent
shivers down the spine of every living thing within a twenty-
mile radius! Like a laser, his eyes glowing with rage, the beast
fixed his sights on the one place he knew for sure he would
find enough children with light enough to sustain him in his
conquest of the grandchildren of King Leonolis: Castle Aerie.

The dragon flew so fast he looked more like a blur than a
distinguishable monster. Streaking southward toward the
great castle of Bren, Luminaud created such a great wind in
his wake that trees toppled as he swooshed above them.
Sounding like a giant arrow coursing through the air toward
its target, the great dragon had arrived before any of the royal
guards had had a chance to sound the alarm. He came to a
thundering halt as his massive talons struck the ground in the
castle courtyard. Many people had become trapped between
the beast and any chance of escape, including ten children
who had just been playing a game of Red Rover.

Huffing and puffing and snarling and hissing as if to make
sure he did not go unnoticed (as if that were possible),
Luminaud began taunting the guards as those surrounding
him from the castle walls released a barrage of massive arrows
called dragon-slayers. These special missiles had been created
for just such a moment. Heavier than normal wooden arrows,

they were forged of iron and launched from larger-than-normal crossbows. With tips of Phrygian crystal, these dragon-slayers began to pelt the monster's scaly body and bounce off without administering so much as a scratch!

"Pitiful! Pitiful efforts of man! Your weapons feel like no more than gnats, buzzing and annoying yet virtually harmless! Go ahead! Shoot if you must, but I dare say there is nothing that you have in your arsenal that could possibly harm me!" snarled Luminaud in defiance.

"Where is your King? Where is the one they call Leonolis?" demanded the beast.

"He is not here!" shouted a voice from one of the castle turrets directly behind the head of the great beast.

Turning around in a flurry of wings and slashing tail, Luminaud shouted back, "Then who speaks on his behalf?"

Adolphus stepped into the window frame. "It is I, Adolphus."

"And who are you who dares speak for the King? And why does he send another? Is he so afraid that he cannot even come to the aid of his own people?" mocked the dragon.

"Even now, he is about the business of the realm and has left me to speak on his behalf to any major needs of the realm during his absence. I am both seer and sage, friend and counsel to good King Leonolis. What is your purpose here?" asked the seer.

"Purpose? My purpose here?" laughed Luminaud. "My purpose is quite simple. You have something I need."

"And what might that be?" asked Adolphus.

Facing the group of children now huddled together near the courtyard well, he curled his long tail around them and completely encircled them with his slithering, scaly appendage. With a hiss of scorn, the dragon said, "These will do."

At the utterance of those chilling words, Adolphus raised the wand he had hidden in his sleeve and pointed it at Luminaud, saying, "Beast of darkness, harm no child! Get thee back to darkness wild!" A bolt of lightning shot from the end of the wand and struck the dragon squarely in the back of his giant head, but the lightning's shock seemed to have the opposite effect on him. While the beast grew brighter red in color, the entire courtyard began to grow strangely dim! Luminaud was somehow taking the magic of light and consuming it!

"Ah! How refreshing and invigorating! Do it again, good Adolphus! *Please* wield your lightning wand my way once again!" laughed Luminaud. Turning his attention back to the children, the dragon tightened his tail like a python wrapping his body around prey. His grip was just tight enough to not crush them but strong enough to keep them still. Leaping into the air, the children helpless in his clutches, Luminaud laughed and shouted, "I will be back for more, but these will do just fine in the meantime!"

Watching helplessly as the beast fled with the captured children flailing, Adolphus heard the wailing and weeping of the adults left dumbfounded in the courtyard below. Mothers and fathers, grandparents, aunts, and uncles of the kidnapped children wept in shock and left the courtyard in a haze of mourning where only a few moments before had been a brightness of joy and activity.

While Adolphus surveyed the situation from above, a mother whose child was taken cried out to him: "Adolphus, seer of Bren! What will become of our children? Where has the King gone? Who will rally the forces of Bren and pursue the monster? Please sir, rally the forces of Bren and rescue our children. Brianna, my daughter, is the only family I have left in this world! She is my one and only! Please do something!"

With great calm and assurance yet in a grave tone of voice, Adolphus responded, "Good woman of Bren. Mother of Brianna and to all kin of these children, I assure you we will take all steps necessary to assure the safe return of your children as the Founders will it so! This very day, not only have your sons and daughters, your grandchildren, your nieces and nephews, your siblings been snatched away from our midst, but the very heart of Bren has been wounded! The loss of a child is deep and devastating to this nation! Even one child is too many! We will not stand helpless! Even now good King Leonolis has set forth on a quest to slay this very beast that has so violated us today! I will relay word to him of today's attack and give charge to general Bek, who will oversee our pursuit of the beast!"

"But how we will find the beast? Where has he taken our children?" lamented another mother.

"He is a creature known to inhabit the waters of Menden Lake. This we have seen. General Bek, rally the forces of Bren and make for the north straightaway!" commanded Adolphus.

General Bek called to the generals, colonels, lieutenants, and captains of those beneath him in rank, shouting, "To Warrior's Canyon at once! Every battalion! Every squadron! Every man and all the legions of the royal forces of Bren! Form ranks at once!"

With each general calling to each colonel and each colonel calling to each lieutenant and each lieutenant calling to each captain below him, the troops of Bren stationed at or near Castle Aerie assembled quickly and orderly in the canyon below Castle Aerie. Simultaneously, General Bek commanded the alarm to be sounded from watchtower to watchtower from the south to the north. Like a well-oiled machine, the fires were set and bells rung in each watchtower, sounding the alarm distinctly known throughout the land of Bren to be warning of dragons, followed by the distinct signal for all troops to gather from the north to the south and to converge upon Menden Lake.

Assembling so quickly that even General Bek was surprised, the troops, to a man, felt the passion of anger toward the beast at the mere thought of harm coming to a single child. With the blast of the battle trumpet, the cavalry went ahead of the infantry by way of the roadway following the River Runland northward toward Menden Lake, while only one squadron of five hundred men remained behind to provide protection for the people of Castle Aerie and its surrounding environs.

Signal fire and bell toll passed from watchtower to watchtower until the entire land was awakened to the threat of the Light Eater. Simultaneously, Adolphus had begun dispatching the Dragon Lily Elixir to every household via special messenger along with a good supply of Phrygian crystal. A garrison of troops accompanied each wagon and messenger transporting the elixir and stones. If one could have seen the goings-on of the entire land of Bren from high above, one would have seen the most beautifully choreographed sequence of events, almost like a dance, a most passionate dance of defenders willing to fight to the death for the life of every man woman and child of Bren.

Passing from homestead to homestead and from farm to farm, from village to village and from cottage to cottage, the messengers rapidly but methodically delivered the elixir and crystal along with instructions on how to use them to every household with children. The plan? Daub the elixir between the upper lip and nose of each child, place a piece of Phrygian crystal in the pocket of each child, and by dark of night, head for the nearest cavern too small for a dragon to fit into. For most, this meant a whole night's journey to the great caverns of the north—near Menden Lake—since the caverns in the south were not nearly as massive or accessible as the many caverns known to exist there.

While the legions of Bren's magnificent army began to race toward and converge on Menden Lake, the families of the land made their way to the nearest caverns at dusk as instructed by Adolphus via the messengers. So silent were the footsteps of the families, from the fathers and mothers carrying babies and toddlers to the young lads and lasses to the teenagers, that even the night-feeding creatures were startled as they crossed the paths of the people during their forage for food. It was as if even the animal realm knew the Light Eater was no respecter of species, feeding on the light of life from wherever he could find it. They, too, were leading their children to safety as if summoned by the magic of Bren to do so.

Lions mingled with deer. Wolves walked silently with lambs. Wildcats scurried alongside field mice. Unicorns plodded with bears. Swine rats scooted aside wolfen. Hawks flew with owl and the occasional chiroptera. Bats and swallows swooshed almost silently toward safety, carrying their young on their backs through the dark night sky. Human and animal realm alike seemed to be headed for a common goal and bolstered by a common purpose, each laying aside former fears for present necessity. Under any other circumstances, such a sight would have brought forth much joy and laughter. But in the here and dangerous now, fear could be seen in the eyes of both man and beast. Though fearful, the common good buoyed the entire land of Bren with hopefulness.

While the families headed for safety and the armies marched to the Light Eater, those without children began to take up arms. Old men with swords that had not been wielded since younger days and young unmarried men full of vim and vigor and in need of a good fight took up sword and spear and went to Menden Lake. Old women carried pitchforks and daggers, and young women brought lances and slingshots to the lair of the beast. Werewolf and wolfen joined forces with hawken and fairy. Glass dragon and chiroptera rallied alongside treesant and ogre. It was as if by some good magic, the entire land had been awakened to its need for one another, regardless of differences. Though they did not speak a common language, they shared one thing in common. Each shared the light of life bestowed upon them by the Founders, and each knew that they could not fight and defeat the Light Eater without the other. The magic of peace filled the realm in a most wonderful and mystical way ... until it was shattered.

Unbeknownst to the people and creatures below, Luminaud had been observing the activities of Bren from high above. With the ten children still held tightly in the grasp of his long leathery tail, the dragon was at once joyful beyond belief and confused beyond reason. Joyful at the thought of all the light he sensed emanating from the living humans and living creatures below, yet absolutely confounded at why he could not smell or sense any children. With confusion overshadowing his joy, the great leviathan began to shriek wildly, partly out of frustration and partly to send fear and terror through the ranks of those below.

One would think that a dragon would have incredible night vision since dragons are known to spend so much time hiding in the darkness of caves by day, but Luminaud's sense of sight was muted by darkness, especially if he had not consumed light of other living creatures in some time. And it had been quite some time since his last consumption. In fact, all that powered his present flight was the light of life in the children trailing behind him, and he sensed that life would soon be used up. He risked falling from the sky.

Assessing his situation, the dragon sensed a massive amount of energy—the light of life—coming from directly beneath him. Diving like a dart toward the earth below, the great beast planted his feet so heavily on the ground it sent a quivering tremor throughout the entire land. So massive was the light of life he now found himself amongst, he loosened his grip on the children. A flock of hawken that the dragon didn't even notice until they were far out of his sulfurous reach quickly scooped them up. Rather than waste his time on pursuing the children, the dragon began feasting on the light of life surrounding him.

One by one, the elk and deer and bison and antelope he had landed amidst fell prey to his hunger. The brave creatures gave their lives to protect the families. Even though they were not children, the light of the lives of these five hundred animals had filled him with invigorating life. The more life came into his evil heart and mind, the more he became filled with rage. While adult lives would do for a moment, it was the light of the life of children he craved most.

With one rage-filled lunge, Luminaud leapt into the night sky and shrieked so loudly it was heard all the way past the great mountains of the north. "Where are the children?" he screamed. And he was gone.

NOT MENDEN LAKE

*A*rnoldo removed the bags and blankets he had used to conceal the children and Ariel. Their eyes had adjusted to the moonlit night quite easily since they had been in complete darkness for so long by the time they arrived at Menden Lake. They saw mist rising from the surface of the waters. Rubbing his eyes, Harry was first to speak.

"I thought it would be bigger?"

"Me, too," agreed Abigail.

"Me, three," snarked Mia.

"You observe well, children. We are not at Menden Lake, are we, Arnoldo?" asked Ariel

"You are right, dear Ariel. We are, indeed, not at Menden Lake. Even as we left the safety of Abysstine, I felt as if we were being watched," cautioned Arnoldo. "I could not shake the feeling that eyes were on me and dared not risk taking you anywhere near the Lake, especially when I heard the screeches and shrieks of the terrible beast they call The Light Eater emanating from the depths of Menden Lake itself. I thought it best to make my way to the trade city of Treacherin. The mist you see rises from the waters of the River Runland that runs through Treacherin. No one would ever suspect a businessman delivering his wares to Treacherin since it is quite common for such loads to be transported during the less busy time of night and to avoid the heat of the day on any perishable wares."

"I sense you have done wisely, good Arnoldo," said Ariel.

"I know it is not the way you had asked me to take you, but I thought it best, and I am sad to tell you that I must go about my business of transporting the wares to the proper vendors before I make my way back to Abysstine or questions will be asked," replied Arnoldo.

"Go. Be about your business, dear friend. It is the will of the Founders by which we are here. There is a reason and a point of view yet to discover in our little adventure. Right, children?" responded Ariel.

Harry nodded to Ariel as he turned toward Mia. Mia nodded to Ariel as she looked to her sister, Abigail, to reassure her ... only to find Abigail responding with eager agreement as she nodded to Ariel herself. After thanking Arnoldo and giving him the best group hug ever, the children and Ariel watched as Arnoldo and his wagon full of wares headed toward the business district of Treacherin and slowly disappeared into the darkness.

Mia broke the silence by asking, "Where to now, Ariel?"

"Let us think about this together, children. I am here as a guide but cannot make your decisions for you. Somehow, the answers you seek will be revealed as you seek and trust the Founders," replied Ariel.

"How do we do that? How do we seek what we cannot see? How can we trust what we sense?" asked Harry.

"Well, that is actually quite simple," replied Ariel. "In the Kingdom of Bren it is the children who understand the concept of the Kingdom even more readily than your adult counterparts. Like it is written somewhere in the deepest recesses of your beings—somewhere deep within your mind —the mystery of the Kingdom is waiting for you to step into."

"What do you mean?" asked Abigail. "We are just children."

"Just children? Just children? Do not sell yourself short of what the Founders say and intend for you. You are each full of wonder at the possibility of the impossible. Within each of you is there not a deep sense of adventure? In the deepest part of you there is a knowing of mysteries yet undiscovered. Even the mystery of the Kingdom is there for you to solve, and in the solving you discover the Kingdom in its fullness. The Kingdom of Bren is far greater than you can see with adult eyes," said Ariel.

"Why can't adults see and solve the mysteries of the Kingdom?" asked Mia.

"Because as humans grow and become adults, they often lose their sense of childlike wonder. They far too often replace childlike faith and trust with reason, logic, and science," said the Nova.

"But I thought reason and logic and science were good things," said Harry in exasperation.

"Oh, they are indeed good things, but even good things can become less than they were intended when used apart from the purpose for which they were created. Reason and logic and science were all created by the Founders to help children discover the keys to the Kingdom and were meant to be used to unlock the mysteries found therein. Simply put: all things were created by the Founders and were intended for use in the Kingdom."

Ariel continued, "Simply put, children, the best way to describe the Kingdom is to simply understand that the Founders rule ... that the Founders are in control even when humans forget that the entire existence of the universe was for the sake of the Kingdom."

"I get it! I get it" shouted Harry. "The Founders waste nothing!"

"Me, too!" replied Mia. "Even bad things that happen can be used for good!"

"Of course!" cried Abigail. "They cause all things to work together for our good and for their purposes!"

"That's right, children! That's absolutely right! But just how does that happen?" Ariel asked.

"Well, instead of seeing with adult eyes and from an adult point of view, we must learn to see with the trusting, believing eyes of children," replied Abigail.

"And just what does that mean, children of Bren?" queried Ariel.

"I know! I know! I know!" insisted Harry. "We must learn to see what the Founders see—to see from the Founders' point of view!"

"Yes! Yes! Yes!" said Ariel with great wonder. "That's it! So what do they see in our present predicament? What do you see, children?"

As if they had made the greatest discovery of all time (and some say they had), the children huddled together with foreheads touching. They instinctively held onto one another in solidarity and began to think about where they were. And then, Mia began to speak to the Founders!

"Oh, great Founders, creators of all that is, we are but children and you are our makers. We trust You, we believe in You, we need You, and we need to see what you see. We see an impossible situation, but You see a way around or through or over or under. We see no way to find our Cullen or the other children, but You know right where they are. We ask that You would reveal to us Your point of view on these matters."

Simple yet powerful, her petition became the collective

prayer of the children and Ariel. And they all waited there, heads still touching, arms still draped around one another's shoulders. A few moments passed, and Mia began to speak again.

"I know this may sound crazy, but..."

"But what, Mia? But what?" asked Harry and Abigail.

Hesitating, Mia looked to Ariel for reassurance.

"Speak, child. Remember the Kingdom ... that the Founders are in control and waste nothing ... not even our hard times ... not even your fears ... not your wonder ... and especially not your faith," said Ariel wisely.

"I see ... boats ..." said Mia, haltingly.

"Boats? Of course you see boats! We are at the Runland!" said Abigail in exasperation.

"Children!" said Ariel sternly, "let her speak. Go on, dear Mia. The Founders waste nothing. What sounds like foolishness to an adult makes perfect sense to the trusting heart of a child. Do not lose your wonder now, children! Be the unlockers of the mysteries!"

"Yes, I see ... I see boats ... but they are not like boats made of wood or metal, but boats I can see through like glass or..."

"Like *crystal*!" shouted Harry.

"Like the crystalline vessels built by the Scavengians of old!" Abigail chimed in.

"Powered by merely thinking thoughts!" exclaimed Mia.

"If only such a boat were somewhere nearby ..." said Harry.

"If only," agreed Abigail.

As the three children pondered the possibilities of what finding a Scavengian boat made of Phrygian crystal might mean to their current situation, Ariel calmly said, "Look, children, toward the river. Look."

Like a ghost floating in complete silence and almost unseen save for the obvious twinkle and glimmer of moonlight shimmering from its crystalline hull, a Scavengian vessel passed by them headed for the moorings in the port of Treacherin. Needing no instruction, the children ran after the boat. Ariel tried to keep up!

The slow-moving vessel came to a perfect stop at a nearby pier and moored. As luck, or the Founders, would have it, the boat's captain was with the Royal Navy of Bren. Several hundred children and their parents disembarked from the boat in silence as if they were trying to stay hidden from some unseen entity. Royal officials of the land of Bren directed the families toward the city. This was evident from the seal of the King emblazoned on the armor of the men attending to and directing the travelers. Once the last family had left the vessel, Ariel and the children approached the captain.

When he saw them, the captain said as softly yet as sternly as possible, "Children! You must go with the royal guards to the great northern caverns! Even now the great beast may be hovering in wait above us!"

"We know, good captain! We know!" replied Mia.

"Then be off at once or you will surely be in more danger! You cannot—you *must* not—stay here!" insisted the captain.

Stepping in to explain their situation, Ariel said, "These are the grandchildren of High King Leonolis! They have been summoned from another realm for the very purpose of ridding the land of the Light Eater!"

"That is preposterous! How can mere children rid the land of such a beast? If these are, as you say, the grandchildren of the King, then that is all the more reason to send them into the protection of the northern caverns," the captain insisted.

"Good Captain Akvo, we are truly the grandchildren of King Leonolis and we are indeed summoned here for the very purpose of ..." began Mia.

"What did you just call me?" asked the captain.

"Why, Captain Akvo," said Mia, sheepishly.

"How can it be that you would know my name when I have not introduced myself to you?" asked the bewildered sailor.

"Your name was whispered to me by ... by ... the Founders," said Mia.

Humbled and speechless, the captain was reduced to childlike wonder and he responded accordingly. "Only the Founders could have told you this as we have never met. How may I serve you, grandchildren of the King?"

"We have need of this vessel," answered Abigail. "Grand-father needs us. The others need us now!"

Without hesitation, because those who know the Kingdom expect such supernatural occurrences, Captain Akvo ushered the children and Ariel aboard the vessel. "We call her Defender."

"Call who Defender, Captain Akvo?" asked Harry.

"This ship. We call her Defender because she is used in defense of the realm," replied the captain.

"How do you know it's a 'she'?" asked Abigail.

"Boats are referred to as 'she' because it is the female body that carries life. Just as a mother's body carries the unborn child, the ships and boats of the land carry those on board to safety over and through the depths of the waterways of the world," replied Captain Akvo.

Satisfied with this explanation, the children huddled together again, much to the amusement of Captain Akvo and Ariel.

"What are they doing?" asked Akvo.

"If I am not mistaken, they are seeking the wisdom of the Founders. We shall see soon enough!" replied Ariel.

A few minutes later, the children broke their huddle and Mia addressed Ariel and Captain Akvo. "We are to head south on the River Runland."

"Of course, to rescue as many children and families as possible from the cities and villages along they waterway," said Captain Akvo.

"We are to go after the seven," said Abigail, matter-of-factly.

"The seven what?" asked Ariel.

"We heard only that as we head southward on the Runland, we will know the seven when we see them ... and the two extras," explained Harry.

"Two extra what?" asked Akvo.

"We will know them when we see them, too!" said Mia as if everyone should have known.

"Then to the south we go," ordered Captain Akvo. "Children, would you like to power Defender?"

"Yes! Yes! Yes!" came three excited, sneaky, squeaky voices simultaneously. "How do we do it?" ask Harry.

"It is quite simple. Touch the helm with your right hand and think thoughts of command that tell the boat to move south," replied Captain Akvo.

Of course, all three children ran to the crystal helm of the crystal ship and immediately touched it with their right hands. With a mighty lurch to the left, the ship made a massive wave across the wide river, sending other ships and boats moored there into a rocking, tossing frenzy!

"Slow down, children! Slow down! After all, we must be wary of the darkness and the hidden obstacles beneath the surface. Even on a moonlit night such as this, we must still travel and move with great caution," urged Captain Akvo.

"Good Captain Akvo," chimed in Ariel, "Perhaps it would be better that you man the helm for obvious reasons.

Children, you have done admirably in starting us on our way, but he is the captain for a reason."

Giggling and chuckling and generally full of wonder at what their thoughts had accomplished, the children were glad to turn the helm over to Captain Akvo. As they moved cautiously southward on the south-flowing waters of the River Runland, the children stood on the bow of the ship in the hope of discovering the seven and the two extras.

Just moments into their voyage, Mia shouted, "Look! Look! Seven trees and ... nothing extra ..." her voice trailing off in disappointment.

"Look there! Seven fireflies and ... ten extra fireflies," said Abigail with dismay.

"And what about those seven people floating down the creek there on the left, and the ogre bobbing along after them, and the little fairy flitting just above their heads," said Harry, casually.

"Seven people? And an ogre? And a fairy?" exclaimed Ariel. "Surely this is more than mere coincidence! Captain Akvo!"

"Already headed that way, good Ariel! Already headed that way!" exclaimed Captain Akvo.

While the captain steered the boat toward the figures, Harry, Mia, and Abigail ran to the side of the boat nearest to the figures in the water and began calling out, "Hello, down there! Hello!"

Much to the children's surprise, their greetings were met with very familiar voices in reply!

"Hello, children!" came a deep voice.

"Grandfather?! Grandfather?! Is that *you*?" said Harry with glee.

"Yes! It is I!" exclaimed Leonolis. "Drop the rope ladder from the side so that we may come aboard!"

In quick obedience, Mia and Abigail and Harry ran to the place on the deck where the rope ladder was coiled and made quick work of dropping it over the side of Defender.

"Hey, cousins! Hey, brother! It's me! I'm here!" came the joyful voice of the always-happy Ronald.

As their grandfather held onto the bottom portion of the ladder, Captain Akvo brought Defender to a dead stop in the middle of the Runland. While he held on with one hand, he reached for Annabell with the other, helping her climb the ladder. Next came Mark, but before he could even extend his hand toward Elliott and Matilda, Elliott had taken her little sister by the hand and transported them both from the water below to the deck above!

Once the children were all safely aboard, giggles and sniggers and chuckles and hugs and high fives and tears of joy all mingled from the mass of cousins and siblings, giving the impression to anyone who may have been watching that some grand celebration was taking place on board a ship in the middle of a river in the middle of a moonlit night! Indeed it was! This went on for several

163

minutes as the children exchanged quick versions of how they had come to be where they now found themselves. After awhile, Harry brought the party-like atmosphere to a serious halt, when he asked, "Where is grandfather? Why has he not come aboard?"

Running to the side of the boat where they had last seen their grandfather, the children saw a most humorous sight. Leonolis' face was smooshed into the butt of an ogre as he tried to help the ogre climb the ladder, lifting with his arms extended around said butt, attempting to shoulder the beast up and into the ship.

Unable to mutter even a sound, King Leonolis strained against the ogre's butt to the point of his face turning bright red, visible even in the moonlight! Elliott jumped from the boat and into the river, surfacing next to the ogre's butt. Reaching out, she touched the ogre and instantly transported him and her grandfather directly onto the deck of the boat. All that could be seen of their grandfather were his hands extending out from under either side of the ogre's massive rear end!

"Oliver! Get up at once! You are crushing our grandfather!" exclaimed Matilda.

Embarrassed that he now found himself sitting atop the high King of Bren, Oliver immediately and spryly extricated himself from the King and began apologizing profusely. "Oh, dear me! Dear me! Your Highness, I am so very sorry for having sat me behind on top of you!"

Coughing and sputtering and gasping for breath, Leonolis

sat upright, leaned back on his hands, and began to laugh! Seeing their grandfather laughing set the children all to laughing once again. Of course, they all ran to their grandfather and piled on top of him, hugging and smothering him with love and affection. Once again, the children found themselves in a giggle pile just as they had when the journey began.

Once they had all gotten their giggles and hugs out, they quickly exchanged stories. Then Leonolis introduced Oliver to Ariel and the rest of the children while the little singing fairy that had led them into the river hovered silently just above Defender, as if guarding over the entire group. Motioning toward the fairy, King Leonolis beckoned her to join them below.

Flitting like a streak of lightning, the tiny fairy hovered directly in front of the King. "Good little singing fairy, what is your name?" he asked.

In her sing-song little voice, the tiny creature sang, "I am Canto. Canto is me. Just call me Canto. I sing what I mean."

"Thank you, dear little Canto, for helping us get to the other children. Turning to the children, King Leonolis said, "Children, we must find Cullen at once, and I am afraid that means we must make our way to Menden Lake while we still have cover of darkness."

Canto kept singing, "This is the way. This way we take. Through the dry creek bed. To Menden Lake."

While the children watched, Canto flitted back toward

the riverbank very near the place they had just come from. Motioning to Captain Akvo, Leonolis said, "Follow her."

As they approached the river's edge, the children could see what appeared to be a dry creek bed—more of a gully—rising from the river and in the direction of Menden Lake. Joining hands as they had all become accustomed, Leonolis said, "Now, Elliott!" And they all found themselves safely transported to the creek bed. "This will be a perfect cover from the eyes of Luminaud," said Leonolis, pointing to the canopy of trees covering the creek bed, giving it the appearance of a tunnel.

"Ariel, why have you not come with us?" Mia shouted as she looked back at Defender.

"I will help Captain Akvo in the transport of children to safety, using Defender to ferry them from village and town along the River Runland. I have taken you as far as I can, children. Farewell and Founders-speed to you all," shouted Ariel.

As the king, the children, Oliver, and Canto watched, Defender headed southward into the river. Once the ship had disappeared, Leonolis warned, "Quiet as possible from now on, children. The Light Eater is about."

After a few minutes of silently following their grandfather, the silence was broken by the soft baying of a ... dog? Ronald ran toward the sound of the dog. He laughed aloud and called out, "Buddy! Buddy? Is that you?"

16

BUDDY THE DOG

*a*s Ronald ran toward the sound of the baying dog, the other children could not help but stand in awe and wonder. It couldn't possibly be Buddy the dog. Buddy the beagle-basset hound mix had been Ronald's pet back in Oklahoma. Many were the days when all Ron did was spend time with his four-legged buddy, Buddy. Running! Jumping! Exploring! Wrestling! Petting! Scratching! Sniffing! Whenever Ron was awake, he was either with Buddy or thinking about being with him. And even when he was asleep it seemed all Ron could dream about were more adventures with his Buddy.

When Buddy had gotten sick, Ronald's concern was deep and compassionate. Seeing him go through sickness and pain had been difficult enough for the boy, but Buddy never got better. When his parents told him that Buddy had died during the night, Ronald was inconsolable and collapsed into his mother's arms. Wave upon wave of grief and cry upon cry went on for several days. It had only been a few weeks since Ronald's grief had finally begun to subside and his boyish joy had returned. Now, his siblings and cousins were all concerned for Ronald and his obvious loss of reality as he continued to run toward the sound of the barking dog, crying out, "Buddy! Buddy! My good Buddy! Come here, boy!"

Out of sincere compassion and concern for her cousin, Elliott was the first to try and intervene before Ronald faced what was sure to be another disappointment once he realized this could not possibly be Buddy. "Ronald! Ronald! Wait, cousin! Buddy's gone!"

"Hurry, guys!" chimed in Harry. "He's gonna be crushed when he sees it's not Buddy!"

Being as close as cousins and siblings can be, everyone knew what kind of hurt such a disappointment would bring to Ronald. They all ran toward the sound of Ronald and the baying dog. Mark and Annabell. Mia and Abigail. Harry and, of course, Elliott and Matilda all outran their grandfather and Oliver the ogre and even the little flitting fairy, Canto! But they had arrived too late to stop Ronald!

What they witnessed around that next bend of the dry creek bed made no sense: a boy and a dog reuniting like two long-lost friends. The boy was laughing and giggling hysterically and the dog was jumping all over the boy, licking and slobbering and whimpering gleefully as only a happy dog can.

It was actually quite difficult to see where the boy ended and the dog began, such a blur of frantic joy and glee they had become!

"Buddy! My Buddy! It's really you!" laughed Ron. Buddy wrestled Ronald to the ground in a flurry of wet dog kisses and happy yelps. Boy giggles and barking! Boyish squeals of delight and unintelligible dog yaps of joy. This went on for several minutes, and just when it seemed they had finally calmed down, the flurry of barks and giggles began again!

King Leonolis stepped toward the blur of boy and dog and placed his hand on the boy's shoulder. In the most compassionate tone the children had ever heard, their grandfather simply said, "Ronald, I'm afraid Buddy is gone, son."

Rather than admit what everyone else seemed to know as truth, Ronald wrenched himself away from his grandfather's touch and returned to the frantically happy dog, showering the pup with love and affection.

"Come on, son," continued his grandfather. "Buddy is gone."

"No way, grandfather! No way! This *is* Buddy!" Ron exclaimed in simultaneous wonder and exasperation that no one could see what he saw. "See the black spot below his right eye? This is Buddy! And see the way his left ear droops lower than his right ear? This is Buddy! And the tip of his tail! See the tip of his tail? It's bent a little! Buddy's tail was bent just like that! This *is* Buddy!"

Feeling overcome with grief for their brother and cousin,

the children all looked to their grandfather as to how to break the news to Ronald that this could not possibly be his dog, Buddy. One more time, Leonolis attempted to comfort Ron and stepped forward to pick the boy up in order to hold him close when reality finally set in. But once again, the boy wrenched himself away from his grandfather and wrapped his arms around the neck of the dog. As he did so, he calmly took hold of Buddy's red leather collar, calmly reached for the small metal tag hanging from the collar, and defiantly held it up for all to see. Then he read the words etched into the tag.

"Buddy the Dog. Owner: Ronald Leon Kay. Address: 217 SW 32nd St., Muskogee, OK. If found, please call 918-555-0115."

Stunned and silent, the children and their grandfather found it difficult to wrap their minds around what Ronald had just read. Their minds stirring with raw emotion and disbelief, they stood in awe for several seconds while Ronald went back to lavishing his love upon his old friend, Buddy.

One by one, each child stepped toward the boy and Buddy. Touching the dog on his floppy ears, Harry said, "Yep, this is Buddy. No doubt about it!"

Before their grandfather could even begin to explain to his grandchildren what they were witnessing, the children began to pile on top of one another in one of their now-all-too-familiar giggle piles. Laughing and giggling and roiling and vying to get closer than the next child, they were overcome with sheer joy and delight at yet another wonder of the magical Kingdom of Bren. Buddy did not seem to mind one bit! The more the children laughed, the closer the dog tried to get to each child. Ronald yelled out, "I told you! I told you! This is my Buddy! Good boy! Good boy! Good boy! I missed you so much, Buddy! Buddy, I love you!"

Tears streaming down his face while he watched his grandchildren writhe and laugh in reckless joy and abandon, Leonolis just let them carry on while Oliver the ogre sat there in wonder at the oddness of human behavior. It was all because of a silly little animal, yet this somehow made even this ogre feel hopeful and wanted. Canto just hovered in the same wonder. The moon above their heads seemed to crest in fullness, causing a moment of pure magic and peace in a world whose very light was threatened by the Light Eater. While the serenity and joy continued to play out, Canto began to sing.

What was lost in one world
Is found in the next
Sorrow gives way to laughter
When dark by light is vexed

Death gives way to living
Faith gives way to sight
Blessing comes in giving
Dark give way to light

>Joy is in the journey
>Journey knows no end
>Death gives way to living
>Life finds a way again
>Life rises once again

Mesmerized by Canto's song and spellbound by the light of the moon, the children had grown silent. Even Buddy was still in Ronald's little-boy-who-never-wants-to-let-go-of-his-friend-again embrace. The kids turned slowly to their grandfather, expecting an explanation for all they were now experiencing. They waited. And they waited. And they waited some more, Finally, Elliott could stand no more of the silence.

"Grandfather? How can this be?" asked Ellie.

Normally ready with an answer, Leonolis stood dumbfounded.

Again Elliott asked, "Grandfather! Grandfather Leonolis! How can this be?!"

"Uh, er, I, I honestly do not know what to say, except ... except..."

"Except what, grandfather?" everyone replied.

"Except I have never seen such a thing in all my days in Bren. There can be only one explanation, dear children. Only the Founders are capable of such power, of such wonderful magic, taking what was death in one realm and creating life in another! Surely this day you have witnessed something I have never seen before but have heard of since I myself was a boy.

That death is not the end, but rather the beginning. I have no explanation beyond that, children. We have but to believe and receive such gifts—such miracles—as reality when they are revealed to us."

"Why bring Buddy to Bren, grandfather?" asked Ronald.

"All I know is this, dear Ron," began his grandfather. "It is for some purpose beyond what we are able to see and understand to this point. I suggest we not try to figure it all out right now. Let us be good believers and simply receive this magnificent blessing for what it is: a gift from the Founders reminding us we are never alone and never forgotten. We may never know all the reasons why Buddy had to die in your world or why he gets to live again in this world. We must simply enjoy that he is here and that the Founders will reveal the purpose as we seek to fulfill the calling placed on us for such a time as this."

"What do you mean, 'for such a time as this,' grandfather?" asked Matilda.

As if on cue, the reverie of this precious, priceless moment was shattered by the blood-curdling screech of something high above. Instinctively, the children all crouched down in the middle of the creek bed and became deathly silent. Straining for where the sound might have come from and trying to discern what had made it, Buddy stepped out from Ronald's grip and ran to the top of the furthest embankment. Standing there, the dog lifted his right paw and seemed to point in the direction from which the sound had come.

The children listened in horror as the sound of swooshing wings and the ear-piercing screech of a wild creature once again sent them crouching for cover. They all knew this could only be coming from one source, and they were very concerned that Buddy the dog was now exposed to the full fury of Luminaud the Light Eater. Without fear for his own well-being, Ron ran toward his Buddy just in time to witness yet another burst of magic.

The dog fearlessly stood his ground, pointing toward the direction the dragon's screeches seemed to be coming from. Ron noticed something else about Buddy—or rather, about his collar. Whenever the beast seemed to draw closer, the ID tag on Buddy's collar began to glow with the faintest of red. Just enough to be noticeable to those within a few feet of the dog.

Ron whispered to Leonolis, "Look grandfather! Every time the beast draws near, Buddy's tag glows slightly red! Buddy is here to help warn us, grandfather! With Buddy along, we will always know when the dragon is nearby!"

Before Leonolis could even agree with his grandson, the boy and the dog were off! Racing onward and upward and further into the dry creek bed, Ronald (led by Buddy) led his brother and cousins and grandfather, and Oliver and Canto, toward the beast!

"Where are they taking us, grandfather?" asked Mia.

"I don't know for sure, but my best guess is that the Founders have sent Buddy to lead us to the lair of the great beast. To Menden Lake!"

"What should we do?" asked Abigail.

"I don't think we have much of a choice, dear one! From what we have just witnessed concerning the reappearance of Buddy, it can only mean one thing! The Founders are speaking and leading. We trust and follow. Trust and follow, children! Trust and follow!"

With that, the entire brave gang headed toward Menden Lake and directly into the dragon's realm. All they could do was trust and follow, so trust and follow they did.

17

CULLEN, ZELLA, AND THE DILEMMA

hile King Leonolis, the children with him, Oliver the ogre and Canto the singing fairy made their way to Menden Lake, Zella fixed her eyes on Rania back in the passageway leading to the lair of Luminaud. She was searching for Cullen. Winding around boulders and twisting between stalagmites and stalactites, up and over piles of fallen stones, Rania the little fairy stealthily led Zella to where they hoped to find Cullen.

Although it had taken only a few minutes to get there, it seemed like hours to Zella, so fearful of what condition she might find her brother in. Would he be held captive by the beast? Would he be tortured? Would he be injured? Or something worse? As her thoughts ran rampantly between all the possible scenarios, Rania snapped Zella back to reality. "Shh-hhhhh!" she said quietly, holding her tiny finger to her lips.

"What is it?" whispered Zella.

"A faint glimmer of light," responded Rania, pointing ahead.

"Do you think it might be Luminaud's lair?" asked the girl.

"There is only one way to find out. You wait here while I fly ahead and survey the area and the source of light."

Rania flitted toward the light. It was all Zella could do to keep from running after the fairy. After all, this was her brother and she had been tasked by the Founders to deliver the key to him. Just as she was about to follow, Rania, frantic, stopped her.

The usually very composed and stoic little fairy now appeared agitated and angry. Her words poured out so quickly it sounded to Zella like another language. "What is it, Rania?! Slow down! I cannot understand what you are saying! Did you find Cullen? Did you find my brother? Is he okay?"

Suddenly realizing she had been more confusing than helpful, the little fairy stopped her flittering and fluttering and agitation and hovered quietly in front of Zella's nose. "Yes, I found your brother, but he is not ... okay."

Zella burst into tears!

"He's hurt! I knew it! He's been captured! I knew it! Or worse, he's had the light of life drawn from him and he's ... he's ... gone!" sobbed Zella.

Once again, Rania's agitation and flittering and fluttering

and gibbering and jabbering returned, only this time her agitation was directed at the girl! Wagging her finger at Zella's nose, Rania spoke very slowly and clearly, "Why is it that you humans seem to always believe the worst. You have gone right to the worst possible outcome and scenario and chosen to believe something you have not the foggiest idea about!"

Like a mother scolding her child, Rania went on wagging her finger at the Zella, now silent due to the sudden change in the fairy's attitude toward her. "Cullen is just ahead, and he is alive and well, but listen to me and hear me well, Zella, granddaughter of the King and Queen. There is something you must know. He has been captured by the dragon, and he is in a most precarious predicament."

"What do you mean 'a most precarious predicament'?" asked Zella.

"It is better shown than explained," replied Rania. "Follow me and remain as quiet as possible. Even though good Abel has cast the spell of delusion upon the great beast, we have no certainty of how long he will remain in his deluded state before he realizes he is under a spell. And there is one more thing. The dragon's lair is guarded by his minions —the dragonflies. But I will deal with them as necessary. Come quickly and quietly."

Though not brilliant like daylight, the closer they got to the light the brighter it seemed to Zella. And the brighter it seemed, the lighter her heart felt. The lighter her heart felt, the more despair was replaced with a sense of hope that all would be well with her brother once she laid eyes upon him.

Soon enough, the fairy and the girl left the cramped passageway and walked into a large dome-shaped cavern. As Zella's eyes adjusted, she was instantly drawn to the center of the room. There was a large indentation in the ground—a dragon-sized indentation. This was obviously the place where Luminaud slept! They were suddenly fully aware of where they now stood. Zella froze, taking in the immensity of the room and the intensity of her sudden fear.

"Your fear betrays you once again, good Zella," said the fairy.

In a shaking, timid voice, Zella responded, "What fear?"

"The fear based on what you see rather than hope based on what the Founders see," replied Rania.

"What do the Founders see?" asked the girl.

"Only you can see for you, dear Zella. What the dragon means for evil, the Founders mean for good."

"Oh, bother!" said the girl, "for once can you not simply tell me what to believe?!"

"That would not require faith, girl. And faith is hoping in what is not yet seen. All I can tell you is to fix your eyes on the Founders and truth and step off that ledge of fear you now cling to and into the realm of faith. Spread your wings and trust the Founders. Don't simply believe what your eyes perceive. Often, truth is just beyond the place of sight, but you will never know until you step out."

Just as Zella was about to step out in faith, she saw a slight movement just above the dragon's sleeping chamber. Jutting upward from the floor behind the chamber was a massive wall of granite that wasn't granite at all, but rather, upon closer inspection, crystal. It was a mixture of quartz and diamond and opal and ruby, at once opaque yet as clear as day! The more evident the wall became, the more it became apparent that the light filling the grey cavern was actually emanating from this wall. But the movement Zella saw was not the slight pulsating light but rather the figure suspended in midair. Hanging from some unseen magical rope was a small ... thing. Since it was suspended so high above the cavern floor, Zella had not quite been able to make out the shape. Squinting, the "thing" began to resemble something less "thingish" and more boyish.

"Cullen!" she shouted. "Cullen, is that you?!"

Before Rania could even attempt to shush Zella's glad yet terrified shrieks, two dragonfly sentries guarding the boy suddenly appeared. Buzzing like enraged bees, the sentries, swords in hand, lunged for the girl. Realizing her mistake, Zella instinctively crossed her arms in front of her face for protection. Closing her eyes and cringing in anticipation of the soon-coming pain, Zella felt nothing. But she heard plenty!

Like tiny bowls of lightning and tiny claps of thunder, one on her right and one on her left, Zella heard "zzzttt... zzzttt." It reminded her of the sound of electricity she had heard once at the science museum made by a Tesla coil being turned on! She opened her eyes just in time to see two tiny puffs of smoke on either side of her as both sword-wielding dragonflies fell in burning little heaps to the ground. Rania symbolically blew the end of her wand as a gunslinger might have done after a showdown in one of those old-timer western movies Zella's dad loved to watch.

Realizing her sudden outburst at seeing Cullen hanging in midair had altered the sentries, Zella felt embarrassed and ashamed. "Just shake it off, Zella," said Rania. "Even the granddaughter of a king can be seduced by fear. Just get back to being how and whose you are."

This rebuke seemed at once loving and firm—and needed—by Zella. Rather than being proud, the little girl simply said, "Thank you for reminding me of who and whose I am. What do we do now, Rania?"

Without saying a word, Rania flew up to Cullen and hovered directly in front of his face. "He has been suspended by some dark magic," she reported to Zella. "Though his eyes are open, he appears to have been placed in some sort of trance. He is alive and breathing, but unable to communicate."

Seeing from the Founders' point of view, Zella simple replied, "There is hope as long as he is breathing. What of the map?"

Rania flew around Cullen several times, checking his pockets and pouch and flew back down to Zella.

"The map is not with him," said the fairy.

"That can only mean it has fallen into the hands of the Light Eater," replied Zella. "What do we do now?"

"We must get word to my grandparents," said Zella. "And we must keep this key out of the hands of Luminaud at all cost."

"Let us go back from whence we came before the spell of Abel has worn off the dragon.

Just as Rania flew back into the small passageway, a great thud shook the ground ... as if some giant had just planted itself in the middle of the great cavern. Sure enough, a great giant—giant dragon, that is—jumped between Zella and the passageway leading out of the cavern, effectively cutting her off from escape ... from Rania.

"Ha! Ha! Ha! Ha! Ha! You thought you could fool me, human, with your little feeble spell. While you were trying for find your dear brother, my sentries—at least the ones you managed to miss—warned me of your presence within the environs of my abode. As you can see, your brother is just fine."

Summoning all the bravery and bravado she could muster, Zella shouted, "Fine? Fine? How can he be fine if he is suspended above the cavern floor? How can he be fine if he cannot even utter as much as one word? He is not fine! Let him go! Let him go *now*!"

"Or what?" said Luminaud smugly.

"Or, or, or I'll summon help!" yelled Zella.

Not waiting another second, Zella began to call upon her gift. She began to zig and zag this way and that, confusing the dragon to no end. The more she zigged and zagged, the faster she flew around the room. She knew that once she zig-zagged fast enough, the great beast would be unable to see her. When that happened, she could escape.

Just as she was about to reach escape velocity, Zella was stopped dead in her tracks at the words the dragon spoke. "The key for your brother. I will change the life of your brother for the key you now hide from me."

"I would rather die than make such a deal with a monster!" shouted the girl.

"That can be arranged!" said Luminaud as he reached for the girl.

But before he could touch her, Zella started to zig and zag around the room and once again, just as she was about to make her way to the passageway and sure escape, the dragon spoke.

"I will surely keep your brother alive until I have that key, vile human child, but I will not be so charitable with grandfather and grandmother."

"What do you mean?" asked Zella.

Luminaud swung his great tail and unfurled it and its contents to the girl. Tumbling and stumbling to the ground for the clutches of the beast's tail were High King Leonolis and High Queen Abila!

"What say you now, child? A key for *three* lives. Such an obvious choice, don't you think?" sneered the dragon.

Gathering her wits, Zella's thoughts were transfixed upon Cullen and her grandparents. Was keeping the key from the dragon truly worth the lives of her brother and grandparents? She loved them too much to allow them to die. Isn't that what the Founders' point of view would be? Was one little key worth the death of the ones she loved so much?

"Your decision is quite simple, girl! Give me the key and I will grant you their lives," said Luminaud.

While Zella thought about what the Founders' might have her do, Luminaud once again took Leonolis and Abila into the grip of his mighty tail and squeezed them tightly. The more he squeezed, the more they gasped for breath. The more they gasped for breath, the more the dragon seemed to take in the light of life from the King and Queen. The King and Queen seemed to grow dim, as if life was being breathed out of them and into the monster.

"Wait!" said Zella. "Wait and I will give you what you want."

"Let them go. Let them all go. Once they are completely safe and within the passageway out of this evil place, you can have the key ... but not before."

Zella knew in her knower that they would all die once she handed the key to the dragon, but she knew losing her own life would be worth the lives of her brother and of her grandparents. So the deal was made.

18

ABILA AND LEONOLIS

*Z*ella reached into the inner pocket of her cloak—
the secret place she had hidden the key—and
said, "Let them go."

"Once you have handed the key to me, I will let them go,"
assured Luminaud.

"I do not trust you any further than I can throw you," said
Zella, defiantly.

"You have no other option, foolish little girl. Either you
hand that key over to me or they all die—your grandfather,
your grandmother, and brother!" snarled the great beast.

"I have been instructed by the Founders to deliver the key
to my brother, Cullen, and to no one but Cullen. Release him
or I'm out of here," said Zella with as much boldness as she
had ever mustered in her young life.

"When you are 'out of here,' as you say, I will consume

the light of their lives," responded Luminaud. "Is one little key truly worth the loss of your grandparents and brother? I think not!"

Mustering as much courage as she could, spurred on by stepping off that ledge of fear and spreading her wings of faith just as Rania had suggested moments before, Zella said, "I cannot—I *will* not—disobey the word of the Founders. All I know is this: you will not have the key unless and until my grandparents and my brother are released. Release them or we are done here!"

Seething with rage and roiling with anger, snorting and fuming with great blasts of yellow, sulfurous smoke billowing from his nostrils, the dragon paced the cavern, flailing Leonolis and Abila wildly back and forth in the grasp of his mighty tail for what seemed like an eternity. Luminaud knew deep inside his black heart that the girl seemed sure in her threat to sacrifice even her family to protect the key and to follow through on her commitment to the task set before her by the Founders. Finally, he relented and released his grip on Leonolis and Abila. With a flick of his writhing tail, he sent them sliding across the cavern floor toward Zella. Rolling and tumbling like the dice the children used when playing Yahtzee with her grandparents, Leonolis and Abila tumbled toward her! Moaning and groaning as their bodies slid across the gravel-strewn floor, they managed to stand from their stupor after a few seconds, rubbing their bruised and scraped knees and elbows while coming to Zella's side.

"And my brother?" Zella demanded.

Again, the great beast began to snort and snot and steam as his massive serpentine body and tail writhed like some giant four-legged snake, fumes and plumes of yellow haze steaming from his nostrils while the red pupils of his dragon eyes, surrounded by yellow where one expected white to be, glared and glowered at the defiant little girl.

Luminaud seethed. "Fine!"

The dragon raised his angry gaze upward toward the suspended body of her brother, Cullen. Turning ever so slowly, the boy began to spiral slowly toward the cavern floor. Just as his feet were about to touch the ground, he stopped.

"The key, girl!" shouted the dragon.

"Not until my brother and my grandparents are safely released and out of this dreadful cavern!" Zella shouted back.

"How do I know you'll keep your word?" asked Luminaud.

"How do I know you will keep yours?" retorted Zella.

As if in one of her legendary staring contests with her brothers, Zella's gaze was locked in defiance with the piercing eyes of the great dragon. Finally, Luminaud released his hold on the boy. Cullen immediately fell into a slumped, crumpled pile onto the cavern floor, dazed but conscious, and asked, "What happened?"

Running to their grandson's side, Leonolis and Abila quickly helped him to his feet, assuring him they would explain what had just happened as soon as they were all safely out of the dragon's reach. With a grandparent on either side, Cullen half-walked and half-slid as they dragged his wobbly feet across the floor toward the small entrance to the tunnel directly behind brave Zella, standing in steadfast defiance of the Light Eater.

As they were about to make their escape, Luminaud slammed his tail down between the tunnel and the threesome, leaving only Zella near enough the exit to make her way out. "The key, girl! Now!" he demanded.

"This key will not be yours until my grandparents and my brother have all entered the tunnel. Then and only then will I hand it over!" said Zella.

Exasperated beyond belief, like a child who does not get his way unless he throws a tantrum, Luminaud shouted, "Fine!"

Lifting his tail, Luminaud allowed them to pass into the darkness of the tunnel and out of his scaly reach, leaving only Zella and the key alone in the lair.

Rather than turning to run into the tunnel as one would have expected, Zella stood her ground in utter defiance of the great dragon. Luminaud slithered toward Zella and lowered his giant red scaly head to mere inches from her face. As he stooped to make eye contact on her level, he reached out his right front paw while simultaneously and stealthily unfurling his serpentine tail and bringing it down slowly and quietly behind her, cutting off any way of escape. Zella stood unflinchingly while the beast tightened his grip around her with his scaly appendage until she could no longer move her hands or feet. The more he tightened his grip, the more strained her breathing became. The more she strained for her next breath, the more defiant she grew. Expecting fear to play into his scheme, the dragon could only marvel at the fortitude being displayed by such a small, brave, little human.

"I must say, I thought you were a bit spunky for a human, even more so for a human female, but I never expected such a display as I now witness! Bravo, little one! Bravo!"

Hesitating as if in awe of this little powerhouse of a girl, Luminaud began to draw the light of life from her. As he did so, Zella whispered to herself.

"What's that you say?" insisted the dragon.

Zella ignored him and kept whispering.

"What are you saying?" demanded the dragon as he loosened his grip enough to allow her to speak more clearly.

Looking him right in the evil eyes, Zella simply stated, "I am not talking to you."

Incredulous at her boldness, the beast forcefully shook her and demanded, "Who do you talk to if not to me? Talking to yourself? Have you simply gone mad? Have you lost your mind at the display of my great power?"

"Don't be so prideful or so foolish! You think I am afraid of you or that you wield some great power over me? The only power you have is that of deception!" averred the little girl.

"I could crush you with one simple squeeze of my tail,

fool! If not to yourself and if not to me, who do you talk to? The Founders?" mocked the dragon.

"Crush me you well may, but defeat me you never will!" said Zella.

"Pray tell—pun intended—what you say to the Founders," sneered Luminaud.

"That is simple: Save me if it is Your will. Use my death to bring life to others if it is Your will. Keep the key hidden from the liar called Luminaud," replied Zella.

"Save you, they cannot. Use your life would be better prayed 'waste your life' and keep the key hidden. How foolish to ask when you yourself hold the key! You have no other options, foolish girl. Foolish human! I will have that key *now*!" roared Luminaud.

"Then you have a problem, indeed," declared Zella, "Because I do not *have* the key!"

The monster hurled Zella to the floor. She slid to a stop against the sleeping chamber of his lair. Summoning the dragonflies that served him as slaves, Luminaud demanded, "Search her! Find the key!"

Out of nowhere, a horde of buzzing, flitting, hissing, biting dragonflies assaulted the girl. Rummaging through her robe, flummoxing her in the process, they peered into her ears, they glared into her nostrils, they even searched her hair and found nothing!

The search ended in futility. There was no key!

"Sire," said the head dragonfly, "the girl has no key!"

"Are you sure?" demanded Luminaud. "Search her again!"

The assault began anew. Once again Zella found herself tormented by the power such a small creature, in large numbers, could wield. Again, the head dragonfly said, "Sire, there is no key. Nothing at all!"

Flying into a great fiery, sulfurous rage, the dragon beat his wings and thrashed his mighty tail and snorted his sulfur-spewing breath and glared at the girl with the yellow and red eyes of a beast gone completely mad. "You lie to me, girl! You lie! And for that you will pay with your life!"

While the great beast lifted his tail and spread his sharp talons to rip Zella's precious little body apart, she talked to the Founders again. Though the beast could no longer hear her because of his own rage, she continued her brave, faithful conversation with the Founders.

"Good Founders, makers of Bren and its people, givers of life, I call upon you now for help. If you will, deliver me. If you choose for me to die, I simply ask for grace to get through it without fear ruling my heart and mind. I am yours, dear Founders. Do Your will."

Closing her eyes and receiving the grace to endure what-ever came next, Zella came to a place of complete rest and was filled with trust in the Founders.

When the dragon saw this response from the little girl, he at once began to consume the light of her life. In pure evil fury, he raised his razor-sharp talons and pointed scaly tail to deliver the death blow. As he thrust his tail toward her and lunged with his talons and teeth bared, the room suddenly shook with the violence of an earthquake, the fury of a giant twister zipping through Tornado Alley back in Oklahoma, and the most brilliant flash of lightning anyone has ever seen before or since. But there was one small difference. The earth shook and the winds blew and the lightning flashed in complete silence!

The dragon was hurled against the side of the cave wall and was rendered unconscious while Zella found herself standing upright and unscathed and surrounded by the carcasses of a thousand dragonflies! As if she had just risen from the longest, most refreshing nap she had ever taken, Zella felt rested and exhilarated and full of wonder at how the Founders had answered her prayer!

And just how *had* they answered?

Zella wanted out of the dragon's lair before the great beast awoke, but she felt a presence in the room with her. She noticed a small boy floating slowly toward her from near the ceiling of the massive cavern. As her eyes adjusted from the brilliance of the aforementioned lightning, she squealed, "Theo! Little cousin, Theo! How did you get here? How did you do that? Did *you* do that?" She pointed to the unconscious dragon.

"Yes, cousin Zella. I did that ... with a little help from the Founders!" responded Theo as they embraced.

"I didn't even know you knew Bren existed!" exclaimed Zella.

"Grandpa Lee and Grandma Mellie have been telling me stories of Bren since I was little. And just today, just a few seconds ago, Grandpa Lee told me to head to the Forest of Bren and that I would find the way and to do just what the Founders impressed upon my heart to do! As I ran between the stone lions at the entrance of the forest, I was suddenly flying! One second I was running and the next I was *flying*, Zella! I can fly! And then a still small voice just whispered into my thoughts, 'Zella needs help! Use your gifts.' Then I found myself up there looking down on you and that ... that ... hideous thing! The next thing I knew, I joined my fists together across my heart and as I pulled them apart, thunder and lightning and wind all flooded the room from somewhere deep in my heart and here we stand!"

"That is your gift, Theo! Silent Thunder! You are Thunder Boy! My cousin is Thunder Boy!" exclaimed Zella.

"What is the key the beast spoke of, cousin?" asked Theo.

"I will explain everything while we get out of here. The key is in good hands. I knew the dragon wanted it so I asked Abel—you'll meet her once we are out of this dreadful place—to keep it hidden for me while I came after Cullen. He and Grandfather and Grandmother are just ahead of us in the tunnel. We can meet them and the others above ground, get the key from Abel, and come back and do what we were sent here to do!"

193

The children made their escape, but Luminaud had awoken in time to hear every word they said while pretending to be unconscious. While the children ran toward the surface and a rendezvous with their grandparents, the beast headed into the cavern entrance beneath the waters of Menden Lake, devising his next scheme.

WISDOM AND HUMILITY

Running through the tunnel between his grandparents, Cullen was becoming stronger and more aware and awake with each step. "How did you find me? How did you get here?" he asked.

"Before we answer your questions, we must stop here. It was Zella who set us free!" gasped the King while trying to catch his breath.

"My little sister? Zella?!" exclaimed Cullen. "She did not even come to Bren with us, grandfather! How can this be?"

"She was summoned and made her way here to you by the help of a guide, Abel, sent by the Founders. Zella's mission is to deliver a special key to you," replied Abila.

"The key! Zella has the key?" responded Cullen in surprise.

"What is the purpose of the key?" asked Leonolis.

"It unlocks Lumen's Hammer from within the stone in Luminaud's lair!" exclaimed Cullen. "I somehow knew Zella was nearby even though I could not see or hear her. I had a sort of ... feeling."

"We call that intuition, son," replied Abila.

"The last thing I remember was being held in the dragon's talons as he lifted me high above his head. While he held me there, he snorted out a green mist from his gross nostrils and I began to float. The last thing I remember was Luminaud releasing his grip on me and I didn't fall."

"I must go back for her," replied Leonolis.

"Go back? You left her there?" shouted Cullen, appalled at the thought of his grandfather leaving his very own granddaughter to fend for herself with such a terrible monster.

"We had no choice in the matter, son," replied Abila.

Before they could stop him, Cullen wrenched himself free from the grip of his grandparents and ran with all his might back toward the dragon's lair. So fast was his pace and so set was his focus that he could no longer hear the pleas of his grandparents to stop. He was so set upon getting to his little helpless sister that he never saw her coming!

Zella and Cullen collided with such force that they crumpled into a heap, heads spinning in a confused stupor.

"Cullen, what are you doing? We've got to get out of here!" exclaimed Zella.

"Zella, what are *you* doing?" asked the exasperated boy.

"I came to give you the key that unlock's Lumen's Hammer!" she replied, excitedly.

"You could have been killed!" responded Cullen.

"*You* could have been killed!" Zella answered.

"I had everything under control," said the prideful boy.

"If you had everything under control, why did I have to rescue *you*?" Zella retorted, a bit prideful herself.

"Children, we have no time for squabbling and we definitely have no time for pride to come between us. Cullen, she rescued you. Zella, you rescued him by the grace of the Founders. Neither of you can afford to forget that. Let us be grateful and move along," said Leonolis.

"Grandfather? Grandmother? How did you come to be here? How did Luminaud capture you? Grandfather, I thought you were with the other children! Grandmother, I thought you were with Adolphus in Castle Aerie!" Zella queried.

Abila answered, "I asked Adolphus to help me find your grandfather and the other children. I knew you were safe with Abel. By the magic of the Founders, I found myself standing in the courtyard of Castle Aerie one minute and in the middle of a dry creek bed the next! And who should I find there but your grandfather and Mark, Annabell, Mia, Abigail, Elliott, Matilda, and Ronald ... and Buddy the dog!"

"Buddy the dog? Buddy's alive?" exclaimed Cullen and Zella in unison.

"Yes, he is quite alive and well and as rambunctious as

ever," said the Queen. And I've never seen Ronald Leon Kay happier!"

"And don't forget Oliver the ogre and Canto the fairy!" said Leonolis.

"Huh?" Zella and Cullen were incredulous. "An ogre and a fairy together? We thought they were mortal enemies!"

"Leave it to the Founders to bring together the most unlikely of friendships in times of trial. They have been an immense help in getting us to this moment," said the King.

"But how did you come to be captured by the beast?" asked Zella.

"I am afraid that was my fault," began Leonolis. "In the excitement of seeing Ron reunited with Buddy and then the added exhilaration of seeing your grandmother suddenly in our midst, I let my guard down. I should have recognized what was happening. I should have seen it."

"Should have seen what?" asked Cullen.

"Buddy's ID tag around his neck. Ronald had just discovered that every time the great dragon drew near, it began to glow the faintest of red. By the time I recognized the glow for what it was, it was too late to warn the children. The Light Eater landed with a giant quaking thud right in front of us. We had no place to run. No time to hide," said the King.

"So, what did you do?" asked Cullen.

"The only logical thing. Or illogical, depending upon your point of view. I caught Annabell's eye and nodded. She reached into her robe, pulled out the bell, and rang it with all her might, sending the dragon into a state of stunned immobility! He was paralyzed in his tracks by the magic of her bell! I shouted to the children, 'Run and hide! Now!' And the children, Buddy, Oliver, and Canto found sufficient hiding places within the many caves along the creek bed."

"But why did you and grandmother not run and hide as well?" asked Zella.

"We knew the dragon would stop searching for you once he had us," replied Abila. "You children represent the next generation of Bren. We cannot afford to lose your generation to evil—to lose Bren. Your lives are worth more than our own in moments such as these.

"We also knew that we were more valuable alive to the dragon and his purposes than we were dead. He took us into his slimy tail and flew us back to his lair. How we survived the underwater passage beneath Menden Lake I may never know, but somehow we did, thanks to the Founders," explained Leonolis.

"Once we were in his lair, we found ourselves in the dilemma of how to save you and Zella, and how to keep the key from his evil clutches," said Abila.

"Zella, you're quite the negotiator!" said Leonolis proudly to his granddaughter.

"Yes, but had it not been for Theo ..." began Zella.

"Theo? Our littlest cousin? Theo is *here*?" asked Cullen. How can this be? He's so ... so ... young ... so ... little ... so ... Theo!"

As if on cue, the hero of the moment appeared. Whistling a nonsensical, made-up tune as was his custom, Theo was suddenly *floating* in their midst!

"Theo! When? How? What the heck?" asked Cullen.

Theo, who had grown up hearing the tales and adventures the others had experienced in Bren, had always hung on every word of every sibling and cousin and of every story told. He respected them greatly and, being the youngest, found it easy to believe them. Having dreamed many times of what Bren must be like, imagine his surprise when his own dreams were finally realized!

He explained with great little-boy excitement what had happened. "All I know is that Papa Lee, who looks and sounds a lot like King Leonolis, by the way, told me to head toward Bren and to trust the Founders. So, I did! The very moment I ran between the stone lions, something deep in me came to life. Something changed! I suddenly realized I did not have to settle for dreaming, but I could actually *live* what I had dreamed of all these years!"

"The next thing I knew, I saw you, Cullie, suspended in the air, and I saw Zella near the entrance to the tunnel we now stand in. I saw our grandparents caught in the middle of it all, and that thing, that ... monster, threatening to kill you all! Something deep in me knew what to do, so I just *did* it!" explained Theo.

"Did what?" asked Cullen.

"I made thunder and lightning and a great wind!" said Theo.

"And then?" asked Cullen.

"And then he dragon was hurled against the far wall and you began to float to the ground and Zella said we needed to get out of there, and here we are!" said Theo.

"And everything he said is true, but he forgot to mention one thing!" exclaimed Zella.

"What did he forget?" asked Cullie.

"He did it all—the lightning, the thunder, the wind, everything—without a sound! It was so awesome! I call him Thunder Boy!"

"Enough, children! There will be time for questions and answers later! We must get to the others before the great beast awakens and seeks his revenge!" said Leonolis.

"How will we find them?" asked Theo.

"I suggest we begin in the place we last saw them," suggested Abila.

So off they went, winding up and down, around and over, until they came to the tunnel entrance near Menden Lake's western shore. After several minutes in the tunnel, it became obvious that Leonolis and Abila were too big to continue. Leonolis instructed the children to run ahead. "Your grandmother and I will find another way to meet you in the dry creek bed," he said. Obediently, the children journeyed on without their grandparents. Once they had made it out into the moonlit night, Theo flew several hundred feet above them so as to get their bearings.

Soon he floated back to the ground and reported, "There lies Menden Lake and there, leading from its western edge, is a dry creek bed that flows from Menden Lake when its waters are deeper, like an overflow."

"Great eye, Theo," replied Cullen.

"Let us carry on down the creek bed. Stay as close to the cover of the overhanging bushes and reeds along its edge so as to better conceal our whereabouts from the dragon," suggested Theo.

Silently, the children sneaked along, hoping to find the others. But they had not heard the slight rippling of the waters of Menden Lake as the dragon moved just below the surface toward the dry creek bed.

After several minutes, they heard a faint and familiar "Who-who! Who-who!" just a few feet ahead of them. It was the signal Papa Lee used when playing hide and seek back in Oklahoma whenever he could tell they were exasperated about not finding him.

Cullen hooted back, "Who-who! Who-who!"

One by one, the children stepped out of their hiding places. Mark and Annabell from behind a large boulder. Ronald and Harry and Buddy from an indention in the creek bank. Mia and Abigail from beneath the massive roots of an old willow tree. Elliott and Matilda from the recesses of a small hidden cave.

Silently, they all embraced while what appeared to be a boulder began to move and take the shape of an ogre! Oliver had disguised himself as a boulder. And out flew Canto from between his giant protective arms. Finally, the entire group was together and celebrating as quietly as children, grandparents, an ogre, a fairy and a dog could. The joy was almost too much to bear.

Leonolis whispered, "Your grandmother and I, by the help of the Founders, found another route out of the cavern. Great job, grandchildren, in finding your way here so quickly!"

They were so happy to see one another that it was almost too much to bear. No one even noticed the red glow on Buddy's ID tag until it was too late!

20

WHEN ATTITUDES GET IN THE WAY

*T*he entire family and Buddy and Oliver and Canto silently embraced in what must have seemed like the world's largest group hug. Occasionally Ron let out a tiny snort of a giggle, followed by Matilda's slightest snicker in response, followed by Harry giggling as silently as he was able, which was not so silent at all, until the group began to sound like a happy breeze of whispered laughter and playful nudges and much-needed hugs of reassurance. But Abila placed a finger to her pursed lips and whispered her all too familiar "shhhhh," which made everyone freeze, not daring to cross their wise grandmother.

Glancing at the children's grandfather in that special way grandparents have of knowing what the other is thinking, Abila's eyes said it all. "Listen."

Everyone stepped a little closer toward one another, if

that were even possible, straining their ears for what their grandmother was hearing.

From somewhere between the western shores of Menden Lake and where they all now stood in the middle of the dry creek bed, they heard what sounded like drops of rain. Not a downpour—more like the sound of water dripping from eaves after a big rain, but without the refreshing feeling one gets after such a shower. It felt like something dreadful was about to happen.

They tried their best not to move or make a sound, but the more they tried to quiet themselves, the louder their breathing became, at least to their own ears. The sound of their hearts beating became so loud and the fear flooding through the thumping rhythm of their hearts made them feel like their hearts would explode right out of their chests!

Theo, being the youngest, was stuffed smack-dab in the middle of the tight familial scrum. Having never been in such a situation, he was not yet accustomed to something that had become familiar to his cousins. So he did what he had to do. Freeing himself from his two Aussie cousins, Ellie and Tillie, he darted straight upward and hovered about ten feet above.

He saw only what was directly below him. A family he loved with all his heart, an ogre he felt would be a good friend for such a time as this, the most beautiful fairy he had ever imagined or ever seen at all, and the dog he had only heard stories about from his cousins. Buddy the dog!

Although Buddy was somewhat obscured by the tangled

group, Theo saw what the others could not. Trying to remain silent, he pointed to the dog while everyone stretched their hands toward him, beckoning him back to the safety of the group.

Theo continued to pointed toward the middle of the group until King Leonolis finally whispered, "What is it, Theo?"

"Buddy!" whispered Theo. "Why is Buddy glowing? Why is he red?"

Buddy's ID tag was once again glowing red, which sent the group into an even tighter formation and into an even deeper dread than the sound of that drip, drop, drip, drop had caused. Everyone except for Theo, who had missed those particular conversations, knew what the red glow meant.

Luminaud was near.

King Leonolis stepped away from the group to stand between them and the sound of the drips. He quietly and quickly unsheathed his sword and said to his family, "Prepare to use your gifts, children. It is not raindrops you hear but the drip, drop, drip, drop of water dripping from the scaly back and wings of a beast who just emerged from beneath the dark waters of Menden Lake. Prepare to direct your gifts toward the beast upon my signal."

King Leonolis never had the chance to give the signal or even utter one word of warning as the Light Eater pounced from the darkness and pinned him to the ground with his mighty talons. It looked as if he would be crushed between the forefeet of the dragon, arms and sword pinned to the side of his body, as the great beast began to draw the life from him.

With all the strength he could muster, Leonolis shouted, "Now, children! Now!"

No sooner had he said those words than the King passed out. He never saw, although he later heard about, the bravery of his grandchildren and how even good gifts and the best of intentions can lead to bad attitudes and bad attitudes can lead to bad choices. Indeed, how pride can lead to the downfall of even the strongest young men and young women.

Luminaud issued a challenge: "To the boy or girl who uses their gifts wisely I will free their grandfather and your name will be heralded throughout the realm as the brave child who saved the life of the High King of Bren." As those words rang through the air, Luminaud spewed out an odorless, colorless blast of a gaseous spell that has since come to be known as the Pall of Pride. A pall is a dark covering of smoke or mist, but this pall was invisible! And the spell spread like the evil breeze pride is among the children.

Cullen immediately leapt from the center of the group and, using his ability to see any situation from multiple points of view, shouted to Mark, "Summon the creatures of the forests! Call out to the bears and the lions and the glass dragons and the unicorns! Summon the hawken and the wolfen and the treesant and chiroptera!"

Mark shouted back, "What do you think I was about to do, Cullen? You're not the boss of me!"

Shocked at the response of his cousin, Cullen shouted to Elliott, "Use your gift and transport us all out of here!"

As only Elliott can do, she retorted, "And just how am I supposed to do that without us all touching? Everyone scattered like roaches when the lights came on and that stupid dragon appeared! And don't tell me what to do! I *know* what to do!"

Elliott then turned to Mia and said, "Mia! Use your lightning and free our grandfather!" Mia, being able to read minds, heard what Elliott was thinking and shouted back, "You think you are the only one who can actually do anything! You think you're grandfather's favorite! *You* shoot your lightning and free him! Oh, I forgot! You *can't!*"

Mia, full of anger at Elliott's response to her, turned her anger upon Ron and demanded, "Fire Boy! Set the stupid dragon on fire! Stop just standing there and *do* something!"

Ronald immediately felt belittled and humiliated and turned his embarrassment and shame upon the next person he saw—his cousin Matilda.

"Tillie! Shoot the beast with one of your arrows and make him think he is supposed to let grandfather go free!" shouted Ron.

Elliott jumped between Ron and her sister, got right up into her cousin's face, and screamed, "No one! No one tells my little sister what to do! Come on Tillie! We are out of here!" And Ellie and Tillie transported to who knows where!

In exasperation, Ron yelled at Harry, "Come on, Speed Boy! Use your speed and strength to free grandfather!"

Harry replied, "I'm fast and I am strong, but I'm not that fast and not that strong!"

"I knew you were a chicken, Harry! I knew it! As usual I guess I'll have to do it myself!" replied Ron, smugly.

Abigail came to Harry's defense. Using her ability to see through the real thoughts of Ron, she said, "Ron! Harry is not the chicken! *You* are! I see your thoughts! You are afraid ... afraid of losing ... your dog?! Buddy is more important to you than our grandfather? Incredible!" she said in a huff.

Turning her attention to Annabell, Abigail asked, "And why aren't you ringing your special little bell? You seem to be able to use it when it is helpful to you, but what about giving us a little ring-y ding-y when we all need it, cousin?"

Annabell, being Annabell, rang her bell not at the dragon but directly at Abigail! The two were immediately transported to a moment where time stood still. Everyone else seemed to be frozen in mid-action with looks of anger or disdain or pain or hurt or anguish or pride on their faces. Truth be told, each face carried a look of prideful arrogance that said, "This is all about *me!*"

Abigail, startled at Annabell's response, yelled and glared while Annabell continued ringing her bell at her cousin! Finally, they turned away from one another in prideful huffs and stormed away from the ensuing battle in opposite directions!

Annabell caught a glimpse of Zella, who seemed frozen in shock at the responses of her cousins and siblings. Laying into Zella, she screamed, "Hey, Zig Zag Girl! Get to zigging and zagging and do something to help grandfather!"

As if waking from a slumber, Zella began to shake and swing her hands back and forth in a zigzag motion. "If it's zigging and zagging you want, take *that!*" she yelled, thrusting her hands at Annabell and knocking her off her feet.

Theo watched from above what was transpiring and was mortified at the way his cousins were reacting and responding to one another! Even though he was used to the squibbling and squabbling back home, it was something he never expected to see or experience in the famed land of Bren.

Hovering there in silence above the confused mess, his attention turned toward the only one not turning on anyone else—his grandmother, Queen Abila. She ran to the dragon and began beating on his rigid scaly talons in a futile attempt to make him release her husband.

With one swift slap of his right forepaw, Luminaud slammed into Abila. She was airborne until her limp body slammed into the creek bank and slid down to the dry creek bed below.

Luminaud spoke: "Foolish humans! So easily deceived by pride. So easily seduced by the promise of power and prestige. Wanting to be seen as valuable, they are more than willing to turn on one another when given even the slightest chance! My spell is working like a charm."

Hovering helplessly above and not knowing what to do, Theo watched in horror as the great beast took the lifeless bodies of his grandparents into his impenetrable talons and leapt into the air with one mighty leap. While the dragon spread his wings and flew back toward Menden Lake, Theo began to cry.

Tears streamed down his face while his cousins continued their bickering and fighting below. He had always been told that the gifts of Bren were to be used for good, but what he saw caused great doubt to come into his heart and mind.

Not knowing what he was doing, Theo began to pray. "Oh Founders, makers and guardians of Bren, we need you! We need you now. If you are real, if you are really real, give me a sign or something. I just don't know what to do."

The prayer felt like more of an afterthought. Theo hovered above the fray, waiting for something ... anything ... to happen.

Then he heard it. Or he *thought* he heard something. Like a still small voice that makes you wonder if what you just heard was really real. Like the first time one hears a real fairy speak, he heard something. The more he listened, the less he heard of the ongoing commotions of his cousins below. The more he listened, the clearer the voice became.

Like the slightest whisper of the slightest breeze on the stillest night, he heard, "Just be you."

"Just be 'me'?" he wondered to himself.

"Again, a voice whispered, "Just be you."

BY DENNIS JERNIGAN

Thinking about all the stories Papa Lee had told him about Bren, he realized he must be hearing the voices of the Founders. Papa Lee had also told him to use his gifts wisely, and that everyone had a gift or two or three. One was not called to Bren to make a name for one's self, but rather for the needs of others and for the sake of the Kingdom. Gifts were to be used with a humble heart, Papa Lee had said, and gifts used to make one's self feel more important than others would always lead to pride. And pride *always* led to a fall! It suddenly made sense to him what he must do.

"I'll just be *me!*" shouted Theo.

The little boy clapped his hands together! As the palms of his hands came together, a silent thunder, followed by a silent bolt of lightning, followed by a strong burst of cleansing wind, sent all his cousins and siblings below into a bumbling, tumbling jumble of little arms and legs! Even Elliott and Matilda were brought back into the midst of the group by the silent wind Theo had created!

Oliver and Canto watched in bewilderment at what was taking place among the humans. Theo yelled at his cousins, now released from the dragon's spell, "Stop it! Stop it *now!*"

"Look what we've done! We have fallen right into the dragon's scheme! We allowed our selfish pride to keep us from doing what we have been called here to do! The Light Eater has taken our grandparents once again!" scolded Theo.

Coming to their senses and feeling ashamed, the children

212

began to seek forgiveness from one another, exchanging their foolish pride for the wisdom of humility.

"He's right," Cullen said. "We have allowed pride to cause harm to come to the Kingdom and to our grandparents."

"What would grandfather and grandmother have us do?" asked Zella, meekly.

"I think we all know, don't we?" asked Mark.

With one voice, the children asked, "What is the Founders' point of view?"

The same children who had been consumed with pride-induced fighting mere seconds before were now huddling together with hearts of humility, seeking the Founders to come up with a plan.

Oh my, what a plan it was!

A PLAN WELL MADE

"**W**hat just happened?" asked Zella.

"It was a spell placed upon us by Luminaud," explained Cullen. "Do you remember that spewing sound that came from his nostrils just before we all turned on one another?"

"A Pall of Pride!" exclaimed Mia.

"A Pall of Pride?" said Abigail, confused.

"Yes, a Pall of Pride. I have heard Adolphus speak of it in one of the gathering of seers grandfather allowed me to attend. A pall is a dark mist and the dragon spewed out a mist of pride, which we all breathed in," explained Mia.

"Except for me!" said Theo, pridefully.

"Are you sure about that, little cousin?" shot back Ron.

"Enough! Let's not fall for the trap of pride again! Let us

humble ourselves and turn our attentions and energy to helping our grandparents—to helping Bren!" said Zella.

"You're right, cousin," said Elliott. Turning to Cullen, she asked, "What do we do now?"

"Does anyone have any idea what the Founders are seeing right now?" asked Cullen. Being the oldest, he often spoke as leader of the group.

"I don't 'see' anything with my eyes right now, but I am 'seeing' something in my mind's eye," said Mark.

"Wow! How cool is that, cousin!" exclaimed Theo, having never experienced such a moment. "What does your mind 'see'?"

"I see ... I see ..." began Mark with some hesitation, afraid his cousins might think him a bit crazy.

"What do you see, Mark? Spit it out!" said Elliott as patiently as she was able to express.

"You'll think this is silly, but I see a giant clock," said Mark, slowly.

"A giant clock?" asked Matilda. "Are we to search for a giant clock in order to rescue our grandparents?"

"No, no, it's bigger than that," replied Mark.

"Just how big *is* this clock you supposedly 'see'?" asked Mia.

"It's bigger than all of us, yet ... small," he went on.

"Wait a minute! Is it big or is it small? Big difference, bro!" exclaimed Harry.

"Why, it's ... it's ... *both*," insisted Mark.

"How can it be both?" asked Ron. "And can you hurry this up? I've gotta pee!"

"Boys!" huffed Abigail and Annabell in mock disgust.

"What does it mean? What do you mean, cousin?" asked Zella.

"Well, it's big enough to hold us all yet small enough to..." started Mark.

"To *what*?" asked Cullen.

"Small enough to hold us all," said Mark

"Well, that explains everything ... *not!*" yelled Elliott.

"Hold on, guys!" said Cullen. "I see it, too!"

"What do you think it means?" asked Abigail, sweetly.

"It means it's a picture of us and how we are to work together!" blurted out Theo.

"What the ...?" said all the children at once, amazed by their youngest cousin.

"Don't you see? We are to see ourselves like a giant clock, each of us being but one small part of that clock. Without even the smallest part—I guess that would be *me*—the entire clock cannot function properly. Don't you see? We *need* one another to save our grandparents and to save Bren!" shouted Theo.

Patting his cousin on the back, Cullen said, "That sounds like something the Founders would say! We are to see ourselves as a necessary part of the big picture, yet we are to see our individual selves as vital parts of the clock in order for it to work correctly! We are to join our individual gifts in order to rescue the land from the scourge of Luminaud!"

Stepping into the middle of the children, Ron said as only Ron can, "I hate to say this, but we are running out of ... time. Just sayin'. Pun intended!"

"You're right brother. Let's ask the Founders to help us see the big picture and how we all fit into it. Here's what I know. We need to get to Lumen's Hammer before we can defeat the dragon. And I'm afraid to tell you this, but Lumen's Hammer lies firmly encased in crystal in the dragon's lair," said Cullen.

"Then the beast already has it?" asked Mark.

"Yes and no," replied Cullen. "Yes, he knows it is encased within his lair but he cannot access it because a key is required to loose it from the crystal encasing it."

"That means we have to go into the dragon's lair, find the key, and take the sword and rescue our grandparents while we're at it. Easy peasy," said Elliott, wryly.

"But we will need the key. Where is the key? Is it in the dragon's lair, too?" asked Matilda.

"No! Zella was sent to bring the key to Cullen!" shouted Theo. "I heard the dragon ask you for the key, Zella, but you didn't give it to him! Awesome, cousin!"

With all eyes on her, Zella sheepishly hung her head and said, "I *had* the key, but I gave it to Abel."

"And just who is this Abel?" asked Annabell.

"She was the special traveling companion assigned by the Founders to go with me so I could deliver it to Cullen ..." she said, her voice trailing off.

"Then we have the upper hand!" said Harry with excitement.

"I'm afraid I don't, and for that I am very ashamed," Zella said.

"What did you do with it? Where is it? Where did you last see it? Why in the world would you be ashamed?" asked Abigail.

"I am ashamed because I did not do as I was instructed! You see, I was never to let the key out of my sight or out of my control. I was to deliver it to Cullen and no one else, but I gave it to Abel," explained Zella. "I reasoned that I would give it to Abel in order to keep it from the dragon. It was my only leverage against the beast! It was all that kept Cullen from having the light of his life consumed."

"What would the Founders think of me now?" asked Zella in shame.

"The Founders would say, 'We waste nothing,' replied Annabell. 'We will not waste your pain. We will not waste your sorrow. We will not even waste your failure. Even what your enemies mean for evil against you, We will use for your good if you give your pain, your sorrow, your failure to Us.'"

"So how do the Founders use what I've done for our good?" asked Zella.

"Well," began Mark, "wouldn't it be prudent to find your traveling companion, Abel? Where did you last see her?"

Just as Mark posed the question to Zella, a figure in a dark robe stepped from the shadows and said, "I am here. I am Abel."

Running from where she had been standing in shame, Zella leapt into the arms of her friend. "Abel! Abel! I'm so glad to see you!"

Bursting into tears while Abel held her close, Zella sobbed, "I disobeyed the Founders! I have ruined everything!"

"Whatever do you mean, brave girl?" asked Abel.

"I am not as brave as you think," said Zella at the now-puzzled Abel. "When I last saw you and we embraced, I ... I..."

"Slipped the key into the outer pocket of my robe?" asked Abel.

Pushing away in shame, Zella was shocked and embarrassed that somehow Abel had known and had just exposed her failure in front of her cousins and siblings.

Crying uncontrollably, Zella simply said, "We need the key, Abel! In spite of my disobedience, we *need* that key."

Zella moved back toward her traveling companion and reached for the pocket. Placing her hand inside, she grasped and groped around into the deepest recesses of said pocket and found *nothing*.

"It's gone!" shrieked Zella in inconsolable disbelief.

Abel once again embraced Zella and said, "There, there, Zella. All is not lost."

"*Everything* is lost!" cried Zella. "I've ruined everything!"

For several minutes, Abel held Zella, during which time Zella's brothers and cousins, along with Oliver and Canto and Buddy the dog, crowded around her, saying words of love and support. Finally, her sobs grew fainter and her tears began to dry. She said, in a faint whimper of a whisper, "I'm so sorry."

Her brothers and cousins gave her ten individual hugs, which took up several more minutes of valuable time.

"I hate to say this again, but ..." began Ron.

"We're running out of time!" groaned his brothers and cousins in unison.

Turning to Abel, Zella asked, "What do we do about the key? It must have fallen from your pocket as you ran from the meadow near Menden Lake."

"I do not have it," replied Abel, "but I *do* know where it is."

"Where is it?" asked Zella.

"Right where I put it," said Abel.

"Where did you put it?" asked Zella.

"Where you should have left it all along," explained Abel.

With an astonished smile beaming from ear to ear, Zella reached into the inner pocket of her own robe and felt the key!

"I've got it! I've got it! I have the *key!*" exclaimed Zella.

Taking Zella by the shoulders and looking her straight in the eyes, Abel said, "You've had it all along, dear girl. As soon as I felt you slip it into my pocket, I slipped it back into yours."

As this truth hit her, Zella shouted, "The dragon could have taken it from me in his lair. I could have been killed. I would never have been so ... so..."

"Brave," said Abel.

"It was not the key nor its absence that made you brave, Zella. It was the love for your brother, the love for your grandparents, your love of all that is Bren that brought out the truth. Key or no key, you acted in love by being willing to lay down your life."

All grew silent now. Even Buddy the dog stopped sniffing around and sat still next to Ron, while Canto rested on the silent shoulder of Oliver the ogre. The silence grew even more intense as everyone recalled the words of the Founders. "We waste nothing, not even your failures."

Tick. Tock. Tick. Tock.

Silence.

Tick. Tock. Tick. Tock.

Silence.

Tick. Tock. Tick. Tock.

"Okay! Am I the only one hearing this or am I losing my ever-loving mind?" asked Mark.

"The clock?" asked Theo innocently.

"Yes! The clock! The *clock*!" shouted Mark.

"I hear it!" said Cullen.

"I hear it!" said Ronald.

"I hear it!" said Harry.

"I hear it!" said Elliott and Matilda at the same time.

"I hear it!" said Mia.

"I hear it, too!" exclaimed Abigail.

"I hear it! I hear it! I hear it!" said Annabell, excitedly.

"The sound of the clock is coming from Menden Lake! I guess that's where we need to go!" said Cullen.

"Wait!" said Zella. "I know the way in to the dragon's lair, but it's too narrow for Abel and for Oliver. The rest of us will all fit easily."

"I will go with you as far as the entrance. Once there, I suspect the dragon will be expecting you all, children. I will cast a spell of allurement and draw him from the lair while you carry the key inside. Once inside, use your gifts like clockwork to free Cullen. Use the key once Zella has gotten it into the dragon's den."

"What do I do with Lumen's Hammer once I have freed it from its crystal encasement?" asked Cullen.

"You will know," Abel said as she bounded up the creek bed toward Menden Lake. "You will know."

Off they went. Like clockwork, each bravely thought about what the Founders would have in store for them, what they would use in mysterious and wonderful ways, to free the land of the evil called Luminaud. Somehow, they all just knew everything was going to work out for the good of the land. They just knew.

What they did not know was that they were being followed.

22

HUMILITY AND THE STAR GIRL

hile the entourage bounded along to keep up with Abel, a near-silent whir of tiny wings could be heard behind them. Flitting and fluttering, panting and sputtering along as quietly as possible, the tiny creature followed. Whenever one of the children turned to make sure no one was following, the little flying thing ducked behind a boulder or a bush.

This hide-and-seek pursuit went on for several minutes before anyone began to suspect they might have others on their tail. Bringing up the rear, Mark had sensed the presence of the thing. Running a bit slower to catch sight of whatever or whomever it was, he strained his ears and trotted as slowly as possible.

Still thinking about how the Founders would have him

use his gift, Mark spoke out a thought to any animals that might be nearby. "Dear creatures of Bren, can anyone hear me?"

He was surprised to hear an answer: "I can hear you, Mark! I can hear you!"

Startled, Mark replied, "Who goes there?"

"It's me, silly cousin of Ron!" It's me!" replied the creature.

A bit exasperated that he did not recognize the voice now thought-conversing with him, Mark thought-shouted, "Me *who*? And how do you know my name? And just how do you know Ron is my cousin?"

"Because I've known you all of your life! Because Ron is always bragging about how awesome and brave and funny and kind and strong you are," said the voice.

"You've known me all my life? How can that be possible when I've never even talked with you before?" asked Mark.

"Silly Mark, I've spent many hours playing with you and Ron and the others. We've wrestled and played tag and I've nipped at your toes and smelled your boy-farts and you've rubbed my belly, making my hind foot kick uncontrollably, all while licking your hands and face as you laughed and laughed and laughed..."

Mark stopped in his tracks when he figured out who he was talking to.

"Buddy! Is this *you*?"

Responding with a playful howl, which sounded like a coyote's howl, just more gleeful than mournful, Buddy ran to Mark and leapt into his arms. "Ow-ow-ow-ooooooooh! It's me! It's me!"

Seeing Buddy run from the front of the procession toward the rear, playfully howling and baying, everyone turned to see what was causing all the excitement. Ron cried out, "Buddy! Buddy, come back here right now!"

Giggling with glee after being tackled by Buddy, Mark shouted back, "He says he's too happy to see me again!"

"He 'says'?" Ron shot back.

"Yes! Yes! Buddy can talk to me! I can hear his words in my thoughts!" replied Mark.

"Of course! That's one of the gifts the Founders have bestowed upon Mark, the ability to converse with animals!" exclaimed Cullen.

"Why am I just now finding this out?" asked Mark, mid-giggle.

"Probably because Buddy did not know you had the gift back in Oklahoma, but in Bren ..." responded Elliott.

"But what made you think to speak to him now, of all times?" asked Mia.

"Because I heard something coming from behind us. I figured I could call out to the creatures of Bren in the area and ask for help, and Buddy answered!" giggled Mark. "This is so cool, right?!"

"So cool," began Matilda, "but what do you mean you heard something?"

"At first it was just a sense that something or someone was there. Once, I thought I could hear a 'whirring' sound like rapidly flapping wings, but each time I strained to listen, it went silent. So, I asked for help and here we are!" said Mark.

"How I wish I could talk with Buddy," said Ron, wistfully.

"Oh, he can understand you, Ron. Every word you've ever said to him, he has understood," said Mark.

"Tell him how much I've missed him, how much I love him," replied Ron.

"You just did!" laughed Mark.

Buddy jumped and ran toward Ron and leapt into his arms so forcefully that Ron fell backward onto the ground. Buddy licked him and howled while tears of joy streamed down Ron's rosy cheeks.

"Wait, guys! Back to what Matilda just said," chimed in Harry. "You heard something following us."

Buddy stopped licking and yipping and turned his attention toward the direction Mark was now pointing. Lifting his highly sensitive nose into the air, Buddy began to sniff. After just a few seconds of sniffing, Buddy tensed, pointing toward a nearby bush.

"What is it, Buddy?" asked Annabell.

Half whining and half quietly barking, Buddy "talked."

"What did he say?" asked Abigail.

"He said, 'It's an insect ... a dragonfly,'" said Mark.

Stepping to the front of the group, Cullen asked, "Verona? Is that you?"

In the darkness behind the bush a teeny, tiny, raspy voice answered, "How did you know?"

"I suppose I just sensed it was you. A voice spoke silently to my thoughts, 'It is your friend, Verona.' I suppose I heard the voice of the Founders," replied Cullen. "Come out so we can see you."

"Wait!" said Ronald tersely as he put his outstretched arm between the dragonfly and his little sister. "Dragonflies mean only one thing!"

"What does it mean?" asked Theo, excited to learn something new about the enchanted land of Bren.

"It means a dragon is nearby," replied Harry.

"No, it doesn't!" interjected Cullen.

"Yes, it *does*," demanded Elliott.

"No, not necessarily," replied Cullen, confidently.

"Not necessarily? Not necessarily? What the ..." replied Ron.

"Verona is a *good* dragonfly! It was he who helped me find the dragon's lair. It was he who helped me discover Lumen's Hammer! He only did the dragon's bidding because Luminaud holds his wife, Fidelia, and his eleven children captive!" shouted Cullen.

"He does the dragon's bidding?" shouted Annabell and Abigail and Mia all at the same time.

"No! No! No! That's not what I meant!" replied Cullen.

"Then what *do* you mean?" asked Ronald.

Interrupting the inquisition, in the sky above a star appeared to be falling behind Verona's hiding spot.

Falling slowly at first, the closer it came to Earth, the greater the velocity. It seemed to be happening in slow motion and instantly at the same time. Like a laser pointer's, it came to a sudden stop just above the bush where Verona still hid, afraid to come out of the darkness.

All stood absolutely frozen in place, mouths agape in amazement as the "star" suddenly took the form of a girl. They stood there dumbfounded as the she slowly floated to the ground.

Theo finally broke the silence with one awestruck utterance, "Whoa."

Instantly recognizing her friend, Mia ran toward the star girl and wrapped her arms around her, saying, "Ariel! I'm so glad you're here!"

Mia explained to everyone, "This is my friend, Ariel. She is of the Nova race of beings, from the land within the land of Bren called Galaxia. They are the people of light, watching over the land of Bren. They are mostly unseen but always in our midst ... a world within our world."

"So, she's an angel," said Elliott, matter-of-factly.

"Yes," said Abel as she stepped to the fore. "In human terms, you would call us 'angels' ... beings of light ... messengers of the Founders ... those who watch over the people of Bren, appearing only when necessary."

"I am afraid that is all the explanation you will get for now," spoke Ariel in a voice that sounded to Abigail like tinkling glass beads.

"I have come with both a message and a mission," said Ariel. "The message is 'Remember the map' and the mission is 'Release Lumen's Hammer'."

"The *map!*" said all the children at once, as if remembering a long lost friend.

"Where *is* the map?" asked Harry as the entire group turned to Cullen.

"It's right here," replied Cullen as he patted the pouch hanging from his shoulder beneath the folds of his outer robe.

As he took the map from the pouch, Annabell made an observation. "Shouldn't it be daytime right now? Does anyone else feel it should be dawn right about now?"

"Yeah! You're right, sister!" said Mark.

"His power grows. The longer we hesitate, the more light he consumes from the people and creatures of Bren," said Abel with sobering gravity. "It *should* be morning light. What you now see is not daylight but, rather, a dimming of true light and life. To the map, children."

Already unfurling it, Cullen held the map for all to see. Straining in the darkness, Ronald stepped nearer to his brother and held out a small flame of fire in the palm of his hand, illuminating the vibrant living colors contained within the beautiful parchment.

While all gazed intently, some unseen hand began to write in light a portion of the riddle that had sent the children on their present journey. Cullen read aloud:

> With boldness born of silver flagon
> Seek out the eater of light, the dragon
> Through fear and doubt, for Bren's dear sake
> Face the beast of Menden Lake

Cullen paused to let the words soak in. Then he went on:

> Be bold, be brave, be love, be fierce
> Be humble, behold, 'til dragon heart pierced
> Return the land, restore the peace
> Who would be greatest, be the least

"With boldness born of silver flagon?" asked Ron. "What the heck is a flagon?"

"A flagon is a bottle, usually crafted of glass, for holding liquids," said Abel.

"Where do we find a flagon made of silver? And does boldness come in a liquid?" asked Abigail.

With a twinkle in her eye, Ariel said, "I can help with that. She reached into her shiny robe and pulled out a small bottle covered with ornate etchings of dragons and beasts and unicorns and fantastic creatures. As the children gazed at the flagon in wonder, Theo blurted out, "Is it made of silver? And why is there a picture of a child raising a sword triumphantly toward the sky? And why does the boy look like Cullen?"

"Indeed, you speak wisely, little one," Ariel answered. "It is crafted of purest silver and the child wielding the sword does resemble Cullen, but the child symbolizes the heart of any child. The heart of a child is both curious and full of wonder. The heart of a child is trusting and loyal. The heart of a child is both brave and protective of those he or she loves. Even the oldest, wisest men and women of Bren carry within themselves the heart of a child. It's just that far too often, they..."

"Forget," Harry interjected.

"Yes. They do often forget the heart full of wonder by allowing the cares of the world to become more of a burden than the Founders ever intended," replied Ariel.

"So, what's in the bottle?" asked Matilda.

"A liquid born of light. In its flow is contained the essence of the heart of a child, full of wonder and trust and loyalty and bravery and true love. The one who drinks this elixir will be filled with power to overcome and power to walk in the humility and freedom found in the laying down of life. This elixir is called the Light of Grace. Each of you are to drink of this grace. In so doing, you will find strength in times of weakness, joy in times of sorrow, power to overcome even when darkness seems to be winning, the point of view those without grace cannot see. You will see from the perspective of the Founders and be filled with bold wisdom from the ages," said Ariel.

As if by some silent command, the children lined up in front of Ariel as she opened the silver flagon of The Light of Grace. Ariel offered the flagon to Cullen and Cullen took a sip and stepped away. Ron and Harry and Zella were next, followed by Elliott and Matilda, followed by Mark and Annabell, followed by Mia and Abigail, and lastly Theo.

No sooner had Theo taken a sip than Abel said, "Trust the power of the Light of Grace, children. I must forge ahead of you and lure the beast from the cavern. Oliver and Canto will assist me. Ariel will take the rest of you to the dragon's lair, where Cullen will use the key and retrieve Lumen's Hammer."

"What then?" asked Cullen.

"First things first, children. Take the first step. And remember, he who would be greatest must be the least. Walk, run, fight, and be fierce. Be brave, be loyal, be meek, be strong, all with a humbleness of heart," replied Abel.

"Children, follow Ariel, except for you, brave Elliott. Even now, your ride and your assignment nears."

While Abel, Oliver, and Canto vanished into the darkness, Ariel led the other children toward Menden Lake and the hidden entrance to the dragon's lair, leaving Elliott standing alone in the darkness of the creek bed. She trembled in a bit of fear, yet trusted the word of the Founders and the power of the Light of Grace.

And then, he appeared. Her heart stood still, and she found herself unable to utter even a simple gasp, much less a single word. Either her greatest dream had just come true or her greatest nightmare was just beginning.

23

ELLIOTT AND THE UNICORN

*E*lliott froze, her heart full of wonder and disbelief at the same time. Could this truly be happening? Was what she was now seeing possibly real? Could her dreams from her earliest childhood memories really be coming true?

From the age of two, Elliott had been visited most nights in her dreams by a creature. It was the most beautiful yet fierce, most humble yet bold, whitest yet most vividly colorful magical beast! In these dreams, she and the creature went on wild adventures full of triumphant victories and momentous deeds where good always triumphed over evil, even if that triumph seemed unattainable at times. It seemed that just as all hope was lost, light would pierce the darkness and she and the creature would come away as conquering heroes.

What was the creature of her dreams? What now stood proudly in magnificent splendor beyond what she had imagined in her dreams? With a long mane of brilliant rainbow colors running from between his perky ears down the length of his slender neck and ending at his shoulders, the creature's beautiful mane ran from deepest violet to royal indigo to deep-sea blue to forest green to sunflower yellow to opulent orange to fiery red. His tail, of course, was so long it grazed the ground with the colors to match the mane. The body of the incredible being was purest white, almost too dazzlingly white to even gaze upon for more than a few seconds without shading one's eyes!

And the horn protruding in a perfect spiral from his horsey head was almost two feet long, colorfully matching the colors of both tail and mane. Even more magnificent than she had ever dreamed, the being standing proudly and majestically and boldly in front of her was the most beautiful, amazing creature she could ever have imagined. The creature of her dreams? A unicorn!

Elliott stood in awe, mouth agape and eyes wider than saucers, gleaming with both joy and wonder. Captivated, she was startled when the creature spoke.

"Brave Elliott, daughter of Bren, we must go at once," whinnied the unicorn in the deepest, most resonant voice Elliott had ever heard.

"You can *talk*?!" said Elliott in amazement.

"Yes, of course I can talk! How else would you have me communicate with you?" asked the creature.

"How do you know *me*?" asked the girl.

"I have been sent by the Founders to provide assistance and protection to the children of Bren, specifically assigned to *you*, dear, brave Elliott," said the unicorn.

"What shall I call you?" asked the girl. Secretly, Elliott (at least in her dreams) had always called her unicorn Rainbow Glitter Sparkles. Oh how she wanted to call him that now! She wondered if she dare say those three magical words, but just as she was about to call him Rainbow Glitter Sparkles, the unicorn responded.

"You may call me by my name. I am sorry. In my haste to be on our way, I assumed you would know it. Forgive me, dear child, but my name is Patronicus (pronounced Puh-*TRAHN*-ih-cuss)."

"Patronicus! What a regal name for such a regal creature!" said Elliott. "Patronicus! Patronicus! Patronicus! I *love* saying your name!" Throwing caution to the wind, along with any royal protocol such an occasion may have called for, Elliott blurted out, "I've always called you Rainbow Glitter Sparkles ... at least in my dreams!"

Laughing and whinnying as only a unicorn can do, Patronicus said, "My friends call me Patty, if that would help, but you may call me *RGB* if you like! I know how much you Aussies love making up nicknames for people and places and things!"

"Sooooo true, Patty! So true, *RGB*! We call sunglasses sunnies! We call McDonald's Macka's! We call ... well you get the idea! But I shall call you by your given name because I *love* saying it! Patronicus! Patronicus! Patronicus!"

"Come now, Elliott! We have no time to waste! The Founders have a very specific task for us—for you. On my back, girl!" whinnied Patronicus.

Elliott transported instantly to the back of the unicorn, grabbing the rainbow mane with both hands as if she had done this her entire life—as she had countless times in her dreams. "Where to and what do we do once we get there?" she asked.

"To Abysstine we go. The plan of the Founders has been set in motion. Once Abel has lured the beast from his lair, the dragon will make his way to nearby Abysstine and begin consuming the light of life from the people. We have been assigned to come between the dragon and the people," responded the now galloping steed.

"Come *between* the dragon and the people?" asked the frightened girl.

"Remember, daughter of Bren. I have been assigned to provide for your needs and to protect you along the way. Once we have come between the beast and the city of Abysstine, you will know what you need to defend the people. With your gifts and the essence of the magical powers endowed upon me by the Founders, we will prevail," said Patronicus. And with those words, the girl and the unicorn seemed as one as they raced through the darkness toward the dim city lights of Abysstine.

Meanwhile, Abel, Oliver and Canto reached the eastern end of Menden Lake. Instructing the ogre and the fairy to remain hidden behind an outcropping of massive stones, Abel began to speak an incantation over the entrance of the dragon's lair that lay hidden beneath the dark waters of the lake.

> Oh, beast of darkness
> Eater of light
> Come forth from depths
> From dark of night
>
> Come forth great beast
> Come seek men's light
> Come forth raging
> Show thy might
>
> Smell the light and life of men
> Let craven pride well from within
>
> Come feast! Come take man's light again
> Come forth and leave thy hidden den

Abel stretched out her hands toward the place in the waters she knew the entrance to be and summoned the great beast with the power of the Founders of Bren. After only a few seconds, the waters began to roil and bubble and swirl and curl until a giant whirlpool churned from deep within the darkness of the waters. Sensing the dragon nearing the surface, Abel hid among the rocks near Oliver and Canto. Luminaud burst from the giant whirlpool like a bolt of lightning! Full of rage and consumed with a deep prideful lust for the light of the life of mankind, the dragon violently flapped his wings and flew to the nearest city where he could easily obtain light. Abysstine.

Once the beast had flown away, Abel and Oliver and Canto made their way toward the small opening on the surface where they met Ariel, the children who had followed her, and Buddy the dog.

"The dragon has been lured to Abysstine," Abel said to the children. "You have but a few minutes before his return."

"Why did you send the beast to Abysstine? I thought we were to protect and rescue the people of Bren?" asked Mia.

"That is exactly what we are doing," replied Abel with great seriousness in her voice.

"But Luminaud will surely consume the light of life from the people! Why would you send him to do that?" asked Abigail.

"Do you not trust the Founders?" asked Abel.

"Of course, we do? Right?" asked Cullen as he turned toward his siblings and cousins for assurance. "But it does seem odd and wrong that the Founders would do such a thing."

"Remember this, children of Bren. See not with human eyes and think not with human understanding. What the enemy means for evil, the Founders will use for good. Who but the Founders could use darkness to bring forth light? See from the Founders' point of view and remember: You have each partaken of the Light of Grace. Let it awaken your hearts and minds to the truth of where real power lies. The power of sacred love!"

Pondering Abel's words, the children, one by one, began to allow the truth of the Light of Grace to consume their thoughts. As they replaced the human way of thinking with the Founders' way of thinking, their feelings of doubt and dread and fear and confusion were replaced by simple trust.

"We are ready, Abel," said Cullen. "Right, kids?"

"Right!" the other children responded.

"Lead on, dear Ariel."

"Good and faithful children of Bren," said Abel. "Oliver and Canto and I will remain here and watch over the land. Should Luminaud return, I will send Canto through the tunnel to warn you, since she is the only one small enough to fit through the narrow passageway."

The children followed the star girl into the darkness of the tunnel leading to Luminaud's den and to Lumen's Hammer. Quickly and deftly, they maneuvered through many twists and turns and hastily made their way into the massive cavern where the beast made his lair.

As if on cue, a luminescent glow emanated from deep within the massive crystal beneath which was Luminaud's bed. The source of the glow? Lumen's Hammer!

Even within its dense crystal encasement, all could see the outline of the magnificent sword. As if suspended in midair, the sacred weapon of old was securely hidden within the opaque stone. And the stone's outer layer was covered in streaks and scratches made by the massive talons of the dragon in his futile attempts to free the sword.

Cullen turned to Zella: "The key."

Zella reached into the folds of her robe and pulled out a pouch. She reached in and pulled out the key. All stood in awe at their first sight of such a simple yet deeply sacred tool. Zella handed it to Cullen and stepped away. Cullen walked toward the crystal mass.

Nervously shaking, his hand trembled slightly as he thrust the key toward the keyhole. But just as the key was about to meet the keyhole, the room began to buzz and whir as hundreds of dragonflies swarmed them!

But the children immediately began operating in the power of the Light of Grace, each using the specific gift they had been granted by the Founders to fend off the horde and give Cullen the chance to retrieve the sword.

Mark called out to the animal kingdom, specifically the bats of the cave realm. "Oh great army of bats, friends of the realm of Bren. We need your help against the legions of the dragon's minions!" Right on cue, bats began to appear from every nook and cranny of the cavern and set about devouring dragonflies, but it appeared to be an act of futility. The more the bats ate the tiny insects, the more new dragonflies appeared!

Mia began piercing them with bolts of lightning from her fingertips! *Zap! Zap! Zip! Zip! Tzzt! Tzzt!* was the sound of the dragonflies meeting their electrifying end, but all that were felled were quickly replaced by many more!

Joining Mia in the firefight, Ronald cast small balls of fire from his right hand and then his left, over and over again, sending dozens of deep-fried dragonflies to the cave floor until the cavern seemed to be covered with a crunchy, crispy carpet of fried dragonfly bodies! Of course, the boys thought this was so cool, while the girls thought ... *not so much*!

Tillie, not one to shy away from action, took up her bow and arrow and began shooting through the swarm, careful not to aim in the direction of any of her cousins. With one arrow, she would pierce up to a dozen dragonflies, leaving them impaled to the cavern wall and ceiling. Still, they kept coming.

Abigail focused her gaze upon the eyes of the little flying terrorizers and paralyzed them in flight. All the tiny flying menaces could do was fall helplessly to the ground, stunned by the magic with which the Founders had endowed her. Still, the insects kept coming!

Zella began to zig and zag around the room in a fearless z-shaped pattern. Not only did this running cause the dragon-flies to freeze and fall to the ground, but her speedy zigzag hand motions doubled the amount she was able to stun and reduce hundreds of dragonflies to heaps!

Still, the room was almost suffocatingly full of the dreadful little creatures, making it increasingly difficult to see and even more difficult to breathe. Finally, Annabell drew the bell from her side and clanged it sharply against the cavern wall. The wonderful reverberations were like music to the ears of the children, but caused agonizing pain to the dragonflies, which suddenly stopped buzzing and hovered, confused and stunned!

At that moment, Theo sprang into action and leapt from the floor and high into the swarm of insects. He began to spin wildly, like a tiny tornado, and caused a great wind to circle around the cavern! The more he spun, the more the dragonflies were swept into the vortex he had created. So high was the speed of the wind, his cousins below were forced to hang on to anything they could find in order to not be swept into the whirlwind.

Just as it seemed all would be swept away by the mighty rushing wind, Theo sped toward the ground of the cavern and hit the floor with a mighty thud of his right fist! The impact was both thunderous in vibration and deafeningly silent, and the air was filled with thousands of tiny lightning bolts! The horde of dreadful little beasts fell suddenly and silently to the ground!

While the children, scattered around the cavern during the battle, sat stunned on the ground where Theo's silent thunder had left them, Harry pointed toward the ceiling and shouted, "Grandfather and grandmother!"

Suspended above the crystal mass encasing Lumen's Hammer were Leonolis and Abila. Theo flew to their sides and looked for a way to free them. Shouting down to his cousins, he said, "They seem to be in some magical trance! They are breathing, but they are just staring into space! What should I do?"

"We must break the spell!" shouted Mark.

"How?" responded Mia.

"Lumen's Hammer!" said Annabell. "Cullen, use the key!"

Cullen placed it in the keyhole slot and turned it ever so slightly to the right. The room began to vibrate with a tone reminiscent of Annabell's bell! Pleasing and deafening at the same time. As it reverberated, the crystal encasing the sword began to glow. The brighter the glow, the more resonant the sound. As the crystal glowed and the sound echoed, the crystal began to magically open. With great reverence and awe, Cullen reached into the opening and slowly pulled the mighty sword called Lumen's Hammer from its resting place.

While the children stood there, mouths wide open in awe and wonder, Cullen instinctively pointed the mighty weapon toward his grandparents and they instantly floated down to the cavern floor, where, by some great magic, they were both laid down gently on their backs. The children ran to their sides and held their heads upon their laps like pillows.

Slowly, the dazed, faraway looks in the eyes of Leonolis and Abila left, replaced by a sudden awareness that they were safe and in the presence of their grandchildren. The children piled onto their grandparents in a grand pile of hugs and giggles that went on for several tearful, joyful minutes.

Once the hugs and giggles settled down, Leonolis asked, "Where's Ellie?" Little did he and the others know of the great peril Elliott now faced in Abysstine. "We must find her at once."

While the children ran toward the tunnel heading out of the cavern, Leonolis and Abila realized they would not be able to squeeze through the narrow opening. Sending the children on ahead, Leonolis instructed, "Cullen, take Lumen's Hammer and find the beast! Everyone else, find Elliott! I fear she is in great need!"

The children found the light-consumed daylight and ran toward the sound of battle coming from Abysstine. Seeing cousin Elliott face to face with Luminaud sent chills down their spines. Would they get to her in time?

They watched in horror as Elliott disappeared beneath the massive body of the terrible beast and listened helplessly at the terrible crashing sound the dragon's body made as it thundered down on top of her. The horrible thud sent shockwaves through the ground and caused the children to fall to the ground as the walls of Abysstine crumbled around the mighty red lizard and Elliott.

CULLEN'S CHOICE

*U*pon seeing his cousin trampled by the giant beast, Cullen didn't hesitate. Lifting Lumen's Hammer high above his head and pointing it toward the dragon, he shouted, "Elliott!" At once, the children ran with all their might toward the melee.

Cullen focused every thought upon finding the dragon's weakness, asking for the Founders to show him their point of view as he ran into the fray.

Mark called out to a nearby eagle and asked in thought-speak, "Friend eagle! The citizens of Abysstine, both human and animal, are under siege by the terrible dragon, the Light Eater, Luminaud! Can you help me get to them?" The eagle instantly flew to Mark's side and said, "On my back!" Mark, with bow and arrow in hand, leapt onto the eagle and sped toward the crumbling castle walls of Abysstine.

Mia ran toward Elliott and began sending small bolts of lightning in the direction of the dragon. As she did so, she discovered something new about her particular gift. If she pointed her hands toward the ground directly beneath her, she could vault ahead several feet much like a kangaroo! She quickly developed a rhythm of leaping ahead and, while airborne, sending electric bolts like daggers toward the dragon, and just as her feet were about to touch the ground again, she would send herself flying ahead with greater and greater speed!

As the children drew to the city walls of Abysstine, they realized the dragon was not alone in his rage. Once again, swarms of angry, hissing, buzzing dragonflies tried to confuse the children and keep them from getting to the dragon or anywhere near the city. Ronald, enraged at the sneaky little creatures who were trying to destroy the land he loved, went into a fireball-throwing frenzy! Ball after ball of fire he sent into the teeming hordes, dispatching thousands into charred little insect corpses that sounded and felt like running through fields of breakfast cereal! Of course, running step for step to keep up with his friend of friends was Buddy the dog, who bayed and howled, occasionally chomping on any dragonfly that flew too close to his face!

On Ronald's heels, Matilda ran to the dragon. She sent arrow after arrow from her mighty bow, screaming with great precision toward Luminaud's ugly snake-like head, causing the beast to become even more irritated. From a distance, it looked like the dragon was swatting away pesky gnats from his face! Harold could only giggle at this as he followed Tillie.

Because of his great strength and speed, Harry soon zoomed right past Cullen and Mark and Mia and Ronald and Tillie and leapt over a pile of stones where the city wall had stood. There, Harry found himself face to face with the Light Eater and saw Elliott pinned to the ground beneath him!

While Zella zigged and zagged her way toward the breach in the city wall, she took out as many dragonflies as she could. Simultaneously, Abigail used her amazing blue eyes and overpowering gaze like a laser to stun dragonfly after dragonfly, sending their tiny evil bodies crashing to the ground.

Behind them, Annabell rang her bell loudly and clearly, sending encouragement to her brother and cousins while sending shockwaves of destruction toward the flying little menacing dragonflies. As the vibrations met the wings of the little pests, they quickly shriveled and crumpled into broken and useless appendages, sending the entire throng to the ground. All was hauntingly silent save for the roars of Luminaud, drooling with rage.

Theo, the newest member of the mighty Bairns of Bren to experience such a battle, had flown directly toward the mighty dragon, getting there first. No one had seen Theo's naive attempt at thwarting the dragon's attack. Flying much too close to the dragon's giant head, Theo had begun to spin, making a swirling vortex of wind, to free Elliott. But the dragon had lifted his right forepaw and swatted the boy away. The force of the blow was so great that Theo crashed into one of the castle spires. So severe was the strike that it rendered the boy unconscious. Theo's lifeless body lay hidden from view on the floor beneath the spire's turret wall.

Try as they might, Leonolis and Abila could not keep pace with their grandchildren. They ran and prayed to the Founders for strength and protection for their grandchildren. At the breach in the wall, what they saw made their hearts sink. Their greatest fear, harm to one of their grandchildren, was taking place before their very helpless eyes.

While the kids pelted the Light Eater with their Kingdom gifts, precious Elliott was lifelessly pinned beneath the immense weight of the dragon's left forepaw. Bodies of people and animals lie around the castle grounds and scattered throughout the entire city of Abysstine. Some seemed completely dark, having had the light of life drained from their bodies, while others had a faint dimness of light because they still had a measure of life within them!

Suddenly, the great beast ceased roaring. The brief silence was eerie. A few seconds later, Luminaud laughed with the most evil, insidious cackle the children had ever heard. "Ha! Ha! Ha! Ha! Ha!"

"As you can see, now that the royal gang is all here, my power has grown too great for you! I am afraid your little seer's spell has had no effect upon me. In fact, things are working exactly according to my plan. Once I have consumed the light of life from the royal line of Bren, especially the Bairns of Bren, the realm will be mine!"

In defiance, Leonolis shouted, "You have defeated no one! In fact, the rest of the Bairns of Bren ... the children of the realm..."

"Have been sheltered away in the caverns and stony recesses of the northern realm!" laughed Luminaud. "Exactly as I had foreseen and planned all along! You have sufficiently rounded up a grand feast for me that will ensure my reign for generations to come! Like stocking up food and supplies for a long winter's chill, you have led the very greatest supply of light I could have ever asked for right into my grand pantry and cupboard! What fools you are! Such is the wisdom of you and your precious Founders!"

In utter shock, Leonolis and Abila stood silently—for a few moments, that is. Then with great boldness and fearless abandon, Leonolis cried out to the Founders, "Oh great Founders of the realm of Bren, we have need of your help! You have said in times past we but have to call upon the name of the Founders and we will be saved! Save us, Oh great Founders! Save us *now*!"

Silence.

"Tsk, tsk, tsk," mocked Luminaud. "I think your Founders are either sleeping or don't care ... or they are simply myths concocted by your royal line to keep your people filled with empty faith and firmly under your royal thumbs of oppression! I grow weary of such fairy tales and myths and am ready to rule and reign. It is time for a new king!"

"You are a false king!" shouted Cullen, sword lifted toward the beast.

"We shall see how false a king I am once I am in complete power, young royal," answered Luminaud.

"True royalty rules with love. False royalty rules by fear! Fear can only be maintained for so long and is always defeated by, and must always bow to, perfect love!" shouted Cullen.

"Perfect love?! Perfect love?! There is no such thing!" shouted the beast, sending a smothering mist of green smelly mist fuming from his mouth and nostrils. "What is so perfect about your love? What makes love any different than fear? Both demand control and dominion, foolish human child!"

"Perfect love rules at the will of those it serves and does not force itself upon anyone," argued Cullen. "Fear rules by threat and forces servitude upon those it would rule over. Perfect love lays down its life for those it serves. Fear *takes* the life of those it lords itself over! You rule in fear! You are a *false* king!"

"Enough!" fumed the dragon. "Once I have consumed the one beneath my feet, you will each have your turn. Trust me. Even now your powers weaken as I draw the life from the one you call Elliott."

Gazing upon the still body of Elliott pinned beneath him, Luminaud began to stare into her face. As he did so, a small beam of light was drawn from her like a wisp of air or a drawing of breath into the nostrils of the great and horrible beast. Exhaling as if to catch his breath, the dragon snorted and began to breathe in deeply, so deeply that it felt to all those who witnessed it that the air of the entire world was sucked into the lungs of the dragon.

All hope seemed lost. The Founders must truly have been sleeping ... if they were real at all. Fear and dread began to replace the hope and bravery the children had all been feeling mere moments before. Until, that is, an amazing thing happened.

Just as Luminaud was about to consume the last bit of life from Elliott, she awoke and shouted, "*Now*, Patronicus! *Now!*"

Before anyone could even begin to make sense of what was happening, there appeared in their midst, directly in front of Luminaud, one of the most beautiful and storied creatures of Bren! Surrounded by a brilliant aura of purest light was the most magnificent being any of the children could have imagined. Of course, they had all heard the rumors of their existence, but none had actually laid eyes on one until *now*!

Rearing up on his hind legs, rainbow mane cascading down his mighty arched neck, massively long rainbow tail billowing as if blown by the wind, with a coat of brilliant white, piercingly blue eyes, and long spiraling rainbow horn, was the mighty unicorn Patronicus!

Mesmerized by the beauty of the unicorn, Luminaud stopped breathing for a moment, the way someone does when they are taken by surprise. Then Elliott did as only Elliott could do. She transported from beneath the dragon's talons, unharmed, to directly between her grandparents!

While the dragon stood there in shock, Patronicus pointed his horn right at his heart. Before the beast knew what had hit him, a great beam of pure glittering light burst from the tip of the unicorn's horn. As it touched the scaly red skin of the dragon, the light of life flowed out of the dragon and back into the bodies of the people and animals that lay scattered around Abysstine. The city was coming back to life!

At the sight of this new life springing forth, the dragon became even more enraged and lunged toward Patronicus. But the mighty unicorn held his ground, keeping the dragon at bay and giving the children the chance to spring into action.

As if on cue, they surrounded the dragon. Mark stood to the left of Patronicus and pointed an arrow directly at the head of Luminaud. Elliott took her place to the left of Mark. Mia stood left of Elliott. Ronald next to Mia, directly behind the dragon. Matilda stood to the left of Ronald and Harold was to her left. Next came Abigail and, beside her, Annabell, bell in hand. And next to Annabell stood Zella, while Cullen stood directly to the right of Patronicus, sword still held high. But there was something odd about the circular configuration.

Between Cullen and Zella, there was a void ... as if there was supposed to be one other child.

Looking around, Cullen shouted, "Someone is missing! Who are we missing?"

And to the horror of all, Luminaud leaned back on his haunches, reached over the turret wall of the nearest spire, and dangled a small, lifeless body from his talons. "Do you mean *this*?"

The children gasped as one. Theo hung limply and precariously between two talons. Taking advantage of the sudden silence, the dragon asked, "Would you like to trade?"

"Trade what?" cried out Cullen.

"The child for the sword you now wield. Lumen's Hammer in exchange for the life of this one you call Theo," hissed the dragon.

Cullen's heart sank. He had been tasked with this greatest of task, to find and wield the sword of legend, yet now he found himself with an impossible choice. Honor the task set before him or save the life of his young cousin. In his mind, he had no choice. Though not easy, he would ...

25

ELEVEN WOLVES

*C*ullen instinctively knew what he had to do. His choice, though dreadfully painful, was part of who he was as a child of the royal lineage of Bren. Stepping in front of Patronicus, he shouted, "I and the sword are one. It is my task and my burden to bear for the sake of the kingdom. Where it goes, I shall go. I cannot give you the sword without surrendering myself to you. Put Theo safely down and I will go with you."

Laughing in a prideful snicker that only evil can produce, Luminaud said snidely, "That sounds like a fair trade to me, fool."

With an attitude of mockery, the giant winged lizard tenderly and gracefully laid Theo's still unconscious body on the ground. Leonolis and Abila rushed to his side. While Leonolis picked up the boy, Abila held his limp head firmly in her gentle grasp as she walked alongside her husband toward the breach in the wall. The other ten children stood their ground, each prepared to continue the battle once Theo was safe and secure.

Once their grandparents disappeared with Theo behind the wall, the children knew a signal would be coming from Cullen, telling them to begin their assault on the great dragon. Tense and intent upon what they must do, they waited ... and waited ... and waited, growing more and more anxious. Finally, Mark broke the silence.

"Cullen! What are you doing?! What is your plan?" shouted Mark.

"I will do as I have agreed," Cullen answered. "The sword and I are not to be separated. If the eater of light wants the sword, he must take me as well. This is the will of the Founders. I just know it somehow. I just know this is what is best."

"But the sword in the hand of evil flies squarely in the face of what the Founders intended! Was it not prophesied that the sword must not be allowed to be in the hands of the dragon?" asked Mia.

"As long as I have the sword, the beast cannot take it from my hands. Don't you see? The sword and I are *one*," pled Cullen.

"He will suck the life right out of you and the sword will be lost to the darkness! Don't do this, Cullie," implored Abigail.

With the glittering light still shimmering from the tip of his mighty horn, keeping the beast at bay, Patronicus interrupted the children.

"Bairns of Bren, your cousin is right. He and the sword are one. The dragon can no more wield the sword than he can fly to the moon! Apart from the sacred touch of the royal lineage, the sword has no power to perform darkness. The only power darkness has is deception and fear. For the sword to be of *any* use to Luminaud, a child of the royal realm must wield it. Light begets light. Darkness cannot make light. Cullen is right to make this choice. Will you trust the Founders or will you trust the fear darkness produces?"

"Cousins. Brothers. Sister. All is well. Trust me, I just ... know," replied Cullen with complete and quiet confidence. Walking right up to the talons of Luminaud's front paws, the boy said, "Here am I, and here is Lumen's Hammer. The sword and I are *one.*"

Laughing from the deepest recesses of his cold dragon heart, the mighty beast pinned Cullen to the ground with his left paw and gripped the tip of the sword with his right. He pulled with all his might, yet he could not separate the boy from the sword! In sheer frustration, the giant lizard picked up Cullen and slammed his body to the ground with all his might, hoping to jar the sword from his grip. Rather than crushing the boy as all who witnessed this horrifying moment thought would be the result, a cushion of light magically came between the boy and the ground, absorbing the impact and keeping Cullen utterly unscathed! Again and again, the beast slammed him to the ground, and every time the light of the Founders absorbed the impact.

As Luminaud realized the futility of his situation, he abruptly picked up Cullen and leapt into the air. With the mighty swoosh of his leathery wings, the beast was slipped into the dark night. As the children watched Cullen disappear, he cried out faintly, "Remember the wolves..."

"Remember the wolves?" said Ronald. "What the heck does that mean?"

"What wolves? There are no wolves among the citizens of Abysstine that I can see!" responded Annabell.

"There were wolves on the map! Remember, guys? We each had a wolf representing us on the map Papa Lee gave us when all this began!" shouted Harry.

Zella quickly replied, "But Cullen has the map! How can we know what he meant by 'remember the wolves' if we do not have the map to guide us?"

"I remember mine!" replied Tillie. "He was pink and his emblem was a bow and arrow, like my gifting!"

"And I remember mine, too!" shouted Ellie. "He was orange and his emblem was a wisp of cloud, representing my ability to transport!"

"So Cullen was simply reminding us to use our gifts?" asked Harry. "Duh!"

"No," replied Mark. "Not just a reminder to use our gifts, but ... but..."

"But what?" asked Annabell, impatiently.

"Listen," said Mark. "Just listen."

With the city of Abysstine slowly coming back to life all around them, the children did as Mark asked. Amidst the hustle and bustle of the citizens of Abysstine tending to the injured and assessing the damages to the city walls, the faintest howling sounds came coming from the southern woods near Menden Lake.

The howling grew ever closer and ever more eerie. Not in a creepy way, but in an adventurous sort of way that makes one feel as if they cannot wait to see what lies around the next bend.

Not fully comprehending what was happening, the children came together near the breach in the city wall. But the howling stopped as mysteriously as it had begun. While the children held their collective breath, their shadows began to move and take the shape of wolves!

Ronald began to count the wolves, while Buddy the dog bayed and barked. "One. Two. Three. Four..."

"There are *eleven* wolves, Ron! Eleven! One for each of us," shouted Ellie.

Tillie chimed in, "Ellie! Remember ... be kind!"

"Sorry, Ronald! We just don't have time to waste!" replied Elliott.

"Can you keep Buddy quiet?" asked Mark.

Before Ronald could answer, the white wolf walked up to Buddy and sniffed his nose. Instantly, Buddy became quiet, as if he and the wolf had come to an understanding that they were on the same side.

"They're huge!" came a voice from the shadows beneath the rubble of the wall.

"Theo! Theo! Is that *you?*" asked Abigail and Annabell at the same time.

"Yes! Yes! It's *me*! I'm okay, guys!" shouted Theo as he leapt to his feet and out of the shadows. "The wolves are so *cool!*"

"What are they doing here?" asked Mia.

"They are here to take you to your next place of battle," replied Abel, stepping into view.

"Our next place of battle?" asked Abigail.

"Yes, and there is no time to waste," replied Abel. "Find your wolf, get on its back, and hold on tight!"

Ronald was first to obey, leaping onto the white wolf marked with the emblem of a flame. Buddy excitedly bounced around in anticipation of joining the journey as part of the pack!

Harry was next, quickly mounting the red wolf marked with the swoosh of wind, representing strength and speed.

Matilda easily climbed onto the pink wolf bearing the emblem of her bow and arrow.

Next came Mark on the grey wolf with the emblem of the herd of deer designating his ability to talk with animals.

Annabell found the transparent wolf due to the emblem of a bell emblazoned upon the scarf around his neck.

261

Abigail was next, recognizing the blonde wolf with one blue eye and one brown eye, the blue eye representing her mesmerizing gaze and ability to read minds.

Not waiting for Mia to find her, the huge brown wolf with the emblem of a lightning bolt nuzzled up to the girl, actually helping Mia atop her furry back.

"There's mine! There's mine!" shouted Elliott as she instantly transported to the back of the orange wolf bearing the wispy cloud emblem!

"And there is mine!" shouted Zella, running to the side of the silver wolf with a lightning bolt in the shape of a Z around his neck.

Theo stood alone, somewhat downcast, feeling left out. "Where is my wolf? Do I even have a wolf?" he said so sadly.

"Of course you have a wolf!" exclaimed Mark. "You are a Bairn of Bren. According to the legend of the map, there should be eleven wolves."

"Then where is he?" asked Theo.

"I'm right here," said a deep, dark voice in the shadows. Part growl and part howl, yet somehow quiet and confident, the creature stepped into the light. A collective gasp went up at the sight of the shiny, muscular black wolf with the symbol of a whirlwind emblazoned on his collar.

"I am at your service, young Theo, the boy who makes thunder. Come! Let us bring a storm of light to the one who would rob the land of that very light," said the black wolf. Theo jumped on, shouting, "Let's ride, cousins! Let's ride!"

Once the children were on their respective wolves, it became painfully apparent that the dark blue wolf with the emblem of a mountain vista on his collar had no rider.

"What about Cullen's wolf?" asked Zella.

"He has been assigned to lead the way," replied Abel.

"Lead the way where?" asked Mark.

"As the emblem of the mountain vista represents the Founders' point of view, the blue wolf of Cullen will know where the next battle awaits. He will lead the way. Your task, children, is simple. Follow where the Founders lead," replied Abel.

"How will we know where that is?" asked Elliott.

"You will know when you get there," responded Abel.

"What about our grandparents?" asked Mia.

"I will take them to where they are needed," replied Patronicus. The King and Queen were already on his massive white back.

"And I will lead Oliver and Canto back to the dragon's lair in case he should come back there," said Ariel, appearing out of nowhere. "There is one of the race of dragonflies who has need of our assistance in freeing his family."

"Verona! It is Verona you speak of!" shouted Zella.

"And who the heck is Verona?" asked Ronald.

"Cullen told me Verona helped him locate Lumen's Hammer, and only aided Luminaud because the evil dragon held his family captive. Verona defied the evil beast in spite of the threat of harm to his family.

"We will help them to freedom," replied Ariel.

"Children," said Abel, "begin the next phase of your journey with the ancient chant of solidarity."

The children gathered their wolves in a circle and began chanting with one voice, "We shall surely overcome! Vict'ry ours when hearts are one! We shall surely overcome! Vict'ry ours when hearts are one! We shall surely overcome! Vict'ry ours when hearts are one!"

As the chant grew to a fevered pitch, the air suddenly exploded with a mighty crash of thunder and the darkness was as the light of day as massive bolts of lightning jutted from the sky above them.

While the thunder rolled down into the valley below and the last tinges of electricity buzzed into darkness, the great blue wolf let out a massive howl and bounded into the darkness. The children held on to the manes of their companions, following Cullen's wolf as he streaked around the city wall of Abysstine and onto the road leading to the heights of the great northern mountains that surrounded the northernmost region of Bren.

To a child, there was not one shred of fear. Not one iota of doubt. Not one notion of turning back. Full of faith and wonder at what they would find at the end of their journey, the children and their wolf-pack, including their honorary wolf, Buddy, bound boldly into the darkness, hearts full of the light that they would need soon enough.

26

ELEVEN WORDS

While the blue wolf bounded up the steep, dark and winding face of the northern mountains of Bren, a faint glow of pale blue light emanated around him, effectively lighting the path for the wolves and children following close behind.

Buddy the dog was right behind the blue wolf, wholeheartedly part of the pack. Even Buddy glowed with a dim pale white light! Ronald was next, atop his white wolf, white glow softly surrounding them. Then came Harold and the red glow of the red wolf he rode, followed just as closely by Matilda and the pinkish glow of her pink wolf.

Careful to not make a sound, the children took their cues from the wolves, silent in their hurried pace up the mountain trail. Right on the tail of Matilda's pink streak was Annabell astride her clear wolf, which glowed with an otherworldly glow, not white but clear light.

Abigail, atop her blonde wolf, streaming a faint yellow glow that looked more like a comet streaking up the trail than a little girl atop a great wolf, kept pace with Annabell. Following her sister, Mia, on her brown wolf, emitted the most pleasing brown aura as she sped up the trail.

Behind Mia, an orange hue was unmistakably Elliott and her beautiful orange wolf. Zella followed closely behind on her silver wolf that looked more like a faint sword heading up the mountain!

Next came Theo on his black wolf. The light produced by the ebony wolf was the most curious of all. It emitted the most beautiful black neon color, giving a radiance unlike the other wolves. It was as if the light of the black wolf somehow enhanced the colors of the other wolves, making for the most glorious beautiful rainbow streak up those dark and winding mountain trails.

Bringing up the rear, Mark rode his great grey wolf, emanating the most royal color of grey light anyone might imagine. And behind everyone, unbeknownst to any of the children but very apparent to the wolves, was a faint white glowing orb—like a tiny star.

Mark eventually noticed the brightness coming up from behind him, yet did not turn to see what or who it might be. The exhilaration of the ride to save his cousin, Cullen, and rid Bren of the menace of Luminaud, filled his heart with great peace —a sort of "knowing" he could not explain. He just knew in his heart of hearts that the bright light following him was a good thing.

Riding at full speed, Mark and the grey wolf suddenly found themselves suspended in midair! Still not fearing, still full of peace, Mark looked ahead to see that all the children seemed to be suspended, too. Before he could make sense of it, the light that had been trailing him flew directly in front of his face and seemed to light the whole world around him. Yet it seemed visible only to him.

In wonder, he reached out his finger to touch the light. That very instant, his mind was filled with a vision of the entire universe. He could see everything that had ever existed and ever would exist in the same moment. Holding his breath in awe, Mark said, "It's a, a, ... it's a ... *star*! I'm touching a star!"

As the words escaped his awestruck lips, the star spoke. "Yes, I am a star." Then the star took the form of a girl. His mouth agape in wonder, Mark asked, "Ariel! Is that you?"

"Yes! It is I," she replied. "I have come to remind you of the meaning of your name before you head into battle. The Founders want you to remember who and whose you are."

"I *do* remember who I am," replied the boy. "It's me! Mark!"

"Yes, but do you remember what the name Mark means?" asked the star girl. "There is power in the word 'Mark' ... power of the universe contained in a word that realizes its fullest potential when believed and spoken out loud by the one who bears it. Your name—the meaning of your name—is 'Tender Warrior'. This means you are to walk and wage war with a merciful heart, yet with the fierceness of one who is invincible. When you find yourself in the throes of battle, speak your name and believe it. It will be as a wave of grace and strength that will flood your heart and mind and carry you through."

The star girl streaked ahead to Theo. Just as Mark had done, Theo instinctively reached out to touch the star girl and immediately saw the entirety of the universe.

"Theo," said Ariel, softly.

"Yes," responded the dumbfounded little boy.

"The Founders have given you a name. You are to bear this name with absolute assurance, even when the dragon speaks to you in subtle and kind tones. When your identity in the realm is attacked, speak the name to your own heart and mind and you will overcome the lies of the enemy. There is the power of the universe in the name, and yours is 'Gift of God.' See yourself as a gift of service to those you encounter who are in need. You are not here for your glory or for your own pleasure, but you are sent of the Founders to serve the realm and serve the Kingdom by the laying down of life."

While Theo sat speechless, Ariel found Zella. Zella touched her and saw the entirety of the universe in the time it takes to inhale one breath. "Zella, the name of the Founders for you is 'Lacking Nothing.' You have everything you need to succeed in life—everything required for the fulfillment of your destiny—in speaking aloud this name to your own heart and mind."

"Yes, I see it," Zella said. "I have everything I need ..." Ariel was now face to face with Elliott atop her orange wolf. Elliott somehow knew before she touched the star that it was Ariel. "Why have we stopped?" she asked.

"We have not stopped, child," replied Ariel. "Time has simply been stopped for a moment.

"What are you doing here? I thought you were with Abel and the others," asked Elliott.

"I *am* with the others yet I am here with you. Don't ask how or why. Just trust, child," said Ariel. "I have come to remind you to use the power of the spoken word granted to you by the Founders. Your word is..."

"Follower of God," replied Elliott before Ariel could continue.

"Yes! Follower of God!" Ariel beamed.

"Why are you telling me what I already know?" asked Ellie.

"Darkness will soon come. When it causes you to fear, remember who and whose you are. Say the word to your own heart and mind, 'I am a follower of God ... I am a follower of the Light.' By speaking the word aloud, you send forth the word and the word does not go out without accomplishing what it was sent to do. Your word will scatter darkness. Your word will light your path. Your word is power spoken out loud. Use it, daughter of Bren."

Ariel sped ahead to Mia. Responding in much the same way as Elliott, Mia recognized the star girl and reached for her, asking, "What are you doing here?"

"I have been sent by the Founders to remind you of the powerful name you are to speak to your own heart and mind when the lies of the enemy try to persuade you otherwise."

"What is my name?" asked Mia.

"You name is 'My Beloved Daughter,'" replied Ariel.

"What does it mean?" asked Mia.

"Speak this name to your own heart and mind whenever the enemy tries to cause you to doubt that you are loved and wanted. When doubt comes to your mind, say it aloud to your own heart and mind and the power of the Founders will scatter the darkness of that doubt and replace it with light and love. Use it often, and remember to say it out loud so all around you can hear."

With that, the star flitted ahead to Abigail.

"Why have we stopped?" asked Abigail as she reached out to touch Ariel.

"We have not stopped," Ariel explained. "We have simply stepped out of the realm of time as you know it and into the pace of eternity. You will understand it more one day. I have been sent by the Founders to remind you of your true name."

"My name means 'Daughter of Joy'!" said Abigail with excitement.

"Yes! And there is great power in that name, especially when spoken out loud to your own heart and mind. When you experience feelings of despair or dread, speak out that name to your own heart and mind and you will change the way you think. When you change the way you think, you will change the way you feel. Say your name into the darkness when those times come. Your joy will spread to those around you like a contagion of laughter. It will be like soothing medicine to those around you."

Without giving Abigail a chance to respond, Ariel streaked ahead to Annabell. Once again—it must be something about the Jennings and their kin—Annabell reached out to touch the star without one trace of fear, saying, "Ariel! I'm so glad to see you!"

"I have come to remind you of the name of power granted to you by the Founders," said Ariel. "Your name is 'Gracious Woman.' This is who you are and it is what you are to speak out loud to your own soul, heart and mind when the enemy spews his hateful lies at you. When you remind yourself of who and of whose you are, you are speaking strength to your own heart and mind. You are a woman, equal in worth to any man, and you are a woman of strength because you bear the light of the Founders to all those you meet. Say your name out loud as often as necessary. This is who you are!"

Matilda was next. "Hello, Ariel. I knew you would be coming," she said.

"I have come to remind you to hold fast to the word of power and truth bestowed upon you by the Founders," said Ariel. "Your name is 'Mighty in Battle.'"

"But I am just a little girl," responded Tillie.

"Great power and might are not determined by physical stature or by gender," Ariel replied. "Power and might come by way of the grace one bears within their heart and mind. And you carry the grace and might and power of the Founders within your deepest heart and mind. Speak this truth to your soul when necessary. Out loud is best because the truth when spoken aloud will strengthen your friends and bewilder your foes. Who are you, Matilda of Bren? What is your word?"

"My name is 'Mighty in Battle,' and I *am* mighty in battle!" shouted Matilda.

Next came Harold atop his red wolf. Not knowing time had even stopped, Harold was a bit startled—in a good surprise-party kind of way—when Ariel appeared directly in front of his face.

"Ariel!" laughed Harold. "What are you doing here?"

"I have come to remind you of the power of the spoken word granted to you by the Founders. Your true name—your specific truth power—is 'Peace Warrior'. You are to say it out loud to your own heart and mind even in the most intense waging of war against the darkness. You have the power to speak peace to your own heart and mind even in the midst of a storm. There is great power when those two simple words are spoken out loud. You *are* a warrior of peace."

Ronald was next. Laughing like Abigail, he reached out and exclaimed, "Ariel! You're here! I *knew* you would come!"

"My dear Ronald, I have come to remind you of the word of the Founders. Your name, which you are to speak to your heart and mind when the enemy lies to you, is this: 'Wise and Powerful Ruler.' You are to rule over others with a servant's heart. You are to see life and its circumstances from the Founders' point of view. In the speaking out loud of your name, power will be granted to your heart and to your mind to endure any hardships that come your way."

Ronald watched in amazement as Ariel started speaking to Buddy the dog. From the moment Ariel had approached Mark, all the way to Ronald who led the way, each child had heard the spoken word of their cousins and siblings and had taken those words to their own hearts as well. Somehow they all just *knew* they were to remind one another who and whose they were and to use the names spoken by Ariel to strengthen and encourage one another when needed.

Buddy nuzzled the star girl. "Buddy," she began, "your name is 'Faithful and True.' You are a friend to all you meet. Your presence is an expression of the presence of the Founders. As you bark out your name, all who hear it will be reminded that they are never alone and that there is power in the presence of the Founders. Bark and bay the power of this word in the heat of battle as a battle cry to rally your children and whisper and coo it as a lullaby of peace as they rest their heads at night. Lead on, good Buddy! Lead on!"

Rising above Cullen's blue wolf, Ariel addressed the group, "Remember who you are! Remember whose you are! Speak your names out loud to your own hearts and minds, and speak them out loud to one another. The darkness is about to grow darker! The battle is about to grow in intensity! But you have no reason to fear. Just speak the name and it will be so! As you think, so you shall be! Follow the blue wolf of Cullen. I must be off to remind Cullen of his word before the darkness consumes him completely!"

The children collectively gasped as they were brought back to the reality of the task at hand: rescuing their brother and cousin, Cullen.

Ariel's conversations with everyone seemed to have taken several minutes at the time, but had actually taken place in the time it takes to blink one's eye! And even as the children gasped, they were once again moving up the mountain trail as fast as the wolves could carry them.

As they ascended the twists and turns of the ever-spiraling trail, they began to hear terrible sounds. Thunderous sounds. The sounds of wailing and screaming. The gnashing of teeth and the ripping of claws against solid rock faces. Interspersed amongst the cacophony of sound were flashes of lightning and the sounds of electrical explosions. It sounded like war ... horrific ... like Luminaud in deepest anger. This could only mean one thing: Cullen was still alive and in control of the sword.

The closer they drew to the chaos, the more adrenaline flowed through their veins. The more adrenaline coursed through them, the more excited they became to join the fray. The more excited they became, the faster the wolves ran. And at the top of the highest ridge of the highest mountain's crest, they saw what they had all hoped they would not see. Cullen was in more trouble than they could ever have imagined.

27

LUMEN'S HAMMER

The wolves and children arrived at the peak and slid to an abrupt halt at the sight of Cullen. Standing atop the precipice, he looked like a little boy yet somewhat conveyed the aura of an adult warrior. With barely enough room to plant his feet, Cullen stood, holding Lumen's Hammer—the great sword of the kingdom of Bren—above his head. With his right arm completely extended, a beam of light, like the most powerful of lasers, shot out from the tip of the great blade.

Although it was the middle of the night, the light of the sword bathed the surroundings with the glow of almost-daylight, giving all who witnessed the fray a sense of dread unlike any they experienced before.

Flapping with ferocity, the wings of the terrible beast caused a gale-force wind with every down stroke, almost knocking the children from the backs of their wolves. Screaming and cursing and screeching and mocking, Luminaud repeatedly assaulted Cullen, trying to topple him from the precarious perch he now held.

The dragon spewed fuming plumes of green smoke from his nostrils in an attempt to cause Cullen to lose consciousness, but the green vapor disintegrated upon contact with the light of Lumen's Hammer. Each time this occurred, Luminaud became more enraged and his frenzy more intense.

No matter where the beast tried to attack Cullen, the boy was able to maintain his balance and keep the beast at bay. From Cullen's point of view, he had to do very little. The sword was directing him as if it had a mind and will of its own! In addition to the beam of light piercing straight from the tip of the blade, a sort of umbrella of light emanated from the sword itself, effectively enveloping Cullen in a protective covering of pure light.

Darting in and out and back and forth, the dragon tried to get to the boy. Each time it seemed the beast was finally close enough to knock Cullen down, the sword repelled him by the power of its light. Again and again, Luminaud came at Cullen. At times, he flew down beneath the boy and attempted to attack from below. He scratched and clawed at the rock beneath Cullen's feet to try and cause the tip of the peak to give way, but the boy and Lumen's Hammer held fast.

Finally, in sheer frustration and weariness, the dragon

flew away into the pitch-black darkness of the night sky. For several minutes, Cullen kept the sword extended above his head, slowly turning just in case Luminaud was still coming for him. Of course, the boy knew the dragon was not done by any means, but at least those few minutes of reprieve gave him a bit of relief from the battle.

Closely watching the sky above, Cullen had not seen his siblings and cousins a few hundred feet below him. The children had watched in silence, captivated by the bravery and skill with which Cullen fought the dragon. Only when the dragon disappeared did they feel the freedom to let Cullen know he was not alone.

Mark called out to Cullen, "Cousin! We are here!" Just as the words left his mouth, time was once again suspended. It was so odd, but the children swore they could see Mark's words stop in the atmosphere between his tongue and Cullen's ear. Of course, they instantly knew what was taking place as they saw a tiny star nearing Cullen's precarious perch.

"Ariel! Is that you?" asked Cullen as he reached out to touch the star girl.

"Yes, son of Bren. It is I," replied Ariel.

"What are you doing here? And why can I see so far into the past? Why do I feel so fully alive in the present, yet how am I able to see what lies ahead in the future? What is happening?" asked the boy.

"You are being granted a view of the universe—of eternity," said Ariel.

"The universe? Everything that exists? All at once? How is that even possible?" asked the boy.

"With the Founders, all is possible. Time stands still. Time is transcended. Eyes are opened. Minds are able to comprehend what they normally could not. What you are experiencing is the place where dreams and reality intersect. In this place, all things are possible. You but have to think it and speak it and it will be so," replied Ariel.

"What am I to do about Luminaud? Even though I can see eternity from where I stand, I cannot seem to find the beast in this moment," explained Cullen.

"You will not be able to see the motives nor feel the intent of that which is of the darkness, but you always have the choice as to how you will respond to that darkness," advised the star girl.

"What does that even mean, Ariel?" asked Cullen.

"It means you can expect the darkness to act as darkness acts. You can expect evil to act as evil does. You but have to walk in the word of your identity as a son of Bren," replied Ariel.

"What is the word of my identity?" asked the boy.

"The truth of your purpose, your destiny, and your reason for existence is quite simple. Your true name is 'evergreen and full of life.' This is who you are. When the darkness returns and evil comes, be who you are called to be. No matter your circum-stances. No matter your temptations. No matter your pain. No matter your sorrow. No matter what, just choose the power of your name. Be evergreen and full of life, son of Bren," said Ariel.

Just like that, Ariel vanished. No sooner was she gone than a mighty swoosh of wind threatened to knock Cullen from his perch. As the air around him began to move with fury, Cullen could not tell which direction the blast of wind was coming from. All he knew for sure was that Luminaud was making yet another attempt at taking the sword.

Suddenly, like a streak of darkness from below and behind, the dragon rushed at Cullen, wings frantically flap-ping and slithering tongue darting in and out between his enormous front fangs. As the dragon slammed into Cullen full force, Lumen's Hammer drew Cullen's hand to face the beast! He struck Luminaud directly on his snarling snout, and the dragon was suddenly dazed and confused. His great body hurtled down the side of the peak, wings flailing and feet clawing for any grip that might slow his fall.

Unable to stop his sudden descent and reeling from the blow of the mighty sword against his scaly dragon nose, Luminaud soon found himself surrounded by eleven brave children, eleven snarling and colorful wolves, and one brave beagle-basset hound mix!

Without a word, the children attacked the dragon! Mark summoned the chiroptera and all flying creatures to join the fray as he sent arrow upon arrow at the leviathan. Soon, the air was abuzz with eagles, bats, sparrows, hawks, herons, and the mighty man-like bat people known as chiroptera. Even hummingbirds joined the battle.

Elliott went into transport mode. When a creature was felled by a swat of the dragon's talons, she was at its side. Taking the creature by the paw or wing, with a simple touch she transported the injured one to safety far beyond the dragon's reach.

Mia, of course, sent bolts of lightning toward the head of Luminaud in an effort to blind him and bewilder him. And it worked! With every streak of light that touched his ugly dragon face, he swatted like a cat swats at a laser, moaning and groaning.

While Mia focused on the dragon's eyes, Ron focused his attacks on the dark underbelly of the beast, sending fireballs to his exposed belly. With each strike, the dragon was pushed farther back toward the rock wall of the peak.

As Ronald sent his fireballs toward Luminaud, Harold picked up boulders three times his own weight and mightily hurled them at the dragon's feet, causing him to stumble precariously and adding to the giant lizard's confusion and anger.

Abigail focused on the swarms of dragonflies that had once again joined the battle in defense of Luminaud. Using the piercing gaze of her blue eyes, she mesmerized the entire swarm into a hovering cloud of uselessness.

Once Abigail had caused the dragonflies to be suspended

uselessly in midair, Annabell took out her amazing bell and struck a nearby boulder, causing such a reverberation that the entire hovering horde fell to the ground. The vibrations caused their wings to crumble and crinkle into oblivion.

No sooner had the dragonflies been rendered useless than Zella began to zigzag back and forth beneath Luminaud's feet, causing him to trip and stumble and sway like a giant tree that is about to crash to the ground. Like clockwork, the children worked together to bring Luminaud to his knees in surrender.

Zella then shouted out to Theo, "Now, little cousin! Now!"

As the terrible beast flapped his mighty wings in an attempt to escape the onslaught, Theo flew into the air directly above the dragon and spun rapidly, creating a whirlwind and a downdraft. The monster couldn't get any lift whatsoever! Spinning and spinning without letting up for even a smidgen of a second, Theo continued until the beast fell on his side with a mighty thud!

Cullen watched it all happen from atop the peak and started making his way down to dispatch the dragon with a final blow from Lumen's Hammer. His siblings and cousins, along with the pack of multi-colored wolves, formed a tight circle around Luminaud, keeping him pinned down by the force of their combined giftings.

From the prophecies contained within the map Cullen carried, the children all knew the dragon could only be slain with Lumen's Hammer. They knew they had to hold the beast until Cullen could get there and do the deed.

Cullen came to the dragon's writhing body and lifted the ancient, sacred sword high above his head with a sure grip. As he was about to deliver the death blow and sever the beast from his head, a voice shouted, "Stop, Bairn of Bren! Stop!"

Stopping in mid-stroke, Cullen was shocked to see Patronicus rearing up on his hind legs, whinnying loudly, "Do not slay the dragon! Not yet! Stop!"

"But the prophecy! What about the prophecy, Patronicus?" asked Cullen, holding Lumen's Hammer against the throat of the dragon.

"The prophecy will be fulfilled as it has been written, but..."

"But what?" asked Cullen, incredulously. "If I allow him to live, have I not failed?"

"Wait a second," interjected Ronald. "Weren't our grandparents with you? Should they not be the ones giving the order not to slay the dragon?"

"That is why you must stop," said Patronicus.

"Please explain, *RGB!*" demanded Elliott.

"When Luminaud fled for those few seconds and it appeared he had flown away, he sought your grandparents, King Leonolis and Queen Abila. As we neared Menden Lake mere minutes ago, he swooped in and ripped them from my back with his mighty talons. I followed him back up the mountain trail just in time to put a stop to Cullen's death blow!"

"But why must he not slay the dragon?" asked Mark.

Writhing in pain while the children held him at bay, Luminaud strained to speak. "I have them ... I have your grandparents ..." His voice trailed off in fatigue.

"Where have you taken them?" asked Cullen.

"If you slay me, they will die. The only way for you to save your grandparents is to release me and give me the sword. The treasure you seek—the safe release of your grand-parents—for the treasure I seek: Lumen's Hammer."

"Wait a minute," interjected Mia. "He used the word 'treasure,' and the word 'treasure' is used in the prophecy of the map Cullen now keeps."

"She's right, you know," said Matilda.

"But what does that have to do with the fate of the dragon? *Now* is our chance to slay him once and for all, to put an end to this terror once and for all," pled Annabell.

"Your treasure in exchange for mine," hissed Luminaud. "Your treasure for mine."

"I will never give you Lumen's Hammer," said Cullen, defiantly.

"Then your grandparents are already dead and it is all your doing," said Luminaud.

"Where are they? What have you done with them?" asked Harold. "Tell me or I'll ... I'll..."

"You'll what?" seethed the dragon, "You'll kill me yourself? The only way to save your precious grandparents is to release me and give me Lumen's Hammer."

Again he hissed, "Your treasure in exchange for mine."

While the dragon spoke, time was once again suspended as Ariel floated from above the children and stood directly on top of Luminaud.

"The beast cannot hear me. You alone, Bairns of Bren, are able to hear what I am about to tell you."

"Cullen, Bairn of Bren," she said, matter-of-factly, "you are to give him the sword."

"But the prophecy!" Cullen argued.

"The prophecy *is* being fulfilled even in the giving up of the sword. I assure you, the power of the light of Lumen's Hammer cannot be harnessed or controlled or contained by the Light Eater. You must see from a different point of view, children. Giving up the sword is much akin to the laying down of life. You will find it is in the laying down of one's life, the losing of one's life, that brings about the finding of life."

"I really don't understand, Ariel, but I trust you," said Cullen. "What am I to do?"

"Tell the beast you will hand over the sword on one condition and one condition alone," Ariel explained. "You are to tell him to take you to the place of treasure. He will understand what you mean even though you don't. The place of the treasure is where you will find your grandparents. All will make sense in time.

"What are *we* to do?" asked Theo, motioning to his cousins.

"You are to heed the true names you have been given and go where your wolves take you. You are to simply trust," said Ariel.

Upon her utterance of the word "trust," time was unsuspended and Luminaud strained against the powerful gifts of the children, demanding, "Your treasure in exchange for mine!"

"Okay! Okay!" shouted Cullen at the beast. "I will hand over the sword on one condition and on one condition alone. You will take me to the place of treasure. And once there, you will release my grandparents. Once they are free and clear of danger, Lumen's Hammer is yours."

With a great sense of dread, the children, one by one, released their grips on the evil beast. Stumbling to his feet, Luminaud ordered Cullen, "On my back, scum of Bren!"

Cullen climbed atop the dreadful creature and securely tightened his knees against the body of the beast. He rode into the night behind the wings of the Light Eater. The dragon never saw the pouch fall from the sky and into the midst of the remaining children.

Cullen had dropped the map!

28

MAP ALIVE

*A*s if by magic, the pouch containing the map fell right at the feet of the great grey wolf. Mark leapt off his back, picked up the pouch, and reached in and grasped the map with great reverence. While the children gathered around, Mark loosened the string that kept the map bound. As he did so, the map instantly unfurled as if under its own power and began pulsating with color and light. It seemed to be alive—breathing! As the pulsations continued and the colorful light beamed upward and outward from the parchment, the children saw tiny animated drawings of each of them and their wolves, along with Buddy and Patronicus.

"That's *us!*" cried Theo as he hovered above the group. "How cool is that?!"

"Very cool," agreed Harry.

"Come on, boys! Yes, it's cool, but what is it trying to tell us? Where are we to go next?" implored Elliott.

Ronald, muttering under his breath, "It's *so* cool," was met with Ellie's icy gaze that said in uncertain terms, 'Silent!' Still, he muttered, "Just sayin'."

"Look!" exclaimed Mia. "We and our wolves are headed down the back side of this very mountain!"

"Where does that trail lead?" asked Annabell.

"Let's watch and see!" chimed in Abigail.

"It leads right to the base of the mountain and enters a ginormous cavern!" exclaimed Zella. "Not another cavern! I *hate* caverns!"

The little green-hatted gnome of the map began leaping up and down, beckoning with his right arm to follow. "I think we are to do as the gnome says!" reasoned Mark. "To the wolves!"

The children bravely jumped back on their wolves and the wolves headed directly down the mountain trail as suggested by the map, as if they had understood every word the children had just spoken. Howling and baying, Buddy followed the pack while Patronicus brought up the rear.

Like arrows of light, the brave children and their mighty wolves streaked down the trail, twisting and turning as they followed the switchback down, down, down the mountain. With great ease, they leapt over fallen boulders or trees that would have stopped a wagon and team of horses in their tracks. It seemed that the more the wolves ran, the more powerful they became. And so it was for the children, Buddy and Patronicus!

Making the trek down in mere minutes (it should have taken at least two hours), the children came to a sudden stop in front of a massive opening in the side of the mountain.

"This must be it—the cavern entrance!" shouted Mark.

"What should we do now?" asked Ronald.

"Elliott," began Mark, "can you transport ahead a few feet into the cavern and report back to us what you see?"

Before Elliott could respond, little Theo flew from the back of his wolf and directly into the gaping maw of the cavern.

"Theo! Wait" shouted Mark, but he was gone!

"What should we do now?" asked Matilda.

"We should go after him!" exclaimed Mark.

The children all followed Mark into the cavern. "Ronald, can you lead the way by the power of your fire?"

"Already on it, cousin!" shouted Ronald as he produced a small fireball in each hand. Holding his hands out in front of him, he and his white wolf led the way through the massive cavern. A few hundred feet in, the fireballs became unnecessary because of the golden glow emanating ahead of them. With a heavenly yellowish aura filling the entire cave, the children stopped.

Ronald extinguished the fireballs in his hands. The kids could see the glow was coming from somewhere around the next bend of the huge cave system. Moving as quietly and stealthily as the wolves they all rode, they strained to see what awaited them around that next bend. Then they heard a familiar voice.

"Come, Bairns of Bren," hissed Luminaud. "I've been expecting you."

What they saw around the bend brought shivers down their spines. They were mesmerized at first by the mountains of gold and silver and precious gems. Diamonds and rubies. Amethyst and jade. Topaz and emeralds. Phrygian crystal and quartz every color in the rainbow.

Mound upon mound of all these riches were quite overwhelming to the children, so dazzlingly beautiful and shiny. One by one, the children, at least for a moment, lost all fear of the dragon and why they had ventured so far. They were mesmerized. Absolutely mesmerized by the sheer amount of rich treasure the dragon had accumulated in the hidden cavern. The taste of greed in the atmosphere was almost palpable until Elliott recognized what was happening.

"Cousins! Sister! Do not be deceived by what we see before us! This is earthly treasure! It's not real and true treasure!" she shouted.

"Looks like real and true treasure to me," chimed in Ronald.

"Looks real to me, too!" exclaimed Mark.

"It's very real!" exclaimed Theo as he flew directly into the mound of gold coins and artifacts nearest him, causing a cascade of coins and trinkets to clank to a stop at the base of the mound and leaving the boy half-buried in the gold.

"That's not the treasure we are seeking!" shouted Elliott. "That's not the treasure we were sent to find! Look!" She pointed to the mound of gold and silver that reached nearly to the cavern ceiling.

"Grandfather and grandmother!" shouted Annabell.

"Why are they just standing there?" asked Mia.

"They are bound; they cannot move! They are bound in chains of gold!" shouted Abigail.

"Let's free them!" shouted Matilda. "Come on, guys!"

"Not so fast, Bairns of Bren!" came the voice the children all knew too well now.

Luminaud slithered out of the shadows from behind the mound of treasure where King Leonolis and Queen Abila were bound. Like a giant serpent with legs, the great dragon came closer to the children and their wolves, causing quite a racket as his huge body disturbed the many piles of gold, silver, and precious gems. Luminaud held something tightly in his right forepaw. That something turned out to be some-one. As the dragon came within a few feet of the children, he sat back on his haunches and held out that someone for all to see.

"Cullen!" shouted Harry. "Cullen, are you all right?"

"Yes, brother! I am fine!" shouted Cullen.

"Enough!" roared Luminaud. "It is time for the exchange.

Your treasure—the sword—in exchange for mine. Your grandparents."

"Don't do it!" shouted Elliott. "Once you give him the sword, he will kill our grandparents and he will come after us next!"

"I am a dragon of my word," Luminaud calmly replied. "I will release your grandparents once the sword is in my hands. And you have my word, I will leave you all here alone."

"We cannot trust him!" Zella shouted to Cullen.

"We cannot trust him, sister. This is true. But we can trust the prophecy of the map. The word is true and will accomplish what it was sent out—what we were sent out—to do," replied Cullen.

"Put me down, Luminaud, and release my grandparents, my siblings and my cousins, and the sword is yours," said Cullen.

While the stunned children watched in silence, the evil beast gently placed Cullen, still clutching Lumen's Hammer to his chest with both hands, on the cavern floor.

"Go to your grandparents, children. You will find the key to the locks that bind them hanging beneath the treasure mound on the cavern wall next to the mound," said the dragon.

The children ran right past Cullen and Luminaud. Of course, Elliott transported directly to the cavern wall, retrieved the key and found her captive grandparents. While the other children scrambled to the top of the mound, Elliott freed the King and Queen. But something was not right. They seemed to be frozen in a trance, staring out into the cavern but not seeing or saying a thing to their grandchildren!

"What have you done to them?!" Mark shouted back at Luminaud.

"I needed a bit of their light of life, so I withdrew enough for myself, leaving just enough in them to keep them alive. Their light will be restored as soon as the sword is fully mine," replied the dragon.

The children held their catatonic grandparents upright and watched helplessly as Cullen stepped boldly toward the great beast. "Here, Light Eater," he calmly said, "my treasure for yours."

Cullen held the sword upward in his hands. The beast nimbly took it by the hilt and lifted it toward the cavern ceiling in victory. The children, while glad to have their grandparents safely by their sides, were saddened beyond belief at what was transpiring before their eyes. The greatest treasure of the Kingdom—the most sacred of artifacts of the realm, the stuff of legends, Lumen's Hammer—was being handed over to the most vile and evil of creatures. They could only imagine what horrors awaited the realm of Bren because of Cullen's most unfortunate trade.

That horror was made real by what happened next. While clutching the sacred sword in his right paw, Luminaud grabbed Cullen with his left and laughed in scorn and triumph. "Ha! Ha! Ha! Ha! Ha! You fools! This day, the source of all light is now mine! The realm of darkness now rules the realm of light! All power, all dominion, all life bows to *me*!"

"Unhand Cullen!" shouted Mark as he placed an arrow on his bow and aimed it directly at the head of the dragon. "You promised none of the children would be harmed if Cullen gave you the sword. What of your word?"

"I am keeping every word of that promise. I am not harming any of you or your grandparents, at least not yet. And I never promised harm would not come to this vile child of Bren. He is mine and he is to be made an example to all of Bren. Cullen and I have an appointment with the people of Bren at Castle Aerie. It is there that I will consume the light of his life for all the land to see. It will serve as a warning to any who would dare stand in my way. The Age of Light has now been exchanged for the Age of Darkness!"

With that, Luminaud, clutching the sword in one paw and Cullen in the other, walked out of the cavern. As he entered the outside world, he flew to a ledge several hundred feet above the cavern entrance and pushed boulders down toward the cave entrance. Before anyone could react, the cavern entrance was sealed with the children and their grand-parents inside.

After the dust settled and the crashing rocks subsided, the children were in total darkness. That is, until Ronald and Mia began producing balls of fire and little bolts of lightning, causing an eerie glow to reflect off the dragon's horde of precious metals and gems.

By this time, both Leonolis and Abila had regained consciousness. "We have to find a way out of here," Mark said. "Theo, fly around the cavern and see if you can find a way out."

Theo zoomed around the cavern several times, only to return with bad news. "Sorry, cousin! The only way in or out has been sealed! I'm afraid we're trapped!"

"No, we are not!" replied Mark. "Elliott, go and find he ..." Before he finished his sentence, Ellie disappeared.

Elliott transported to the valley leading to the cavern just in time to see Luminaud disappearing into the southern sky, headed to Castle Aerie. As she was about to follow, she heard a voice. "Elliott! Is that you?"

Elliott turned and saw a welcome friend. "Abel! I am so glad to see you—and Oliver and Canto and Ariel! The children, my grandparents, the great unicorn, Patronicus, the wolves, and Buddy the dog are all trapped inside! We must help them, but I must get word to the people of Castle Aerie that Luminaud is headed their way and plans to execute my dear cousin, Cullen, once he gets there!"

Oliver the ogre immediately began tearing away at the massive pile of debris and boulders that now blocked the cavern entrance while Abel addressed Elliott. "Go, dear child. Warn the people of Castle Aerie and rescue your cousin. We will work on freeing the trapped ones."

Elliott answered, "He has the sword. Luminaud has Lumen's Hammer."

Abel softly replied, "I know, child. It is as has been prophesied. But remember this: darkness cannot wield the power of the light. But the power of the light will always find a way to overcome the darkness. Go, child. Go."

Instantly, Elliott was within the walls of the great hall of counsel, in the very center of an ongoing counsel session of the leadership of the realm of Bren. Shocked, the wisest men and women in Bren found themselves listening to the wisdom and warning of a brave little girl.

29

THE POWER OF WONDER AND CONSUMING LIGHT

*E*lliott wasted no time explaining the situation to the wise men and women of Bren. As she addressed the counsel, the castle guards sounded the dragon alarm and prepared the castle defenses for the arrival of Luminaud. Massive dragon nets were loaded into the many catapults atop the castle walls. Immense dragon harpoons were readied and loaded into the large crossbows around the castle. The walls were lined with the special castle forces—men with large dragon-piercing spears and huge dragon-piercing arrows in their dragon-battle-bows.

Within minutes, the entire population of the castle was thoroughly prepped and ready for whatever came next. The cavalrymen, atop their mighty Brennolinian steeds, surrounded the outer walls of the castle, ready to engage the beast from atop their mounts.

Once these tasks were set in motion and the castle forces were in place, Elliott was gone in an instant, back to the cavern where her cousins and sister and grandparent were trapped. By the time she arrived, Oliver, Canto, Abel, and Ariel had managed to move most of the debris from the cavern entrance. Just as she was about to help them, a slow rumbling started inside the cavern. As the group on the outside felt the quaking, they stepped back from the pile of rocks toward safety, assuming an earthquake was causing the ground to shake.

A rush of dust and wind flew out of the cavern, but the tremors suddenly came to a stop. Then a voice inside the cavern shouted, "Watch out below! This is the last one!" Rather than waiting to find out what to watch out for, Elliott and the others ran to the side of the debris pile just as a large boulder came hurtling from the cavern like a giant cannonball piercing the dust. A cloud of dirt swirled like smoke behind the flying rock!

"That should do it!" cried the voice. Like a ghost appearing from out of nowhere, a figure walked out of the cavern and into the dust-filled air in the valley. "Ah! Fresh air at last!" exclaimed Harry. Harry shouted back into the cavern, "Come on guys! The coast is clear and the air smells great!"

"Harry! You could have killed one of us! Next time you're going to throw a boulder our way, give us little more of a head's up!" scolded Elliott as she rushed to embrace him.

"You are so strong, crazy boulder-throwing cousin, but you could be a bit more careful."

Now all the children made their way out of the cave along with their grandparents. Laughing as Elliott told them of the way the boulder had almost taken their heads off, the cousins and siblings and friends and wolves and Buddy the dog did what they always did. In what must have seemed like the world's largest group-hug ever, they became a tangled mass of arms and legs and giggles and snorts and tears as only the Jennings grandchildren could become.

King Leonolis stopped to ask Elliott, "What of Cullen? What of Castle Aerie?"

"Grandfather, the map!" interrupted Mark. "The map is trying to tell us something!"

The southern end of the map became a moving image of Castle Aerie, revealing people preparing for battle, walls lined with soldiers, and flags flying on each turret.

"What's that?" asked Annabell as she pointed to a dark streak, like a mixture of light and dark, heading straight for the castle.

"I am afraid that is Luminaud. He is the darkness, and Cullen is the light. And they are almost there," explained Mark.

"We've no time to waste, grandfather! We must get to Castle Aerie at once!" exclaimed Elliott.

"Then you must take us there, Ellie! Remember last time? asked Leonolis. (He was referring to an episode in the story called Hide and Seek when Elliott had transported the entire group from one place to another simultaneously.)

"Yes, of course I do, grandfather!" shouted the girl.

King Leonolis explained to the group very plainly, "We have no time for explanation. Now is the time for trust and obedience. Elliott will take my right hand while grandmother takes my left. Mark joins hands with grandmother. Annabell joins hands with Mark and she takes hands with Ronald." They took one another's hands until all were in a chain. Ronald to Harold to Zella to Mia to Abigail to Matilda to Theo.

Theo's other hand held Abel's, who held Canto's, who held Ariel's, who held Oliver's, who grabbed Patronicus' outstretched right front hoof! Before giving the go-ahead nod to Elliott, King Leonolis yelled out, "Is everyone connected?"

"What about Buddy the dog? shouted Ronald in earnest.

"What about the wolves?" asked Mia.

"Buddy will ride Patronicus," said the King. Buddy climbed atop the magnificent unicorn and sat proudly on his back.

"As for the wolves," declared Leonolis, "I have a feeling they will arrive in time without being a part of this chain." And with that, a pack of eleven colorful bolts of lightning combined into one unmistakable laser-focused jolt of power and ran south to Castle Aerie.

King Leonolis shouted, "Hold tight, everyone! To Castle

Aerie and to victory we go!" He nodded to Elliott and they were gone in a flash.

Moving at supersonic speed, the children could not help but feel the exhilaration of the pace. Yet they were equally in awe of the way time also stood still.

"What's going on?" asked Theo. "What's happening to us?"

"We are witnessing time and absence of time in the same instant," explained Ariel.

"That hurts my brain," said Ron.

"Mine, too," said Theo, "but it's still so cool!"

Mark felt the map begin to vibrate, as if it were trying to get his attention. "What do I do, grandfather? I cannot keep hold and read the map at the same time."

"But I can," said Ariel. She reaching into the deep pocket of Mark's robe and unfurled the map.

The children looked back in the chain to see Ariel still holding hands with Canto and Oliver. " How is this possible?" asked Mark.

"Remember, Bairn of Bren, I am of the race of stars. I am pure light. I am both here and there at the same time," explained Ariel.

Mouth agape, his eyes darting between Ariel holding the map and Ariel at the back of the chain of hands, Mark asked what the map said.

"It appears to be lighting up the final verses of the riddle, as if saying, 'Read me.' So I will read," said Ariel.

Be bold, be brave, be love, be fierce
Be humble, behold, 'til dragon heart pierced
Return the land, restore the peace
Who would be greatest, be the least

Seek the treasure marked with gold
This treasure's worth the likes untold
Is found where death meets life, the measure
'Tis life laid down will find the treasure

"What does it mean?" asked Abigail.

"It means we must all be prepared to lay down our lives," Ariel explained. "It means that in the laying down of life we will find the real and true treasure of the realm of Bren."

"Are we all going to die?" asked the youngest of the cousins, little Theo.

"All must die, but all will live," said Ariel.

"But I am afraid to die," responded Theo, lips quivering and eyes brimming with tears.

"There, there," said Queen Abila. "What we now face we must all face at some point in our lives. The good news is that our lives will not be wasted, but will accomplish what the Founders have sent us forth to do. And better still, we do not face death alone. Do not fear, child. We are not alone. Even now the Founders are with us."

The dark world around them was suddenly full of light. And not just any light! This light was moving. Not streaking straight ahead like one would expect of a laser beam, not jagged and scattered like a lightning bolt, but like flowing water!

As the sky filled with brilliant waves of undulating light, the green-hatted gnome of the map jumped up and down and pointed toward both the northern sky and the southern sky. The children gasped in awe of what they saw next.

In the northern sky, wave upon wave of brilliant green and gold curling light cascaded like waves from the darkness of outer space into the realm of the earth. At the same time, wave upon wave of curling light filled the southern sky, like waterfalls of brilliant blues and purples, cascading from the darkness onto the earth.

"What is it?" asked Annabell.

"In your world, we call them the Aurora Borealis—the northern lights—and the Aurora Australis—the southern lights. Science would say they are caused and created by your sun, but the reality is they are created by the Founders. What you are seeing are a portion of the people of Galaxia."

"You are witnessing the forces of Galaxia—the many races of the star people—joining forces with the people of Bren. They come to wage war on the Light Eater and to infuse the great weapon of old, Lumen's Hammer, with the power of the universe."

"But Luminaud now holds the great sword!" exclaimed Theo.

"Yes, he holds the sword, or so it may appear. But which

holds which? Does the dragon hold the sword or does the sword hold the dragon? You see, dear Bairns of Bren, darkness cannot control the light, and darkness cannot drive out darkness. Only light can do that. The greatest light is found in the times of greatest darkness—a time such as this."

Suddenly, Ariel was no longer speaking, and the children and others had come to a standstill, right in the middle of the courtyard of Castle Aerie! As their eyes adjusted to the light, dawn seemed to be about to break. But when it seemed the sun was about to pop up from the eastern horizon, the light of the realm dimmed back into the darkness of night!

And then they saw him. Cullen on his back and Luminaud pinning him with the tip of the blade against Cullen's chest. The boy defiantly shouted, "Darkness cannot overcome light, but light will overcome darkness!" By sheer willpower, the boy kept the sword from piercing his heart, and this enraged the beast all the more!

Needing no instruction, the children and their traveling companions surrounded Luminaud, gifts ready to use against the great beast.

"Cullen! We are here!" shouted Mark. "All of us! We are here. You are not alone!"

Mark ran to Cullen's side and did the unthinkable. He laid down on top of his cousin, between the sword and Cullen, and pushed back against the sword and the monster who wielded it.

Elliott ran to the boys and laid down beside them, and

pushed back against the power of the Light Eater. One by one, the children all piled on top of one another. Annabell on Elliott. Matilda on Annabell. Mia on Matilda. Abigail on Mia. Ronald on Mark. Harold on Ronald. Theo on Harold.

While the children pushed back against the dragon, Leonolis and Abila shouted encouragement: "Remember, he has no real power since he is of the realm of darkness, from the realm of lies!"

But Leonolis and Abila could not help but notice the light of the land of Bren was growing ever dimmer and so were their grandchildren.

Crushed by the weight of the darkness of Luminaud, Cullen shouted to his siblings and cousins, "He cannot wield the sword! He can only draw life from those who believe his lies. We know the truth, and truth requires we lay down our life to find the true treasure of Bren. I have seen the true treasure! The treasure is ... the *people!*"

As if a light went on in the head of each child, they were suddenly emboldened with a power they had not yet realized they possessed, and they knew what they must do. From Theo at the top of the pile to Cullen at the bottom, they became still. It was as if they were no longer resisting the dragon.

With as much bravery and volume as he could muster, Cullen yelled out, "Are you ready, cousins and siblings?"

Their response? "Ready, Cullen! Just say the word!"

While the King and Queen and the entire population

and forces of Bren watched from around the castle and its environs, Cullen shouted, "Now!"

And while that one word echoed in slow motion around the great Castle Aerie, the dragon plunged the sword into Theo's chest, piercing his and every heart between he, the youngest, and Cullen, the oldest, of the Jennings grandchildren. Then all was still and utterly dark. All hope, and all light, was gone.

30

A CONVERGENCE OF LIGHT

In that moment, every sense went numb. At least that is what the King and Queen felt when they realized their grandchildren, all eleven, were suddenly no more. So deep was their anguish, they could feel nothing. So dark was the darkness, they could see nothing. So profound was the shock of loss, they could not tell if the air they breathed was hot or cold. So great the pain of watching their grandchildren die, they could no longer taste the dragon's bitter sulfur breath that permeated the atmosphere. So devastating was their grief, they could neither hear their own sobs and anguished moans nor the screams and blood-curdling cries of the wounded that lay around the courtyard. All was dark. All was silent. All was numb. It was as if time and existence had been reduced to nothingness.

Literally knocked senseless by the loss to their family and

to the realm, all Leonolis and Abila could do was hold each other in the darkness. They wrapped each other in that same embrace they had practiced since the day they were wed so long ago. Warm, wet tears poured endlessly from their eyes. Although numb, they sensed the deep pain of loss together and found comfort in the most familiar embrace a man and a woman can know after forty years of marriage. The only thing they longed for more than this embrace was the embrace of their grandchildren.

Like the way Cullen and Ron and Harry and Zella always gave group hugs. The way Ronald always introduced himself to his grandfather with a handshake, saying, "Hi, I'm Ronald Leon Kay. Have you met my brother Harry?" Such bittersweet memories somehow buoyed the heart of Leonolis.

Like the way Annabell always preferred to be held first by her grandmother while giving that side glance, twinkle in her eye, to her grandfather that said, "I love you, too, grandpa, but grandma is all mine." Like the way Mark always remembered that his grandpa had told him, "You make me happy, Mark" and the way Mark always reminded his grandfather, "I make you happy, right grandpa?"

The way Mia always pretended to be afraid of grandfather because she knew he would chase her around and around the castle halls while she ran in mock fear, only to be wonderfully captured and held by him as she giggled with glee. The way Abigail always spoke to her grandmother in the sweetest little voice that made her grandmother's heart melt, even if she had just been caught sneaking a cookie out of the royal cookie jar!

Like the way Elliott lit up the royal throne room just by her grand entrances, often pretending to be the prima ballerina of Bren who just happened to love unicorns ... pretending her grandfather was a unicorn while she rode on his back through the castle courtyard. Like the way Matilda could melt the heart of her grandmother by simply saying, "I love you, G'Ma."

Like the way Theo had captured the hearts of the entire family because he was the youngest and because his laughter and enthusiasm for life seemed to be contagious. He had been born with the gift of joy and he was the human embodiment of sheer joy.

The memories flooded like a tsunami through the minds of Leonolis and Abila, yet they buoyed them, even in their sorrow, like a ship anchored to a solid rock in the midst of the most violent of storms. And this was certainly a storm the realm of Bren had never seen before.

Luminaud had accomplished what he had set out to do. He had consumed the light of life of Bren. So intense was the darkness that one could not know whether it was noon or the dead of night. All was suddenly still. All the Kingdom stood for was lost. All they loved and lived for ... gone.

While the King and Queen embraced, they felt a small tremor beneath their feet. "Of course, what else but an earthquake ..." whispered Abila to the King.

King Leonolis replied, "The Founders waste nothing. There must be some purpose for the ground to now quake. Let's get to safety, dear wife."

While they stumbled in darkness toward the safety of a nearby doorway, the quaking grew in intensity and ferocity, as if everything, not just the earth beneath their feet, was being shaken to its core. The more the tremors grew, the less sporadic they seemed. As if someone were keeping time with the world's largest drumbeat!

And then the rumble of quaking stone and earth began to take on the sound of voices. A mighty and majestic choir singing in the most emotional and beautiful depth yet the with the most angelic purity. It sounded like a mighty chorus of men with the tone and timbre of a children's choir.

The King and Queen strained to hear where the singing might be coming from. Then the northern skies began to glow and flow like a mighty ocean wave toward the castle courtyard. Before their eyes could adjust to these northern lights, there appeared a similar wave of light flooding and cascading from the south. From the mighty flow of light in the north to the mighty flow of light in the south, darkness was invaded by the most brilliant colors—ones not even found in the normal human spectrum!

Greens so deep they brought to life every barren place they touched. Blues so rich they filled the rivers, streams and lakes with deep blue crystalline waters. Yellows and golds so brilliant with power they filled every nook and cranny with newness and cleansing. Reds and oranges that seemed more dazzling than the sun, yet so pure that one could look directly into their depths and see pure redemption and grace. Color upon color. Peace up peace. Yet in the midst of all that peace, an obvious and definite power that made one think the waves of light were somehow alive!

Mesmerized by the array of color and display of majesty from the heavens, the King and Queen called out to the Founders with one voice. "Oh mighty Founders, Creators of Bren, invade death's deep darkness and rise up again!"

At that moment, the tremors shook even more violently and the resulting shockwaves took on a most definite cadence. And the words of that mighty choir rang out clear:

> We shall surely overcome! Vict'ry ours when
>   hearts are one!
> We shall surely overcome! Vict'ry ours when
>   hearts are one!
> We shall surely overcome! Vict'ry ours when
>   hearts are one!

The third time the chant was sung, the entire Kingdom of Bren was filled with an intense explosion of light as the northern lights converged with the southern lights, the light piercing from the hands of Cullen as he held Lumen's Hammer above his head.

When the lights had exploded out from where the children had laid down their lives, Luminaud had been knocked backward and lost his grip on the sword, which Cullen, very much alive, caught!

When Cullen regained control of the sword, he was suddenly surrounded by his very-much-alive siblings and cousins, who began focusing their powers on the stunned and dazed dragon.

Mark shot arrows at his writhing face. Annabell rang her bell and the sound waves subdued the beast. Ronald and Mia sent fireballs and lightning into his great red leathery body. Abigail sent thoughts of confusion to his dragon mind. Harry hurled massive stones at him. Elliott transported soldier after soldier from outside the castle walls where they had been stationed into the castle courtyard, where they joined the attack on Luminaud. Matilda used her bow and arrow to send even more confusion into the mind of the beast, shooting arrows of pure light into the darkness of his small dragon mind. Zella ... well ... Zella zigzagged so rapidly that she caused the dragon to lose his balance. Theo floated in midair directly above the beast, creating a downward vortex that kept the dragon's wings pinned to the ground. Like a giant clock that keeps perfect time with its many moving parts, the Bairns of Bren kept up a relentless bombardment.

The others, who had been so instrumental in helping the children throughout their quest to rid Bren of the Light Eater, joined the fray. Patronicus pierced the dragon's hindquarters with his horn so the beast couldn't stand. Oliver finished the task, binding the hind feet in a massive chain.

Canto began to sing. Before she had finished her first refrain, a horde of fairies added the light of their magic essence to the massive convergence of northern and southern lights. Directing the mighty cascade of light was none other than Ariel. Like a conductor leading an orchestra of sheer light, the star girl directed waves of light to points of weakness in the dragon's body while Abel sent word throughout the realm that the great beast was being subdued at Castle Aerie. The forces of Bren, from wherever they were stationed in the land, came streaming in to defeat the darkness of Luminaud.

While the children and their friends joined forces with the convergence of light, Cullen began to speak. The power of the light kept growing in intensity while the atmosphere grew strangely—no, reverentially—quiet. The screams and groans of the injured were no longer audible. The screeching and writhing and gnashing of dragon teeth was suddenly silenced. The rumbling and rattling of the quaking, tremoring earth could be felt but, oddly, not heard. The light, in all its power and splendor, roared a silent roar that reminded the children of the hum of electricity pulsating through high electrical lines in the countryside back home in Oklahoma. Sheer power, coupled with regal reverence, set the perfect stage for what Cullen was about to say.

Sounding more like a young man than a boy, his voice was

familiar yet deeper. A voice to be respected. Everyone, even Luminaud, listened.

"Dear people of Bren. It was foretold in the prophecies of old that this day, and many more like it, would come. Those prophecies began with the sacred account of how the evil one known as the Liar would arise from the pit of darkness and that One, Christophe the Atoner, the One we know as Lumen, would wield the sword that we now call Lumen's Hammer. What we must remember of that day so long ago is this: true love involves the laying down of life. Christophe did that. He laid down His life for the Kingdom of Bren. For three days it appeared the Liar had won, but then, we all know what happened next!"

"He rose again!" shouted Mark.

"That's right, cousin! He rose again, and in His rising took back Lumen's Hammer and used it to subdue the Liar, casting him back into the eternal pit of darkness from whence he came. But it was always understood throughout our history that the Liar would send his demons, his minions, his beasts, and his dragons to try and take back Lumen's Hammer and force his evil ways upon the good people of Bren.

"We are in the midst of one of those episodes of prophecy even now. It was foretold long ago that a great dragon—a Light Eater—would come into the realm and try to consume the light of the life of mankind. But it also foretold a remedy for just such a moment. The great seers of old wrote these words in the sacred writings of Bren:

"Only a child may bear this sword. Only a childlike faith will find the sword. Only by a child can the armor of the Great Dragon be pierced. As the saying goes, 'A child will lead them.'

"This day, we have found and released Lumen's hammer," Cullen continued, pointing the sword toward the heavens with his right hand.

"This day, a child—many children if we count all my cousins and siblings, and I do!—will lead them," he went on while the people of Bren gathered around the writhing body of the fearsome dragon nodded in silent agreement.

"And *this* day! This day!" he shouted with righteous honor, "Only by a child can the armor of the Great Dragon be pierced!" Cullen lifted the sword, hilt upward, tip downward, as high above his head as he could reach, and plunged it directly into the dragon's chest, piercing the leathery scales of the beast and finding the heart!

Luminaud, the monster, let out a last gasp along with a whisper, "This is not over. I will be back." And the Light Eater lay dead, sprawled in the courtyard of Castle Aerie.

In the very moment the beast drew his last breath, the brilliant vortex of converged lights, mixed with all manner of fairy lights, formed a column that reached up from the castle courtyard farther than anyone could see with the naked eye. The column spun faster and faster, consuming the darkness that the evil Luminaud had brought into the land. As the darkness was drawn into the vortex, the column of light moved higher and higher until it was completely gone!

And then it was suddenly day! The reverential silence turned to cheering and clapping and laughing and dancing and all manner of celebration! Even those who were not present at Castle Aerie that day can tell you the exact moment the beast was slain because, all across the realm, the darkness was gone!

"You know what you must do next," King Leonolis said to Cullen.

"Yes, grandfather. I do."

While his cousins and siblings and grandparents and friends and the people of Castle Aerie watched, Cullen raised the sword one last time and cut off the dragon's head.

THE JOURNEY HOME

*I*n the days that followed, so many celebrations were held throughout the land of Bren in honor of the children and their friends that they all grew weary of being treated and feted and celebrated. What they missed was time with their grandparents, time with one another, and home.

After one such celebration that seemed to go on forever, Zella and Abigail and Annabell decided to sneak out of the party and just be together. Sneaking through the festively adorned hallways and past the castle sentries, they hid behind the castle well and giggled at the way they had accomplished their mission to escape.

The more they giggled, the more they snickered, and the more they snickered, the more they snorted. Once the snorting started, nothing but full-on little-girl screeching laughter filled the courtyard's nearly silent night.

As Zella snorted for the umpteenth time, someone said, "Who goes there? Who is snorting like a pig? Oink! Oink! Oink!"

Zella instantly recognized her brother's voice. "Ronald! What are you doing here?"

"Don't you mean what are *we* doing here?" asked Ronald. "Come on out, guys."

While the three girls watched in disbelief, out from the shadows came Cullen, Mark, Harry, and Theo. "What are you guys doing here? You're supposed to be at the party!" scolded Zella.

"As are you and Annabell and Abigail," retorted Cullen.

"We are tired of all the attention. And to be honest, we just miss home," replied Abigail.

"Well, for crying out loud!" came a familiar voice from the shadows near the royal stable.

"Mia! Is that you?" asked Annabell in surprise.

"Yes, it is me and Elliott and Matilda!"

"And we are quite tired of all the celebration, too," said Elliott. "We just want some time to be..."

"Children?" suggested a deep, manly voice.

"Left alone to play?" answered a very familiar woman's voice.

"Grandfather! Grandmother! We are so sorry! We will go back to the party at once," said Cullen, sadly.

"You will do no such thing, young man!" replied Queen Abila.

"You've done more than your fair share of representing the realm throughout the Kingdom. And we could not be more proud. It is clear to us that you need no more celebration. Even celebration can at times rob us of joy, of time to just be together," responded the King.

"And your parents probably miss you dearly," suggested the Queen.

"And we miss them, too," said Theo, sheepishly.

"I believe the time has come ..." began their grandfather.

"The time has come? What 'time' grandfather?" asked Harold.

"Time to go home," said the King with just a touch of melancholy as a tear welled up in his eye.

"We love being with you," said Elliott.

"We know, dear. We love being with you. But there is a time to come and a time to go, and I think we all know the time for you to go has come," replied the Queen.

"How do we get home?" asked Theo.

The King simply turned slightly toward the castle gate and beckoned, "Come ... come now."

Stepping out of the shadows as if they were actually a part of those shadows came eleven wolves.

"I believe you know these beautiful creatures. They will take you home now," said the King.

The children and their grandparents melded into one

massive group hug, complete with tears and sobs and snorts and snot. After a few minutes of this, Leonolis said, "Children, to your wolves."

Each child was approached by his or her own wolf. Nuzzling the children affectionately, they used their snouts to help them atop their shaggy backs.

"Before you leave, there are a few who would like to wish you a good journey," said Queen Abila.

Bumbling from the darkness came Oliver the ogre. "Children, it has been my honor to serve you and to call you friend."

"We love you, Oliver!" said all the children.

Flittering out from the darkened stable door came Canto, who sang amid tiny fairy tears, "I love you dear Bairns of Bren, and I will miss you dearly!"

"We love you and we will miss you, too, dear Canto," wept the children.

Just then, the night sky was filled with snorting and pawing and prancing and a glinting shiny mane and tail as Patronicus appeared. "Dear Bairns of Bren, thank you for laying down your lives for the realm. Thank you for your friendship. And if you are ever in Bren again..."

"We love you, *RGB*!" exclaimed Elliott.

"And we love you, too!" giggled all the other children.

As the children laughed, a tiny light floating down toward them from the night sky. The children recognized her at once and exclaimed in unison, "Ariel! Good and faithful Ariel! We love you and we will miss you so much!"

"And I love you, Bairns of Bren, but I will be as near as the next shooting star, as near as the northern lights, as near as the southern lights, as near as that next ray of sunshine. I will be watching over you."

From somewhere behind the King, a familiar robed figure stepped into the courtyard light. "Abel!" said the children. "We love you and will miss you dearly!"

"And I have loved you since first we met. I have a question for you."

"What is your question, Abel?" asked Cullen.

"When you were each beneath Lumen's Hammer, when he plunged it into your hearts, when you gave your life for the realm, what did you see?" asked Abel.

"We saw life. We saw that death is not the end at all. It is merely the beginning of the next part of the journey," explained Cullen.

"We saw past the past. We saw the deepest reality of the present. We saw the extent of life that goes far beyond what the human eye can see. The life we live is but a shadow of what is to come," added Mark.

"And we saw that life is to be lived in the present, in the here and now, and that real treasure is not of this earth. The real treasure of life is to know and to be known," said Elliott.

"We saw life from a different point of view. We may see an insurmountable mountain, but the Founders see a mere molehill. We found wisdom is seeing and living life from the Founders' point of view," replied Mia.

"We saw that from the Founders' point of view, nothing is ever wasted," replied Ronald. "They will not waste our sorrow. They will not waste our pain. And they will not even waste our failure. They cause all things to work together for our good, and that includes such sad moments as this. They will somehow use even our sorrow for something good."

"Before you go, there is one more who would like to say goodbye ... several more," replied the King.

Out of the darkness and into the faint light of the castle courtyard came a small swarm of dragonflies.

"Oh, no! A dragon must be nearby!" exclaimed Theo.

"Hold you horses and put your sword away, Theo! This is Verona and his family!" explained Queen Abila.

"Dear Verona!" shouted Cullen. "You are free! Is this your family?"

"Yes! Yes! Yes!" shouted Verona. "This is my wife, Fidelia, and our eleven children! We would not be here had it not been for you!"

"And we would not have been victorious over Luminaud without your bravery! Thank you, good and faithful Verona!" replied Cullen.

Once again, the children all shouted their love and good-byes to Verona and his family amidst tears and laughter and joy and sadness.

"I am afraid the time has now come, children. The time

for goodbye," said the King. You have learned well, dear children, my Bairns of Bren. I send you home with the power of your true names.

"Cullen, go and live your life and enjoy it fully from the Founders' point of view." With that, the King swatted the wolf's behind and Cullen disappeared into the night.

"Harry, be the man of peace with a warrior's heart you have been called to be." And Harry was gone.

"Mia, always remember that you are the beloved daughter of the Founders. Live like you believe that!" And Mia vanished.

"Abigail, live your life in joy as you learn to see and respond to every circumstance of life from the Founders' point of view." Abigail and her wolf were gone.

"Zella, remember you have everything you need to live a full and joyful life because you are a daughter of Bren." And away went Zella.

"Theo, young warrior, you are a gift of God. Never forget that. Give your life away to those in need and all your needs will be met." And Theo was gone.

"Mark, you are tenderhearted warrior, fighting for what is good and true and right and virtuous. You are a son of the realm. Live like you believe that!" Mark disappeared.

"Annabell, you are a woman of grace, full of strength and beauty, both inside and out," said Queen Abila. "Extend that grace to those in need around you." The queen nudged the wolf and Annabell was gone.

"Elliott, dear Ellie," began the Queen, "you are a follower of God. Seek first the Kingdom of God and His righteousness and you will lack for nothing." And Elliott and her wolf were gone.

"And Matilda, my Tillie," said Abila, "you are both princess and mighty warrior. Battle for what is good and allow the strength of the Founders to guide you." The queen swatted the backside of Tillie's wolf, and they bounded away.

Turning to Ronald, Leonolis said, "I saved you for last for a reason, son. There is one more who wishes to say goodbye to you."

Ronald burst into tears and exclaimed, "Buddy! Come on, boy! Let's go home!"

Knowing how much Ron loved Buddy, the King gave him a few extra minutes to say goodbye.

Ron and the dog rolled around on the courtyard floor and laughed and giggled and howled and barked for what felt like a long time to the King and Queen, but not long enough for the boy.

"He's coming with me, right?" asked Ron. "He's coming home, isn't he, grandfather?"

"Dear boy, Buddy *is* home. His home is here in Bren now. I know you have missed him very much, and I can tell you he has missed you just as much. But he cannot go where you go. His home is here," replied the King.

Sobbing and blubbering and holding Buddy tight, Ronald

did not want to let go. But a few minutes later, he knew he must let go. So he did.

With the help of his grandfather, Ronald climbed back on his white wolf as tears streamed down his face. "Will I see him again, grandfather?"

"Why, yes! Of course, Ronald! He is as near as your next dream. He is as near as the next part of your journey. I will keep him safe until you are able to make your way to Bren again," said the King.

With that assurance, Ronald said, "I've missed you, Buddy, and I will always love you." Then Ronald and the white wolf faded into the night.

The children all slept well that night, waking the next morning at home, in their own beds, wondering if they had merely experienced a dream ... until they found them under their pillows. For each child, tucked safely inside a small red velvet pouch was a small gold chain. Dangling from the end of that chain, like the small golden treasure it was meant to recall, was a tiny, perfect replica of a mighty sword they had all fought to secure. The sacred weapon that had defeated the Light Eater ... well, you know the rest.

THE END

MORE FANTASY ADVENTURE AWAITS

What if your dreams became your reality?

Young Lee Jennings, constantly bullied by local boys, suddenly finds himself transported into a world of fantasy and adventure and plunged into a whole new identity as the son of a king! How he traverses this new world and endures captivity at the hands of the realm's resident evil lord is also the journey of self-discovery that will one day serve Lee in his adult life. Full of fantastic beings and magical creatures and wrought with many twists and turns, Captured is just the beginning for Lee Jennings in this fantastic saga of one boy's journey to manhood.

Learn how King Leonolis become ruler of the Realm of Bren in Captured, the first book of The Chronicles of Bren. Find the book at all online book vendors.

BECOME A DJ INSIDER

Would you like to receive email newsletters from me? You'll receive periodic news, updates, offers, and prayer requests. There's no obligation and I'll never spam you. Don't miss out on another update! Visit www.dennisjernigan.com/news-letter to sign up.

You can also join me on Patreon to get daily devotions, music, new releases, and exclusive updates. Check out all the benefits at www.patreon.com/dennisjernigan.

DID YOU ENJOY THIS BOOK?

Did you enjoy this book? You can make a big difference by leaving a review.

Reviews are one of the most important ways authors reach new readers. I don't have the funds to reach new people through advertising, but I have something more valuable, a group of individuals who support and believe in my ministry.

If you enjoyed this book, would you consider leaving an honest review? It doesn't need to be long. Your review will help other readers find this book.

To leave a review, simply visit your preferred ebook vendor and leave a review for The Light Eater (The Bairns of Bren Book Two).

WHO IS DENNIS JERNIGAN?

Dennis Jernigan is a songwriter and author who, with his wife Melinda, makes his home in northeastern Oklahoma very near where these stories were first inspired. They have raised nine children together and now enjoy many grandchildren.

Known foremost for his Christian praise music, Jernigan has extended his creativity to the realm of authoring books.

Fantasy reached him with hope during a very rough period of his life, and he feels a sense of urgency to write stories that will inspire others. The stories found within the pages of these books are a legacy to the generations to come.

For more information:
www.dennisjernigan.com
mail@dennisjernigan.com

facebook.com/official.dennisjernigan

twitter.com/dennisjernigan

instagram.com/dennisjernigan

youtube.com/dennisjernigan

Made in the USA
Coppell, TX
18 November 2024

40521047R00187